THE DAKOTA WINTERS

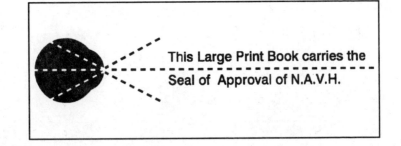

This Large Print Book carries the
Seal of Approval of N.A.V.H.

THE DAKOTA WINTERS

TOM BARBASH

THORNDIKE PRESS
A part of Gale, a Cengage Company

Farmington Hills, Mich • San Francisco • New York • Waterville, Maine
Meriden, Conn • Mason, Ohio • Chicago

LIBRARY OF CONGRESS CIP DATA ON FILE.
CATALOGUING IN PUBLICATION FOR THIS BOOK
IS AVAILABLE FROM THE LIBRARY OF CONGRESS

ISBN-13: 978-1-4328-6006-6 (hardcover)

Published in 2019 by arrangement with Ecco, an imprint of
HarperCollins Publishers

Printed in Mexico
1 2 3 4 5 6 7 23 22 21 20 19

For my family

And ye lucky livers, to whom, by some rare fatality, your Cape Horns are placid as Lake Lemans, flatter not yourselves that good luck is judgment and discretion; for all the yolk in your eggs, you might have foundered and gone down, had the Spirit of the Cape said the word.

— HERMAN MELVILLE,
"ROUNDING CAPE HORN"

August 21, 1979

Dearest Anton,
I hope you're sleeping better and finding the food more to your liking, though I must say I envy the choices you have, corn mush or fufu or roasted snake. I picture you in one of those grass and bamboo huts, sleeping under your mosquito netting, reading by a kerosene lamp. Remember you'll never again have an experience quite like this, and most great men begin great lives by getting out of their comfort zone. I'm glad you liked the books I sent, and yes I agree about the Alan Moorehead. It's an old-fashioned sort of book, but there are sections of it that are as good as anything and it'll be good for you to have read it.

Your brother is doing pretty well, though he misses you terribly. He's getting up early to do push-ups and sit-ups. He's playing in a few local tournaments this summer, and is slowly mastering the psychological game. No more racket throwing. He's been working with the Zen master tennis coach I told you about, and cleared out the negativity. It's inspiring to witness.

For myself I'm still — yes *still* — trying to find my balance, and more and more each day I am. My travels have done wonders for my spirit and my mind, not to mention my middle-aged body, which is more toned than it's been since you were a young kid. And still I feel at times like I'm walking unsteadily. I miss the routine of the show, and am at the same time happy for all the hours in the day I have now to do other things. Sometimes I imagine us having conversations about our experiences and the people we meet. In a sense we've done this (albeit erratically) through letters, though I can't wait to see you in person. We all can't wait. Your mother keeps planning your meals and which movies she wants to take you to. Kip wants to kick your heinie on the tennis court and Rachel wants to take you riding in the park, like you used to.

Everyone has his or her theory about what I've been through. Nice that they have such a broad term, isn't it — nervous breakdown. Covers a lot of things. It feels to me like a fever I've broken through, and now I'm out of bed with the salt on my skin and the wind in my hair.

Oh incidentally, I saw John L. in the elevator a month ago with Sean. I'd told him about your travels and filled him in with a few juicy details, and now he asks about you regularly. I told him of your digestive problems — maybe I exaggerated them a bit, but he had a similar story to tell. We walked all the way to the zoo. His boy is adorable.

As for work, I've got some stand-up lined up, and I'm a bit anxious about it. We might even think about sneaking in a pricey phone call somehow so I can go over material.

I won't burden you with more and, really, Anton, I'm in good shape. The best physical shape I've been in in a long time. I'm swimming again. Playing tennis, as you know four times a week. Joblessness is great for your ground strokes.

So be good, be alert. Eyes, ears and

mind wide open. Eat a roasted snake for your old man. I love the story about all the village kids surrounding you wanting your autograph, and not knowing at all who you were, only that you were from America.

Cherish how far away you are. What an adventure!

Talk to you soon.

Love,
Buddy (aka Dad)
P.S. The Mets are stinking it up, sadly.

1

To begin with, there was the malaria.

I had been in Gabon in the Peace Corps, where my job was to help people improve their nutrition and access potable water. I helped design and implement a water filtration system and was in the midst of building a community center with a large kitchen and a bare-bones medical clinic. I swam with hippos, danced myself, with thirty others, into a trance state, read a lot of Ian Fleming novels, and lost almost twenty pounds. I went ten months without so much as flirting with a girl and then had a consciousness-expanding weekend at a hotel in Libreville with the twenty-year-old daughter of a State Department official.

I had the sense I was figuring things out over there, far away from my friends and my parents, but if my trip was a movie, I'd been yanked out of it in the first act, while things were still building, and before I knew what all the plot threads added up to. I felt like I was on the verge of a significant breakthrough, or within sight of the verge. I was only gone for thirteen months, but the city looked different when I got back. It was beautiful under the snow and dreamy, though that might have been because I was dreamy. I took walks and pretended I'd come from a small village, thousands of miles away, and imagined what all this would look like.

A lot of my time, though, was occupied with being sick. I once had pneumonia in high school, and I'd had a few nasty colds, but nothing to prepare me for this. I think I can remember the precise moment when the infecting occurred. I remember lying under my mosquito netting and realizing there was a mosquito trapped in there, and then being unable to get her out (*only the ladies bite,* my doctor said), and fearing if I ripped the netting all of the mosquitoes in the room would attack me, and anyway I was so tired. I was in and out of sleep. It took a while for me to get sick and then I had all the classic symptoms: a shirt-drenching fever, deathly chills, hallucinations that would begin again each time I closed my eyes. The doctor who treated me in Bongolo Hospital in Lebamba said I could have died. If I'd waited another day I would have. And in truth I did think about death in my misty, hallucinatory state. I pictured people at my memorial service, and I imagined them saying incredibly kind things about me.

I was sent back in a Pan Am 707 that stopped for refueling in Paris. I don't remember much about the flight over the Atlantic. There might have been a movie. I drank half a beer. The woman next to me wore nice perfume and was reading *Sophie's Choice*. My parents met me at the airport, and my father kept hugging me and staring at my face. "Malaria," he said, as though getting used to a new name.

My illness became a story Buddy liked to tell people, that his older boy contracted malaria in Africa, and he'd list the luminaries who'd had malaria: Dante, Caravaggio, Lord Byron, who'd all died from it; and others who'd just had it, like Hemingway, Lincoln (in his Kentucky childhood), and John Kennedy in World War II while in the Solomon Islands. Not much was asked of me in my first days back. I remember watching some of the NFL play-offs — the Rams upsetting the Cowboys; Vince Ferragamo threw for three touchdowns — and I remember reading about, and seeing on television, details about the hostages in Iran, and then the Soviets invading Afghanistan. I was emotional about things I read in the paper. For instance, I was undone for around two days by the news of the death of Joy Adamson, the author of *Born Free.* The story said she'd been mauled by a lion in Kenya. She'd been out for a stroll and was due back to listen to a broadcast of the BBC. Her body was found a hundred yards from the camp. She was sixty-nine years old.

We saw that movie five or six times when we were growing up, and during each viewing I'd wept. I'd also developed a crush on Virginia McKenna, the actress who played Joy Adamson, and had thought about her in my own days in Africa. I had wanted to meet someone like her, blond hair and a starched thin khaki shirt, and fall in love and stay, or take her back to New York with me.

"Live by the sword, die by the sword," Buddy said, but the news had upset him as well.

I was also wrecked by the plight of the hostages in Iran. A photo ran on the front page of the *New York Times* with two hostages reading letters from the U.S., a large pile of mail strewn on the floor in front of them. Clergymen went in there with Christmas cookies, rosaries, and Bibles and said everyone was in good health, though there were also stories of them being blindfolded and tied to radiators.

The Shah of Iran, whom I'd met once at a party at Rowan Rose's house, was exiled to an island in Panama that we'd gone to on vacation. He was staying in a house my father had once rented. There were pictures of him wading in the ocean with armed guards watching him from the beach.

It felt like the world was in the midst of some kind of seismic upheaval, and in retrospect it was. There was a revolution in Rhodesia, an assassination in South Korea, another in Afghanistan, and then the Soviets were rushing toward Kabul and thumbing their noses at our stumbling Southern president, who kept appearing on television to make threats and to seem strong and presidential.

"Such aggression will not be tolerated," he said, and said again, with all the force of a parent telling a small child that if they pull the cat's tail again they'll go without dessert.

I'd read the paper cover to cover and watch the news, and at night I'd dream about revolutions and disease and marauding animals; one night one of them had a face that looked disturbingly like my father's.

"Don't want to get ahead of myself," Buddy was telling me, "but we might be back in the thick of it soon."

We were at Café Un Deux Trois in Midtown on a Thursday night. My mother was home reading and helping my brother with his homework.

"How so?"

"One of our old producers has been floating the idea of a new show and getting some interest. It turns out people's memories are short, he says, so long as I'm up for it."

"And are you?"

"I don't know. Maybe."

"You definitely are," I said.

Reginald "Buddy" Winter, my winsome father, had a national talk show that ran from 1968 to 1978, gained a vast and devoted viewership, and won two Emmys. The list of guests included Salvador Dalí, Muhammad Ali, Gore Vidal, Woody Allen, Luciano Pavarotti, Elizabeth Taylor, Paddy Chayefsky, and John Lennon, the mainstream and the avant-garde. And then Buddy walked off in the middle of a broadcast and had a nervous breakdown, the details of which were written about in a long and largely misleading article in *Manhattan* magazine. Since then he'd become an item of curiosity and fascination, though many of the stories about his intercontinental voyage of recovery were pure fiction and glossed over how truly lost he was.

My mother, Emily Winter (Em, Buddy called her), had spent a month with Buddy in the Greek islands, where they ate fish and stomped grapes and behind sunglasses read books together on the beach. It felt, she said, like they'd gone back a decade, which was both an affirmation and a relief, as she hadn't known who it was she would find when she landed in Athens.

"Anyway, nothing concrete, but it might be time to get back in game shape."

"And mend a few fences," I said. "Who was the producer?"

"Elliot," he said.

Elliot was one of the few who had landed a good job, at ABC Sports. When *The Buddy Winter Show* ended, it wasn't just us out on the street. There were producers and cameramen, gaffers and production assistants, the green room staff, most of whom had planned to stay with Buddy for the run of the show. A lot of them resented the shit

19

out of Buddy for walking out on them, and, by association, me. Our old cameraman, Jay Schwabacker, a gift-bearing uncle to us in the good days, spotted me on the subway once and walked to another car. The saddest was Buddy's agent and college roommate, Harry Abrams, with whom he had a nasty fight, and hadn't talked to since, and whose daughter I was friends with and sort of dated.

A man in his midforties, with silvering hair and a vacation tan, bent to Buddy's side to speak: "I don't want to interrupt your dinner, but I watched you every night until you went off the air. I conceived at least one of my children in front of your show."

"I'm sorry," Buddy said, "but I think that makes *me* the father."

The man broke out laughing and said, "Good to see you holding up so well."

Buddy asked him, "What does that mean?"

"I mean you look great."

My father was a lanky, athletic man still a few months from fifty, six feet two, with strong cheekbones, and lines around his mouth when he smiled (a cross between Edward R. Murrow and George Peppard, someone wrote). This time his smile was strained.

"How should I look?" he asked.

"Exactly like you look," I said.

The man looked at me as if to say "You take it from here, kid."

"You're the *best*, Buddy," the man said, patting my father's shoulder lightly and holding his glance before retreating.

"Yeah, yeah. You too."

Buddy sat there for a while staring at his plate as though there was a message for him in his mashed potatoes.

"You've got to get a little better at things like that," I said.

"You're right, you're absolutely right," he said, and when the waiter returned my father asked him to send a bottle of wine to his admirer's table.

We walked together up Broadway, then past the old theater that had served for more than a decade as home to *The Buddy Winter Show*. His spirits were bright, and he acted unfazed by the incident at dinner. A play had let out, and the audience was dispersing outside, buttoning coats, adjusting their winter hats then raising their arms toward passing taxis.

"You think they liked it, Anton?" my father asked.

"They don't seem ecstatic."

"That's *exactly* what I was thinking," he

21

said. "They're thinking, It beats TV, but I'm not sure it was worth the sixty bucks."

I was relieved none of the theatergoers recognized Buddy, and more likely they were in their own thoughts but I was happy to be just with him for a while. We passed the Stage Deli, where we used to escape to after the show, and O'Donnell's Tavern and other dark bars I'd been to countless times with Buddy or other crew members. Usually Buddy wanted to get back to my mother before it got late, but more than a few times someone would sneak me drinks, and we'd all get buzzed, and at some point it would dawn on Buddy that I was sixteen and had school the next day, and he should probably get me home.

At Columbus Circle I began to tire. I'd had a couple of glasses of wine and, mixed with the medication the hospital sent me home with, I felt dreamy again, like the colors around me were leaking.

"I should have visited you in Africa," Buddy said. "I would have, you know. We'd have had a few adventures, wouldn't we."

"We still can if I go back," I said.

"You're not going back."

"I might go back," I said, because it was my right to say that.

"You can't," he said. "I need your help."

■ ■ ■ ■

The Dakota, where Buddy moved our family when I was four, is among the most famous apartment buildings in the world. It looks like a Hapsburg castle because, like the Eldorado and the Beresford and the San Remo, it was built to be one. The idea at the time was to build in the then remote Upper West Side of Manhattan — which resembled the vast plains of the Dakotas, said the developer Edward Clark — a lifestyle to match what you'd get in a luxury hotel. The sort of place in which Marlene Dietrich, if she'd been alive then, would have been comfortable. The list of people who've lived there or gone to parties there is a who's who of the last hundred years of American culture. The old *New Yorker* cover, which had the rest of the world as tiny dots around a small spot of Manhattan, should have had as its glorious center the Dakota, because during the time of my growing up it felt that way.

Which isn't to say it was a snobby place — it never felt that way. It feels more like a European village — in, say, Luxembourg — open, friendly, grand, with stories everywhere, and the right people to tell those

23

stories and to go out and live them. Not that I noticed that as a kid — when you're a child you believe your experience is everyone's. Still even at five or six I recognized that I was lucky, and maybe unusually so, though I'm sure there are other kids across the world who feel that way, and probably not because of a building.

In the old days on the mazelike roof, there were tents and awnings and gazebos. And on any given weekend the parties would spread to the rooftops, and you could hear the sounds of people playing music all the way out to Central Park.

We lived in an apartment owned once by Boris Karloff that has five fireplaces and two kitchens. That's excessive certainly, but all the apartments in the Dakota are like that, with high ceilings, parquet floors, and amazing old fixtures, odd little touches you kept discovering over time, like the servants' bells in every room that let the servant — or maid in our case — know what room you were in, and the dumbwaiters, used in the old days to whisk your dirty dishes back down to the kitchen.

The building wasn't that expensive for a good long while. It was on the Upper West Side after all, and the Upper West Side was a rough place in the old days, with gangsters like Dutch Schultz and Joe "The Boss" Masseria, and scary empty lots, and supposedly the highest concentration of drug addicts and newly released patients of shuttered mental institutions in the country to go along with all the movie theaters and bookstores and left-wing politics.

At the front desk Hattie Beckwith waved us through. Hattie was from a small town in Ireland and had worked the front desk for fifty years, receiving and sorting the tenants' mail and working the switchboard, usually during the days, but every once in a while at night. She had curly gray hair, and as long as I can remember wore in winter one of three cable-knit sweaters, one red, one kelly green, and the navy one she now had on.

"Who's the *stranger*?" she asked my father and smiled my way.

"One of your many admirers," Buddy said.

"Oh, listen to you. He has your eyes."

"You need a new prescription, Hattie. His are brown."

"Oh well, maybe they are," she said. "Nice to have you back. Your dad needs taking care of."

She always held a soft spot for my father, as did most of the building. We had a party each year in the courtyard, all around that brilliant fountain, and my mother would cook for days, and Buddy made some sort of pastry, or brought out some good wine, and he'd sit at one of a dozen long tables with Rowan Rose and Betty Bacall and Jason Robards and Ruth Ford. In later years John and Yoko would be there with Sean. And Yoko would bring sushi, and John would grab a chair at my father's table, and I'd go run around somewhere else — with no need to be around the action, because it wasn't like the action would run off and leave us.

Until of course it did.

The Dakota elevators are ancient strange things that have been around since the beginning of time. They're water-powered, maybe the last in the city. Occasionally they drip down on you.

It's in the elevators where you meet your neighbors, and we ran into a guy named Paul Loeb who wrote about architecture for the *Times*.

"You're back," he said to me.

"I've been back two weeks now."

"How was it?"

"Great. I got sick, though."

"Doesn't everyone?"

"You have any openings at your paper?" my father asked.

"Maybe," he said.

"It's the *Times*," I said. "It's like asking Billy Martin if there's an opening on the Yankees."

"You *have* been away. They fired Billy months ago," Buddy said.

It was Loeb's floor. On his way out he said, "Seriously, Anton, give me a call and I'll see what I can do. I can't promise anything, but you never know."

"As soon as I can get through a day without feeling dizzy."

He smiled. The door closed.

My mother and my fifteen-year-old brother, Kip, were inside watching the start of a Rangers game on the West Coast. "Did you finish your homework?" my father asked.

"Yes," Kip said. "You want to read it?"

"Read what?"

"My paper on *Siddhartha*."

"Give it to your brother," Buddy said, plopping down next to my mother.

"You want to read it?" Kip asked me.

"When is it due?"

"Tomorrow. There's a lot of sex in the book."

"I don't remember that."

He read, *"They played the game of love. . . . Her body was flexible like that of a jaguar or the bow of a hunter; he who had learned from her how to make love, was knowledgeable of many forms of lust, many secrets."*

"Got it," I said.

"What do jaguars and the bows of hunters have to do with sex?" my mother asked.

"You have to be more flexible to figure it out," Buddy said.

My mother gave him a smile that said *not terrible.*

I followed Kip into his room, which was adorned with sports star posters, primarily tennis players — Connors leaping the net, Borg poised for a backhand passing shot, and Vitas Gerulaitis lunging for a service return, and then pretty boy Ron Duguay of the Rangers slipping the puck by Bernie Parent of the Flyers, and Dr. J levitating for a dunk.

"How was he at dinner?" my brother asked me.

"Good, why?"

"Nothing."

I waited.

"Do you think he's all better?" he asked.

"Yes."

I sat down at the desk in his room, turned on the little shaded lamp, and started reading. "Can I mark this up?" I asked.

"Go to town," he said.

And I did.

The paper was full of good points that needed to be reordered.

"I like that he's around all the time," Kip then said. "That when I get home he's here, and when I wake up, he's already out there reading the paper."

"You're lucky," I said. "When we were little he was gone all the time."

"But he might get a new show, right?"

"We'll see. I hope so, but I think it'll be a while."

"You want him to get a new show, don't you?"

"Sure, but it's not up to me."

"Aren't you going to work on it with him?"

"That isn't the plan."

"He thinks it is."

"He told you that?"

Kip nodded. "A friend of mine said if your father cracks up, there's, you know, a decent chance you will too."

"Your friend's a douchebag," I said. "Now rewrite this thing and go to sleep."

I would stay a month, I thought, and then go back to Gabon, and finish what I started. I didn't want to get sucked back in again.

Couldn't, wouldn't, shouldn't, won't, I thought.

2

On Monday, I went to the tropical disease doctor down at Bellevue Hospital to check on my progress. I rode the subway downtown listening to the Walkman my parents gave me for Christmas, and the cassette tapes Kip had made for me, the Waitresses and the Au Pairs. The lines at the parasitology department went out the door and out into the hallway.

I signed in on a chart and waited for my name to be called. Many of the patients were African immigrants (an influx of which caused the long lines), including a teenager next to me who said he was from Zaire, and I felt at home among them, more so anyway than with your average New Yorker.

The doctor was a handsome, curly-haired guy in his early thirties and had traveled everywhere it seemed. He'd had malaria twice, he told me, dysentery three times, and dengue fever once.

31

"That's the worst," he said. "What were you doing down there?"

"Peace Corps."

"I wish I'd done that."

"I'm going back in a few weeks."

"Let's see how your recovery goes," he said. "So let me guess, I'm betting you stopped the chloroquine."

"I did," I said.

"And then the fever comes on very suddenly, am I right?"

"Yes."

The night the fever kicked in, I was drenched with sweat, and went from hot to freezing cold, and then violently thirsty. Then I was extremely dizzy, as though the hut was spinning.

"If you're from there, it isn't a big deal, but the first time you get it, it is. Now there are a lot of benign kinds. Yours was the deadly sort. And it's true, Anton, you came close."

"I know."

"How are you about that?"

"What do you mean?"

"It's not easy to experience something like that. It's a complicated thing psychologically to recover from, a near death experience."

"I've had some recurring nightmares."

"I'm not surprised. Are they like your hallucinations?"

"Yes. I also had a dream I'd died and I was at my own funeral. And everyone was telling me I should go up and say something."

He wrote a couple of lines in his notepad.

"You might want to find someone you can talk to about this."

"How about you?"

"A psychologist, I mean. I would. I have."

He went on, "I'm going to test you for a few other things — dengue fever, African sleeping sickness."

I told him about the dysentery, and how humiliating it was to need to shit so often for such a long time.

He looked at me sympathetically.

"My first trip to Africa I remember shitting in my pants — right there in my pajamas. That had never happened to me, and my supreme wish is that it will never happen again. I remember waking up with shit all over me."

He tested my hearing for tinnitus and my muscles for neurological abnormalities. My lower right leg felt often like it had fallen asleep. He said that would get better over time but to check back with him if it persisted.

He said relapses weren't uncommon even six months out.

"How will I know if I have one?"

"You won't. Not right away. But if you're yellow and puffy and dehydrated and then drenched with sweat in the middle of the night, you get yourself back down here."

"It's a plan," I said.

He walked out of the room. I wondered for a moment if I should become a parasitologist. That's how rudderless I was.

When he returned, he said, "I just saw your address on your chart. Your father isn't Buddy Winter, is he?"

"He is indeed."

"Tell him I miss his show, will you?"

The light was gone from the day. The days were so short. The snow was filthy and the birds looked cold. There were twigs in the ice. It smelled cold and dirty.

I took the subway home from the clinic, the R, and then the uptown No. 2. The subway was covered in graffiti, crude black Magic Marker stuff on the seats and windows, and the doors. The stations themselves were old and cramped and poorly ventilated, with formerly bright blue columns filthy with grime.

The man next to me was talking to himself. He had clearly peed his pants, and was complaining about a woman who'd taken his money and needed to give it back if she goddamn expected to see him again.

Two guys around my age in red berets stepped aboard, one wearing an army jacket, the other in a white thermal underwear top. They were Guardian Angels, a group that started while I was away with the mission to prevent rapes, assaults, and muggings on the subway. They'd begun with thirteen (the Magnificent 13, they'd called themselves), and now they were over four hundred. They traveled in teams of eight or so and fanned out to different cars.

"Good afternoon," the guy in the army jacket said to the car full of passengers. "I'm Joseph and this is Hector, and we're here to make your ride home safe and enjoyable."

Now that he was closer to me, I could see they were younger than I'd guessed — seventeen or eighteen.

Two years back I had my life threatened on a Brooklyn-bound No. 2 train for making eye contact with a man with a mangled ear. "The fuck you looking at?" he said, and when I said, "Nothing," he pressed his face so close to mine I could see inside his pores, and said, "Damn right, nothing, I will *kill* you, motherfucker."

"For what?" I actually said aloud.

He smacked the book I'd been reading onto the floor.

"*Dead* man," he said, his eyes wild with rage, and after a chilling ten seconds of staring he walked away, and glared at other passengers.

New York felt more on edge than any place I saw in Africa, or anywhere else on my travels. When I left for any length of time, I always forgot how stressful it could feel just getting around at certain hours and on particular streets.

In middle school we heard stories about a guy named Charlie Chop-off, one of those urban legends based on someone real. Boys were dragged into alleyways or dark hallways to be stabbed and in some cases raped, and then their genitals removed with a switchblade. We all had nightmares about Charlie Chop-off. And in the playground we'd joke as someone left for his home in the dwindling light, *Watch out for Charlie Chop-off.* Or at a friend's house you'd pull a knife from the kitchen drawer, stare at your friend's crotch, and shout, *It's Charlie Chop-off!*

At least seven kids fell victim to Charlie, maybe close to twenty. Then there was the Son of Sam, who did his work in the other boroughs but could have stricken anywhere, and Calvin Jackson in our neighborhood who killed and raped women and stole their household appliances. (When caught, he said he "*liked* killing.")

I remember seeing a guy creeping down the street who resembled my nightmare version of Charlie Chop-off. He looked at me funny, and I took off running. Whenever I sensed danger, I'd walk or run on the street side of the cars until I felt safe again, like playing high-stakes tag with a base out there, or swimming by sharks to a raft. Our block was relatively safe, but right there on Broadway and Seventy-Third was Needle Park, where the addicts hung out. They were brutal to see, the vacant look in their eyes, hands out, everything in a sort of warped slow motion.

Then in a minute's walk were blocks of well-tended brownstones, new restaurants and cafés and even a few clubs. Up Broadway a little farther were beloved revival movie theaters — the Thalia and the Regency and the New Yorker — and bookstores, classic and metaphysical, head shops and hardware stores, bakeries and a traffic island bench with two nattily dressed Holocaust survivors sharing a bag of chestnuts, a greasy-haired man in a cable-knit sweater

37

reading Henry Miller, a woman nearby selling paperbacks and LPs. The things you'd want in a city. Life.

Just before my stop, the woman on the other side of the peeing man whispered in my ear, "The world is full of terrible people."

3

I tried to eat as much as I could stomach to get my weight back. I am six feet, and I weighed 145 when I got home, which made my clothes hang funny on me.

I walked around a lot, across the park and then down to the public library, and then on the way back I'd go to the Central Park Zoo and watch the seals do their flips and dives, the only part of the zoo back then where the animals weren't depressingly incarcerated. I went to movies, because I wasn't working, and often Buddy came with me, and we'd order a huge tub of popcorn, Milk Duds, and a couple of Cokes.

I saw *Apocalypse Now* twice, once with Buddy and a second time by myself, and both times I lived the movie more than I watched it. I'd been suffering from feelings of dislocation in the mornings, uncertain of my surroundings. I *was* Martin Sheen waking up in a fevered sweat in that Saigon hotel room. He even looked malarial. His internal voice was my own, and I wasn't sure whether or not it was an auditory hallucination. *"Every time, I think I'm going to wake up back in the jungle."*

My god, I thought. He's me.

"I've been here a week now, waiting for a mission, getting softer."

I was waiting for a mission.

Getting softer.

When I told Buddy about this, he said all the movies we'd seen were about us.

"For example," I asked.

"Take *Kramer vs. Kramer.*"

"That's about maternal abandonment."

"Or man loses job, bonds with his son while plotting his next move."

"The kid's eight, but all right."

"Or *Breaking Away.*"

Directed by one of our Dakota neighbors, Peter Yates. About kids in Indiana, and cycling. I didn't see the connection.

"Lanky and charmingly affected young man, caught between two cultures."

Along with movies we'd go to museums, the Met, or the Whitney, or the Museum of Modern Art. At each, two or three people would recognize him and ask what he was up to, and sometimes he'd give them an honest answer, that he'd been clearing his head and feeding his soul or something of that sort, and they'd nod appreciatively, as though a character in a beloved book had climbed out to become their friend.

When my mother got home, the four of us would head out to dinner, and twice my sister, Rachel, joined us. It felt sometimes like it was the old days again, and other times a little strained, as though we were in a play about a family who all hold secrets from one another. In the past, Buddy had largely orchestrated the conversation, and now he picked his spots, and at times tuned the rest of us out. My mother would ask, "What's up, kiddo?" And he'd raise his eyebrows and say, "Wouldn't *you* like to know."

My mother had been an accomplished actress in her teens and twenties. She grew up on West End, and her father, my grandfather Will Simmons, owned a music store in the West Fifties. She got her B.A. in theater from NYU, and was in a dozen movies, usually playing the star's best friend, to strong reviews. She had a lead role in three films, one of which, *High Seas Charade* (with Lee Marvin and George Kennedy), became a cult hit. I'd watched many of these with her at revival theaters like the

Thalia or the New Yorker, and she'd whisper things to me like *"Check out the girl in the backseat of the convertible, the one in the sunglasses."*

It was strange to see her that young, and slapping Van Johnson in the face, or screaming at the sight of a dead Walter Pidgeon at the bottom of a staircase. She also had a recurring part on *Peyton Place,* performed in several off-Broadway plays, and was in a handful of commercials, once for Playtex Living Bras, where she floated around at a party as a series of creepy men in turtlenecks swiveled their heads to admire her.

Over the last two months she'd been fund-raising for Teddy Kennedy in his run for the Democratic presidential nomination and had been enlisted to escort Joan Kennedy, a longtime friend, around the city and to a rally at the Park Tavern restaurant.

"Sometimes he seems so strong and magnetic," she said, when we were out at our local pizza place, Al Buono Gusto on Columbus. "And then other times, it's as though he can't be bothered to make an effort, like he's irritated he has to explain to anyone why he should be president."

When I had been in Gabon, I followed the campaign on occasional broadcasts from the BBC and from Buddy's letters, and liked thinking about another Kennedy being president. He'd then had a disastrous interview with Roger Mudd, which Buddy had described at length.

"Death by prevarication," he'd diagnosed it.

The race was muddied by the hostage crisis, which had enabled the president to hide out in the Rose Garden, make presidential speeches, and imply that to be campaigning was uncouth in these perilous times. Amazingly it worked, and his approval ratings were still high despite all his evident shortcomings.

"The Kennedy curse," Buddy said.

I think my mother saw parallels in Teddy's and Buddy's quests to overcome their complex pasts, though she would add, I'm sure, that at least in Buddy's case no one died. I'd say they both needed to find their mojo again, and to reconnect with their constituencies.

As soon as I'd finish a slice, a new one would appear on my plate courtesy of my mother.

"That's four," I said.

"And you could eat four more and still look like a UNICEF ad," she said.

"If I have one more, I'll throw up the rest of them."

"I'll eat whatever you don't," Kip said.

"The human tapeworm," Buddy said.

Kip had shot up in the year I was away. He was nearly my height (he'd been a head shorter when I left), with broader shoulders, and legs made strong and wiry from jumping rope in the vestibule at all hours.

He'd saved up dozens of dirty jokes for me while I was away and he shared them at the table, though my parents had heard them already.

His favorite was about a game show, *The Object in Question,* where they blindfold the contestants and then bring an item out on a tray. The contestant asks questions in order to determine the object's identity. The first item brought out is a severed penis from a moose.

"The blindfolded contestant, an old lady from Applewood, Wisconsin, asks, 'Can you *eat* it?' " Kip says in his best old lady voice. "And the judges confer and say, 'Well, yes, ma'am, the judges say you certainly can if you wanted to.' So the next question she asks is 'Is it a *moose cock*?' "

I cannot say why that joke hit me the way it did, but the beer I'd been drinking sprayed through my nose.

"I love that," I said.

On our way out he said, "Can I ask you

something?"

"Sure."

"In the hospital, did you think you were going to die?"

"I sort of did."

"What was that like?"

"I was pretty out of it. But I do remember thinking, Maybe this is it. Maybe I'm going to die, and it seemed strange to be in such a random place, so far away from everyone I know and dying."

"I'm glad you didn't," he said, "because no one laughs at my jokes like you do."

"There you go, I'm good for something."

I felt part of them, and all alone at the same time.

Mostly I felt disconnected, the way one feels in an airport layover. I hadn't yet called a lot of friends or committed myself to any activities beyond the next week or two. What was easiest now was to tag along with Buddy, who was also between things, and to get to know my mother and brother again.

It was nice to see my parents holding hands and walking like two people dating.

"You're pretty skinny," Kip said.

"I can still kick your ass."

"In your dreams," he said.

I pounded his arm, and he yelled and then

pounded mine. It hurt like a motherfucker, but I pretended it didn't.

4

As the weeks went on, I felt increasingly adrift, though not unhappily so. The city kept offering up surprises. I retained the sense of being an outsider in my hometown, and I tried to see the people and the buildings through the eyes of a visitor from Gabon. Mundane observations became fresh insights, like the thought that Manhattan, when you got down to it, wasn't that big. You could walk the whole island, north to south, in an afternoon. Its size was vertical, and the concept of piling millions of lives atop one another felt almost comical.

On balance, my return was an erasure. All my stories were swallowed up by Buddy, either because he told them before I could ("And when he swam to the surface he saw a hippo no more than ten yards away . . .") or because people were more interested in his next move than mine. It was like the party scene in *The Graduate,* but in our version everyone asks Benjamin about his father's health, and what he might next do.

My own story was, in TV terms, still in development. I was recovering, and I'd have to wait until I was fully healthy to go back, which might be in a few weeks or a month. In the meantime, Buddy said, it was a chance to do the things we never had time for when he worked six days a week. We read the *Times* together each day, exercised at the gym or went swimming twice a week, and took walks all over. On these walks I told him about my year away and the people I'd grown close to, and the drought we suffered under for three months, and then the deluge that came after like something out of the Bible, and the fetish priest brought in to heal a dying boy, his head rolling and lolling to the beating of drums before the priest took possession and then healed the boy through the power of suggestion, and the soccer games I organized, and the frustrations I'd felt trying to get things done and not having the resources. And he listened and beamed at me proudly and told me what a great experience it had been, and that he would support my returning to finish my assignment "if that's what you want."

We'd *both* been sick, he said, and now we were both unemployed, and it was a short period of time we'd never get back. And so we treated New York like a far-off world we'd flown to, which in my state of dislocation felt true.

Part of feeling unsettled was lacking my own place, and sleeping each night in my old room under my New York Knicks blanket. A solution emerged when an old magazine writer we knew, who lived on the ninth floor and was heading to Spain for the year, suggested I might want to sublet his two-room place, for a nominal sum, with the expectation I'd collect his mail, water his geraniums and philodendrons, "and do some stateside errands" for him when needed.

A curious aspect of the Dakota is that two separate worlds exist within, the first seven floors with the high ceilings and countless fireplaces, and the famous tenants, and the top two, where on dingy carpeted hallways rows of tiny, often windowless rooms and apartments, with hot plates for stoves and shared bathrooms, were occupied with a few exceptions by people whose names no one knew, and whose faces you wouldn't recognize if they sat next to you on the subway.

I said I'd tell the writer, whose name was Robert Fielding, before he left for San Sebastián on the first of February, but I'd

49

already made up my mind to take it.

On a cold night in late January I met up with my childhood friend Alex, who since college had gotten serious about acting. He was taking classes with Stella Adler. So far he'd been in two low-budget plays and had a walk-on part in a soap opera, which had been extended for a few weeks. He'd played a waiter, which ironically he wasn't — the only actor in New York without a menu in his hands, he said.

We went for dinner at an Indian place on Sixth Street where you brought your own wine, and the meals cost around six bucks. The food was decent, though half the time you'd get the runs after. It was possible to eat cheaply those days if you knew the right places. It had started to lightly snow. Alex wore a black thrift-shop overcoat and baggy black dress pants over red Converse All Stars.

Alex had watched the movie *The Misfits* in his acting class and was talking excitedly about it. It was one of Buddy's favorite movies and I'd seen it four times. They'd done a whole *Buddy Winter Show* on it in fact, with the writer, Arthur Miller, the director, John Huston, and several members from the crew.

"Amazing how many careers ended after that," he said.

"You mean how many lives. Everyone died."

Sadly true, Clark Gable and Marilyn Monroe died within the year, Montgomery Clift not long after.

The story goes that Arthur Miller was in Nevada for six weeks because of their lax divorce laws. He wanted to marry Marilyn. He rented a cabin on Pyramid Lake and made friends with two of the cowboys who were making their living catching wild horses — mustangs — which they'd sell to turn into dog food. They lived on the margins of society — outside of any real community — and Miller wrote a short story, published in *Esquire,* and later the movie script about them.

"I led the discussion on Marilyn and the tree," Alex said. He had a good face for an actor, longish brown hair parted on the side and a cleft chin. His normal expression was a squinty scowl, but he broke into a sly smile when the moment called for it.

The Catholic Church in New York wanted to ban a scene of Marilyn dancing around a tree, "because they said she was *masturbating,*" Arthur Miller had told Buddy on the show. "I said we'd keep the scene and if you

51

object I'll report the conversation to the *New York Times.* That ended *that.*"

"Without that scene you lose half the movie," Alex said.

The food came, tandoori chicken and chicken tikka masala.

"Can you imagine being on that set?"

It was over 100 degrees and they filmed on a dried-up salt lake.

Clark Gable had to wear heavy clothes to protect him while being dragged by the horses. He was exhausted and overheated and he died shortly after finishing the film.

They shot it in black and white, Miller said, so that the scenery would look like drying bones.

That show was what Buddy did and no one else. No empty plugs to drive ticket sales. Here was a discussion of opposing aesthetics and a marriage falling apart, and a great star at the end of her short life hiding out all day long in a hot car with her acting coach.

It was someone's birthday at the next table, and when they sang Happy Birthday Alex joined in loudly. They'd brought at least three bottles of champagne and shared some with us.

"I know three songs in Hindi," Alex said.

"Why don't you sing them? I'm sure the

waitress would love them."

He considered it, until he saw me suppressing a laugh.

"Fuck you, Winter. They're beautiful songs and you just blew your chance to hear them."

We talked then about Gabonese food, which had been a mixed bag at best for me. I began as an adventurous eater, I said, eating bush meats like antelope, wild boar, and monkey.

"Oh my god. You ate Curious George?"

"His cousin."

"What did he taste like?"

"He was a little tough and a little greasy. Like goat meat, or llama."

I told him how I ordered chicken once and heard the squawks of it being killed in the back of the restaurant.

"That's when you know it's fresh," Alex said.

"I thought hard about becoming a vegetarian."

"Speaking of which, have you seen them?"

I was actually impressed that it had taken that long for Alex to ask. He wanted to know about John and Yoko, who lived two floors above us and were friends with my parents. John spent his days as far as I knew in a blue and white kimono, reading, making macrobiotic meals, watching TV, and looking after Sean, his son. Yoko worked downstairs on the first floor in her office, where she bought things: apartments, a couple of houses, two dairy farms with prize-winning cattle, one of which they would famously sell for $250,000.

"A few times, yes," I said.

"In the elevator?" he asked.

"Yes, and at a party."

"What did you talk about?"

"One time we talked about dysentery."

"Nice."

"He's been very interested in sailing actually. He wants to buy a boat."

"Did you tell him how you're king of the high seas?"

"Buddy did."

"You need to get out on a boat with him."

The thought had occurred to me. The Lennons had recently bought a house in Cold Spring Harbor. They'd taken trips down to Palm Beach too, Buddy told me. I'd been sailing since I was a kid visiting my grandparents in Maine.

"Did he say anything about Paul's arrest?"

"Didn't come up," I said.

"Interesting," Alex said.

Paul McCartney had recently flown to Japan for a tour and was flagged at customs for carrying seven ounces of pot. They put him in jail for nine days and he had to cancel his tour.

There were lots of angles to this, first the stupidity of carrying weed into Japan when you'd been busted for smuggling hash into Sweden and two other times for pot possession. Then there was the rumor a neighbor disclosed semiseriously that Yoko had cast a spell on Paul for the crime of booking her favorite hotel suite.

The saddest thing I read was a story of an unhinged Beatles fan turning up at a Miami airport reservations desk demanding a ticket to Tokyo so he could free Paul. True story. When they refused, he pulled a toy gun from the rucksack he'd packed for his trip and was shot dead by a security guard.

Alex hadn't heard about this.

"What was he going to do once he got to Japan?" he asked.

"Get Paul out of jail."

"That's so fucking sad, giving your life for someone you don't know."

"It's like war," I said.

"Yeah, I guess it is," he said. "Let's go get stoned."

We walked through Washington Square Park and then through the Village to Seventh

Avenue. You could smoke out in the open back then without fear of arrest, and there were shops where you could call in your order like at a delicatessen and pick up a wide assortment of buds from around the globe: Dutch, Afghani, Nigerian, Jamaican. Alex liked Colombian the best. Along the way we talked about how Buddy and I were spending our days.

"On the bright side it takes the pressure off you."

"How so?"

"In most families there's a black sheep, and everyone else is off the hook. It's like having a brilliant fucked-up older brother who swallows up all the attention."

There was truth in this I recognized.

"He'll be out of the woods soon enough," I said.

"That's for sure. People want him back on the air, I can tell you that."

"You want him back on because you know him."

"No. It's almost a cult thing, Anton. I think people like him even more now that he's gone. At least the people I know."

"We'll see," I said. "Did I tell you I might have a place to move in to?"

"Where."

"In the Dakota actually. On the ninth

floor. A writer we know wants to sublet it to me."

"That's the floor that smells weird."

"It doesn't smell that weird, but yes. It's like one of those old rooming houses for itinerant workers."

"Remember we used to play ghost up there with Rachel?"

"That's why I like it. It feels like leaving home, and still being there."

"I'll take it if you don't. My place is fucking scary at night. I swear I've heard people getting killed outside. I've called the cops three times in the last six months, I'd guess. What I'd do for a moat and some gargoyles and a big-ass iron gate."

Alex lived in Alphabet City, a Lower East Side neighborhood that was still a long time from turning, and made the worst parts of Amsterdam Avenue seem inviting. Whenever I visited, he had to drop a key down to the sidewalk from his fourth-floor window, and then I'd open the front door and walk up.

We stopped in at Joe Allen on Forty-Sixth Street to have drinks with acting friends of Alex's, a guy named Miles, his actress girlfriend Sophia, and then a friend of hers, Stephanie, who worked at the Helen Hayes Theater.

Joe Allen was a self-styled hangout for actors and theater-goers. The red-brick walls were covered with photos of stars like the Marx Brothers and Mae West, and posters of plays, primarily ones that bombed like *Via Galactica* and the musical version of *Breakfast at Tiffany's*.

"I know everyone tells you this, but your dad's my fucking hero," Miles said. Miles bartended part-time at the West End Café, where I had drunk nightly when I was in college.

"Not everyone," I said. "Thanks for saying that."

"Alex says you're going to get John Lennon and Paul McCartney to come on the new show."

"That's news to me."

"It's just an idea," Alex said.

"He doesn't have a show yet."

"He will," Alex said.

"I'm not sure how long I'll be in New York," I said.

"I heard you have malaria," Sophia said.

"Don't worry," I said. "Most of the time it isn't contagious."

"He doesn't have it anymore."

"True, but the symptoms can come back at any moment over the next year."

"I had mono at Vassar," Sophia said.

"A requirement for her major," Miles said.

"It isn't funny," Sophia said. "I had to drop two classes."

"Is that why you're so thin?" Stephanie asked.

"That was the dysentery," I said.

"Yum," Alex said. "Anybody hungry?"

"Can I tell you my favorite all-time *Buddy Winter Show*?" Miles asked.

"Sure," I said.

People liked doing this around me, like arguing over their favorite *M*A*S*H* episode.

"It was the night he had Tennessee Williams on, in that big plaid suit and those big black-framed glasses. And they talked about the transatlantic trip he took with his grandparents."

"It was just his grandfather," I said.

Miles continued, "He had his first drink on the boat, he said, a mint julep, and it made him so sick he had to stay in his cabin for five days."

"Crème de menthe," I said. They hadn't splurged for first class and so his cabin was stuffy and small, with no porthole.

"Then he got better and took dancing lessons," Miles said. "He got the dance instructor in trouble with her boyfriend, right?"

"She wasn't teaching him," Alex said. "She just liked dancing with him. She'd been flirting earlier in the trip with the captain. I even remember his name, Captain DeVoe."

"Then he went to Paris and lost his mind," Miles said. "That was strange, wasn't it?"

It was the most intense and memorable part of the interview, but I didn't want a conversation right then about celebrity breakdowns, so I told Stephanie, "I love the Helen Hayes."

No lie there. It was one of those great old theaters with murals on each floor, and a terra-cotta façade outside with lots of turquoise, gold, and old ivory.

"We're doing *Strider,* a 'delightful horse operetta,' " she said.

"Excellent. There've been far too many sheep operettas lately."

"Exactly."

"What's it about?"

"What *isn't* it about? The star is a piebald gelding; it starts with them about to slash his throat, and then we go back in time and watch him go from a carefree foal to a living ruin in the dewy meadow."

"Who wrote it?"

"Tolstoy."

"That guy has a future," Alex said.

"They're tearing it down," Stephanie said.

"Tearing what down?" I asked.

"The Helen Hayes."

"You didn't hear about this?" Alex said.

"No."

"They're putting up a monstrosity of a hotel. And it's not just the Helen Hayes. It's the Morosco and the Bijou. Just like I was telling you."

"We've been out protesting it," Stephanie said. "They say they'll build a huge theater at the hotel, but it'll be big and sterile like the Minskoff, where the audience is a mile away."

"Hate that shit," Alex said.

Eventually, once the bill was paid, Miles said, "We're going to Studio. You guys want to come?"

"Last time I was there I actually saw two people fucking on the balcony," Alex said.

"Only two people?" Sophia said.

"Remember Brandon Mayer from high school."

"Unfortunately."

"He's one of those guys who gets up on the speakers and dances all sexy."

I had been to Studio 54 a bunch of times with friends and once with my parents, who'd been dragged there by a movie director who was on the show. It was, if you never saw it, a fantasyland of pounding music, sexy models, shirtless bartender boy toys in creepy little gold shorts, moguls in Bill Blass suits, fashion designers, rock stars, Ralph Lauren preppies next to a guy in leather underwear and a dog collar, and an open flow of coke and amyl nitrate. The owners had weeks before been thrown in jail for tax evasion.

"Come on. You gotta go," Stephanie said. "It's so much fun."

"You go," Alex said. "I hate that fucking place."

"I think we'll pass," I said.

We walked uptown as a group.

"I hear you live in the Dakota," Stephanie said.

"When did you hear that?"

"Just now."

"I do."

"That building gives me the creeps."

"Why?"

"From *Rosemary's Baby* for one thing. And also all the soot, I mean it's so beautiful, but it always looked like a big haunted house to me."

"It actually is," I said.

"Anton, Stephanie wants to ask you about one of your neighbors," Miles said.

I braced for the inevitable John Lennon

inquiry. It was why I often avoided telling people where I lived.

But instead she asked, "Have you met Leonard Bernstein?"

"He's a friend of my parents'."

"Oh my god, what's he like?"

"He smokes a lot and has thick eyebrows. And he has an incredibly deep voice."

Miles asked, "Do you ever, I mean when you're in the elevator with him, just start singing, 'A boy like that, who'd kill your brother' . . . ?"

"Just once," I said.

" 'One of your own kind. *Stick* with your own kind!' "

I'd forgotten that Miles could sing. Sometimes it felt like everyone in New York other than me had a secret talent.

When we reached the crowds outside the velvet ropes of Studio, we let them go and said goodbye.

"It's like heaven's gate, isn't it," Alex said. "They should have another club across the street for those who can't get in."

"They could call it Consolations."

"Or Losers," Alex said. "Speaking of which, you didn't get her number, did you."

"Should I have?"

"Uh, yeah."

"You think she would have given it to me?" Alex looked at me semiastounded.

"You're so clueless sometimes, Winter, I wonder how you get through life."

On our walk uptown I told Alex how Buddy had asked me not to return to the Peace Corps and to stay here and help him get a new show.

"Well, yes. Of course."

"Why 'of course'?"

"Because *of course* that's what you're going to do. I know how you're seeing this, that you went away to make your own life, but you did and you will. You're writing a new ending for your father's career, so he doesn't spend the rest of his days living down the moment he walked offstage. *Fuck,* if you don't help him I will. I'd love to be Buddy Winter's right-hand man. I'd put everything aside right now to do it."

"No you wouldn't."

"If I were you I would."

"Okay then," I said.

We went and saw the Dead Boys at Hurrah's on West Sixty-Second. The lead singer's finger was cut open somehow and he kept playing in the spot where it was cut, and he began to bleed onto his shirt and eventually the blood splattered his face.

I wanted him to stop bleeding and at the same time there was something intoxicating about all the blood.

"He's going to pass out soon," Alex said. "He'll spend the night in the hospital."

But he didn't pass out, though someone in the audience did, and there was an ambulance that pulled up outside the club to take her away.

The pills Alex had us take kicked in within ten minutes of our being there. My heart raced and the walls squeezed in. I had a flash of being back in Africa in my sweltering room at the clinic; of my calling out for help and no one hearing and being sure I would die.

I still didn't feel completely right and wasn't sure I ever would.

Alex and I worked ourselves into sweaty messes on the dance floor, which was crowded with punks. A girl with heavy black mascara and torn fishnet stockings grabbed my ass at one point, and when I turned to look at her, she said, "Don't say a fucking word, just keep doing what you're doing."

And then she danced to another part of the room.

As we were leaving, Alex said, "Stay in New York. Whatever was left undone down there, you're needed here now."

He was right, I thought, for now anyway. I wanted to be here, and to help my family in whatever way I could, and for all I'd miss out on, I wanted not to be on death's door and sweating again under a mosquito net. It was a relief to have figured this out.

5

A few nights later I hung out at the Oak Bar in the Plaza Hotel, with an old girl-friend, Claudia, the daughter of Buddy's ex–best friend and agent, Harry Abrams. I wanted to see her, and to ask about her dad, whom I missed. One of the first orders of business in getting Buddy back on the air, I knew, was somehow finding peace with Harry.

I arrived first and corralled two seats at the bar.

The room was stocked with bankers and young advertising types just out of work and a few well-heeled stodgy folks likely heading soon to the opera, and I caught snippets of conversations on firings and hirings, a boss who got his secretary pregnant. The man seated to my right asked the bartender to guess how many times he'd gotten laid in the last month.

"Four?" the bartender guessed.

"Zero," the man said, "but that's why I love you."

Claudia, after she sighed and fretted about her workday, seemed pleased to see me, if concerned about my health. I reassured her as she assessed my arms and face like a doctor might before drawing blood.

"You look like Anton's sick twin," she said.

"You should have seen me three weeks ago."

"I'm glad I didn't."

We had Bombay martinis and ordered the fried shrimp and caught each other up, on her work for a housing advocacy group and my time in Africa. I told her I was looking for a job but had little clue what I wanted to do with my life.

"How sick were you?"

"They'd just picked out my headstone," I said.

"Seriously?"

"I didn't just have malaria. I had amoebic dysentery too. I had some wild hallucinations, and I felt incredibly weak."

"You poor thing. And what's it like being back here? New York must seem strange to you after a year down there."

"Like Mars," I said.

"Where are you living these days?"

"Back home, for now."

"How is it?"

"I like having a well-stocked refrigerator," I said.

I told her about my plan to move up to the ninth floor, and how it was like one of those old rooming houses for temporary workers.

"It's like a reverse *Upstairs Downstairs*," she said.

"Yes, I'm one of the footmen," I said.

She smiled in a way I couldn't read.

"You're still somewhat good looking," she said, which was the way we used to talk to each other *(That wasn't the worst kiss I've ever received. You don't look terrible in the moonlight).*

"What's your lawyer like?" I asked.

She laughed. "That's funny."

"What?"

"You asking about my lawyer, and not my boyfriend."

"Your lawyer boyfriend?"

"He's good," she said, and then moved her finger on the bar, as though smoothing out a crease. "He's smart. I'm just not always sure we have enough to talk about. He talks about sports. He talks about money. He complains about the dirt and crime in the city. He thinks Carter is an ass, but he thinks Kennedy is just as bad."

"And you?"

"I like Kennedy. Your mom's working for him, isn't she?"

"Yes."

"My mother told me about it. She said it's her third Kennedy, and there was something about that I found so *sad*. I mean, don't you worry a little that if things go well, I mean if he wins the nomination, that something might *happen*."

"You mean he'll get shot."

"Well, yes."

"He won't," I said, though I thought the same thing.

I asked about her older sister, and her nieces who we'd babysat for once. She said they'd watched *The Wizard of Oz* together.

"You know what freaked me out?"

"What?"

"The flying monkeys."

"Nasty fuckers. I used to have nightmares about them."

"That and the cyclone."

"They made that with a stocking," I said.

"What do you mean?"

"The special effects man had a brainstorm. He strung up a woman's stocking and twirled it around with a fan and, presto, a cyclone."

I told her I knew this because I'd met

Mervyn LeRoy once at a party. He told me other things, how the munchkins all lived in a hotel in Culver City, and how they went wild every night, like salesmen at a convention. There were fights and munchkin orgies, and the cops had to rush in almost nightly to keep them from killing one another.

"Are you seeing anyone?"

"Nah."

"That's hard to believe, I mean someone who knows all you do about munchkin orgies."

"I've never actually been in one," I said. "Or not while sober."

Then I did something that surprised me. I put my hand on her leg. She took it in her hand and started stroking my wrist. I had a sudden deep desire to spend the night with Claudia Abrams and to wake up in her arms. Flirting with an old girlfriend who'd moved on to someone else had the effect of making me feel lonely.

"You're really so *thin,*" she said.

"I know. I'm trying to eat as much as I can, but so far it's not working."

I downed my martini and motioned to the bartender. When he looked my way, I tapped my glass and motioned to Claudia's.

He brought us new cocktails and whisked

away the shrimp plate.

She looked down at her watch. "I really should be going," she said, but she'd inched closer to me.

"I love this place," she said.

"You know they shot a scene in *North by Northwest* here."

"Really?"

"That scene near the beginning where Cary Grant has drinks with friends and then he's called out of the room for a phone call. The bad guys page Roger Thornhill, and he walks by them. They think he's their man and they kidnap him. That happened right here in this room."

"You told me that last time we were here," she said.

"No, I didn't."

"But you did. You said that you were thinking of having yourself paged."

I remembered.

"I went and rented the movie the next night," she said.

She was meeting the lawyer boyfriend at a bar on the Upper East Side where he'd been out with friends.

"Walk with me," she said.

"All right."

We walked over to Madison, then up

through the Sixties on our way to Seventy-Fourth Street. On the way we passed a bus shelter with an ad for Fortunoff with Lauren Bacall and the caption beneath: *If you find me drowning in water pearls, don't rescue me.*

"I kind of hate the East Side," she said.

"Why do you live here then?"

"Because Bruce lives here and he had the nicer place. But I miss living on the West Side. Good thing is I work there."

"How's your father?"

She paused.

"He's good," she said. "He has other clients than Buddy, you know."

"I know. He's the best around."

"Buddy was a shit to him."

"I know. He feels awful about it."

"No, he doesn't."

"He actually does. And he's better now. He needs your dad."

"Good luck with that."

"He's that pissed off?"

"Buddy blamed the whole thing on my father. He told him he was always jealous from the first time they met, and that agents were all parasites."

"Oh god."

"I know."

"He doesn't think that anymore."

She nodded.

"He wants to make amends."

"You know I saw him perform one night when you were gone."

"Where?"

"At Catch a Rising Star. Bruce loves those comedy clubs. Anyway, the MC said, 'We have an extra special guest tonight, a star of television and film,' and the extra special guest was Buddy. I tried to say hi to him when he passed our table, but I'm not sure he recognized me. The whole routine was about his breakdown and then his travels. The room was uncomfortable at first, because it wasn't like a normal bit. . . . It wasn't what I expected at all. It was actually really moving, and funny when you wouldn't think it should have been. Everyone in the room felt sort of weirdly close to him, and honored that he'd shared stuff with us. It was so personal, you know? I don't think Bruce really got it. But he misses a lot of things. That's another story, though."

We'd reached the bar then. Bruce the lawyer spotted her in the doorway and motioned Claudia over.

"You want to meet my man?"

"Nah, that's okay," I said.

"Good looking, isn't he?"

"His shirt looks very crisp," I said, because it did.

I waved hello, then I left and walked across the empty park toward the Dakota, wondering along the way why I hadn't heard any of the intimate material my father had chosen to share with a room full of strangers.

6

In his years atop the talk-show world, Buddy was inaccessible from breakfast until he arrived home at night, which was the reason in high school I begged my way onto the set. It was the only way, I figured out, to spend time with him.

We were one of those families like the Osmonds and the Bradys and Chastity Bono who grew up on America's television screens, appearing in silly skits on Buddy's show at one age, then reappearing playing instruments at another. By the time I was sixteen, I was doing odd jobs and chores like stocking the green room with drinks and food, and at some point I began doing pre-interviews of guests and writing up notes for the host. It must have looked amateurish at first, a kid doing a grown-up's job. But it came pretty easily to me, and soon they stopped seeing me as the boss's kid, and more as someone there to make their lives easier. I'd bring my home-work to the set, and I was likely the only high school junior who discussed his World War II paper with George C. Scott, and his biology midterm with James Watson.

Buddy had limited time to be a dad on set. And to ensure I'd fit in, he asked that I call him Buddy at work and Dad at home. I got so used to it that I'd slip and call him Buddy at home and he didn't notice the dif-ference.

The studio was a classic old Broadway theater on Forty-Ninth Street, where *Guys and Dolls* played for years, and *The Odd Couple* after that. I loved the staged inti-macy of the set, how a few armchairs, a strip of carpet, and a table with a lamp could look like your living room, and yet just beyond view were the cameras and booms and the tiers of lights, and across the stage the five-piece Buddy Winter Show Band, led by the Cherokee bluesman Lester John Woods.

And Buddy Winter sitting cross-legged, outwardly poised while his thoughts moved at warp speed. He'd nod attentively while in that instant weighing whether to change the subject or if there was still time in the segment to start something new. I could read his thoughts when guests prattled on too long. He'd be smiling with interest, but dying inside, because with less than a minute to break, his guest was just *getting going,* and if Buddy didn't interrupt he'd have to push into the next segment, which would stress out the next guest whose time would be shortened and who we had to pull strings to get on the show, and yet there was one last thing he *had* to ask his rambler to make the segment work, and, well, you get the idea.

To the naked eye it looked painless and easy, and often it was, but on some nights it was like cooking blindfolded, he liked to say. Instincts and memory saved you from a nasty burn.

You couldn't spout clichés on *The Buddy Winter Show* or be too scripted, or too safe; that was a different audience. Our viewership was notoriously smart and current, a prized demographic for sellers of upscale alcohol, cars, and clothes. The guests were the wild card of course, which was both the magic of it and what caused problems — ones who came in drunk, or tired, or medicated, or manic, or, in the case of Shelley Winters, all of the above. On a few nights, it felt like you'd closed down the bar with my father (imagine him wiping the bar) and, say, Lauren Bacall as she excoriated Frank Sinatra, who romanced her after Bogart died, and eventually proposed but told her, she said, not to tell anyone. At a black-tie event she told a friend in confidence, who managed to whisper it to Swifty Lazar, who that night wrote about it in the *Examiner.* She called Sinatra after the story ran, and he told her what was done was done, but they'd have to "lay low" for the time being.

"It's like you robbed a bank."

"In his eyes I had."

"Then what happened?" Buddy said.

"Oh," she said. "Well, he never spoke to me again after that."

Someone gasped. Lester, I think.

"He'll get his," Buddy said. "Time wounds all heels."

Nearly every night something notable happened: brawls between guests, actors breaking out in song, astounding exhibitions of magic and sword swallowing, and Ping-Pong playing; politicians, sport stars, musicians, and revolutionaries; and once a guest actually died on stage during the commercial break of an unwitnessed cardiac arrest, and that show never aired, and is something that haunted us both, how someone entirely alive one minute could be gone the next.

■ ■ ■ ■

The breakdown was simmering for a long while. We just didn't see it right away. He started to get agitated over small things, couldn't let them go, and around the house he was restless. And he got weirdly upset on the tennis court. He accused his opponents of cheating on meaningless points. And he accused all of us of undercutting him, or insulting him in conversations, when we mostly were having trouble following his thoughts.

It was stress, he said. He'd be better.

Later he would say it was like bad weather in that you couldn't plan for it or keep it from happening. You could have a month of clear days and then two months of storms. He'd had two months of storms leading up to the day he walked out on his show.

He'd started getting into it with guests. At first it was overlooked, because he was responding with his sharp wit, and one critic said it was thrilling to see Buddy Winter laying into the most coddled of movie stars and rock stars, and pampered politicians. I thought he looked like a bully, which he'd never ever been. He started drifting in conversations. Not everyone would notice this but I did. I prepped him the same as always, but he started going off script, and baiting good people into pointless disagreements. A comic sued him for stealing his material, a solid but unmemorable joke about a blackout looter breaking in to Alexander's and finding nothing worth taking. While the case went nowhere — the guy told a joke once about a discerning criminal — Buddy seethed at having to hear accusations of his piracy from tabloid reporters, and a tuxedoed stranger who called him a thief from the window of a passing cab.

Then there was the Leona Helmsley joke that fell worse than flat. He'd always poked fun at the letters that ran as ads in the *Times Magazine,* supposedly penned by the hotel queen.

He said in his monologue one night to my horror that "it's too bad the Son of Sam didn't gun down old Leona instead of one of these young kids. I'd write the letter for that one."

Overnight he'd replaced his signature charm and grace with something mordant and mean, and audiences were confused and then put off. On what would be his final show, he actually slept in late. One of the guests canceled. He scrambled to find someone to fill in. When his monologue found silence and even a buzz of disfavor among his audience, he looked just over their heads, said "What the fuck am I doing here?" and walked offstage, through the theater and out the front doorway. And then he left town.

We heard from him only sporadically over the next three weeks from various hotels and motels and bars and gas stations. Then he was at some kind of meditation place in northern California, and then he was picking fruit, then he was tending bar in Oregon, and then for a while there was nothing other than a postcard saying he loved us and hoped we were okay.

And then at the three-month point we heard from him a lot, and his trip became something else — a quest for experience, a journey to a deeper state of understanding. "A pretty bow on a nasty box of shit," my sister, Rachel, called it. I took it as a personal betrayal, and as a sort of theft. Someone from another galaxy had seized the brain and body of my brilliant father and made him into something unrecognizable and detestable.

It took a while for me not to feel that way about him.

On the sort of early February day that had

become our routine, Buddy and I went down to Ellis Island, and afterward up to the Stock Exchange and Federal Hall. And then we went to Windows on the World for lunch, all these things my father in his enlivened spirit said a real New Yorker needs to do. We walked over the Brooklyn Bridge, which in my postmalarial state exhausted me and which I hadn't done since I was six, and we rode the subway later up to Grant's Tomb. Every day we explored somewhere new.

One morning at breakfast he asked me, "What happens when we run out of places?"

"Then we both get jobs," I said.

"That's the saddest thing I've ever heard," he said.

Unless we work together, I thought surprisingly.

7

The best adventure was the one he dreamt up for the four of us, a trip to Lake Placid for the Winter Olympic Games. "They don't call them the Winter Games for nothing," he said. He bought event tickets and booked rooms, and along with all the fun we'd have going to events, our thought was of the network types we might run into, with Buddy looking new again, blood in his cheeks, snow in his hair. I imagined the mountain air, and the buzz of the games and us having cocktails with the right person somewhere, and their hearing my father's silvery voice, and seeing the glint in his eye and thinking, There's no one out there like this guy, not even close.

The drive up I-87 to Lake Placid in our '63 Mercedes took seven hours. We left the city at two and drove in the dark much of the way. I love riding in a car at night, and it reminded me of earlier car trips, when we played word games like Botticelli and stinky pinky, and listened to the radio (everyone singing to "Me and Julio Down by the Schoolyard"), or the reassuring sound of my parents' voices, and we'd stop at the sort of restaurants we'd never go to normally as a family, like the one outside of Albany we stopped at on this night for dinner, a family-style place called Hugo's.

A man with a waxed mustache named Hugo came by each table to drop off menus and to chat. "You look like Olympic athletes," he said to me and Kip.

"What makes you think they aren't?" Buddy said.

My mother had bought us new arctic blue ski parkas for the occasion and felt-lined boots to tromp around in, and with his face reddened from the cold, Kip could pass for one. I was too malnourished still.

"We're in the two-man luge," Kip said.

"Ah," Hugo said, "that's where the money is, isn't it?"

"And the groupies," Buddy said.

We ordered our meals. Everyone but Kip drank beer, though Kip had several sips of mine.

Buddy prepared for the games as if he might be asked to fill in alongside Jim McKay. There weren't enough buses the first few days, he told us, and people suffered frostbite waiting in the cold. And for weeks before the games there'd been almost no snow. It was the first Winter Olympics to be skied and sledded on primarily artificial snow. Phil Mahre, our shot at a medal in the Alpine skiing races, had dazzled in practice runs, and our best bobsled runner, Willie Davenport, a famous hurdler, had trained at the sport less than a year and sidelined as a big-money blackjack player.

"But the big story is Heiden," Buddy said.

Eric Heiden was the American speed-skating phenomenon.

"Thighs like trees," Kip said.

"Like oak trees, yes, interesting back story too."

It was a line we all used, initiated by Buddy. We'd mention someone, and then we'd say, "Interesting back story too." We'd say it about people on the subway, or a waiter, or a bartender. Heiden was from Madison, Wisconsin, and a world-renowned road cyclist as well. He was handsome and cereal-box wholesome. His sister was also an Olympic skater. He wouldn't win just one gold, Buddy said, he'd win five.

"You heard about the figure skaters," Hugo said as he served us our dinners, a honking brick of lasagna for me and Kip, and a garlicky chicken parmesan for our parents.

"Yes," my mother said and sighed.

The American figure skating team, Tai Babilonia and Randy Gardner, who'd been a cinch to win at least the silver, had dropped out of the competition. Gardner fell twice on simple jumps.

We'd heard the news on our drive up. Gardner, they'd said, had pulled his groin a week before the competition.

"They shot him up with lidocaine to get him through," Hugo said. "Think of all that training, all those hours in the rink leading up to this moment, and then *splat,* nothing."

The television, mounted in the corner of the diner, had showed a slow-motion replay of Gardner falling when we first sat down.

"Imagine," Buddy said, "breaking down like that, and on national television."

It had begun to snow outside the window, a welcome sight. With artificial snow the flakes were actually different, Kip said.

"I call bullshit," I said.

"No, seriously," Kip said. "Machine-made snow is crystalized water, and they're all the same round shape."

"Snowball clones," Buddy said.

I'd seen the portable hoses at ski places

blasting out snow like an oil gusher.

"Real snowflakes are hexagonal and no two are exactly alike," Kip said.

"Like fingerprints," my mother said. "How lovely."

In our room at the Mountain Home Inn that night we ate fresh-baked chocolate chip cookies the desk clerk gave us and watched the nightly recap of the games on ABC. Our parents had a room next door and they came into ours to watch our TV. We could hear the sounds of a raucous party going on in the lounge downstairs.

"A sleepy village no longer," Buddy said.

We watched Heiden, decked in gold, sprint past the Russian, Yevgeny Kulikov, in the 500 meter race. Kulikov skidded slightly at one point and Heiden sprang past him as though launched by a slingshot.

Keith Jackson interviewed him afterward, and in his rainbow-striped wool hat (a gift from his Norwegian girlfriend, he'd later say) and shoulder-length hair, he appeared relaxed and preternaturally confident.

He's two years younger than me, I thought. *Motherfucker.*

I did this to myself back then, compared my accomplishments at twenty-three to those of spectacularly successful people

88

(Picasso at twenty-three was finishing his Blue Period; Mick Jagger was writing "19th Nervous Breakdown"; Joan of Arc had rescued France, been burned at the stake, and been dead for four years). I'd heard that Heiden wore nylon socks or no socks so he could have a more intimate feel for the ice. As a result, his feet bled. His ankles were bloody pulps after an event.

The wrap-up was followed by a fifteen-minute report on the hostage crisis, with Ted Koppel gravely opening the show, saying "Day 104, America Held Hostage."

Bearded young men in skullcaps crowded the streets in Tehran, swinging chains over their shoulders in symbolic self-flagellation. Others burned the American flag, or Uncle Sam in effigy. Kids as young as four or five wore shrouds and held up signs with pictures of the Ayatollah Khomeini. In the guise of news, they were broadcasting a victory parade.

We debated for a while which should go first, the Olympics or the hostages.

"Hostages definitely second," Buddy said. "Otherwise you've got too much guilt watching people bobsledding and skiing and kissing their medals. You'd be thinking, That's nice for *you.* But when fifty people are blindfolded and tied to radiators, do we

89

really care about a perfect double axel?"

"But wouldn't it be nice to go to bed hopeful?" my mother asked.

The news that night was actually more hopeful than usual. The hostages could be released as early as the following week, according to U.N. Secretary-General Kurt Waldheim.

"Don't count on it," Buddy said. "They'll want us to serve the Shah up on a skewer and we're not yet ready to do that."

Kip and I stayed up late watching a slasher movie with Clint Eastwood playing an easy-listening DJ terrorized by a crazy fan. The woman, whose name was Evelyn, kept turning up at Clint Eastwood's house, or at a restaurant when he was out having a business lunch with his boss.

"She reminds me of the hand-puppet lady," Kip said.

"My god yes," I said.

Buddy had a stalker who insisted on talking to him through a hand puppet, which vaguely resembled the stalker and would say she loved Buddy and wanted a kiss. Buddy thought it was creepy but a little funny at first, and one time he kissed the puppet, and the woman made a motion with her hand like her puppet was swooning.

A month later she turned up with a second

puppet that looked and dressed like Buddy and asked him to wear it and go for a walk with her to the Central Park boat pond. When he declined the puppet yelled at him, Buddy told us later, and wouldn't stop until the doorman intervened and told her to move on or he'd call the police.

The puppet kept protesting in a high-pitched puppet voice, "But I *love* you, Buddy Winter. I love you!"

Buddy rose at five the next morning and went for a long walk in the falling snow, then came back and meditated in the empty hotel lounge (lotus position, jeans, barefoot). Then he read the *Times* front to back, and when I ran into him it was at breakfast next door to our hotel, seated at the counter with Kip, who told me I'd been talking in my sleep again.

I guess I did this from time to time. A girlfriend in college once told me I'd said, *The door is broken.*

"What did I say?"

"Something like *Rindle bindle.* You were mumbling."

"You feeling okay, Anton?" Buddy asked.

"Of course," I said.

He slid to me a plate of linked sausages. I wolfed down two of them.

"You know what's wrong with all those highlights we watched last night," Buddy said. "Way too much about the Americans. And we're only a small part of this. In the next hour or so I want the two of you to have a list of five athletes from foreign countries that you're following closely. No Americans. Heiden and the U.S. hockey team have enough fans."

I'd already done that. I had around ten different participants I was interested in following, and only one American — Heiden, of course.

Buddy had circled in the paper two items he thought might interest us.

Kip was reading them first.

"Oh my god," Kip said. "John Denver shot a dog."

"Intentionally?" I asked.

"Kind of. It was digging through his garbage. Didn't kill him it looks like."

"It was only a BB gun," Buddy said. "But as any movie character knows, you can shoot who you like, just don't hurt the dog."

The other article was about Richard Nixon moving to an apartment in the East Sixties. He'd been spotted eating at Lüchow's and had sent a bottle of champagne over to a couple who had given him a piece of their anniversary cake.

"If that doesn't melt your heart, what will?" Buddy said.

We had decided to split up for much of the day. Buddy and my mother were planning to go snowshoeing in the acres of wilderness behind the resort then meet up with us at the biathlon at noon.

Buddy did a bit for us about the biathlon, which he said was the Olympic event most clearly designed for James Bond.

"Ski racing with a rifle strapped to your back, that's not a sport; it's *The Spy Who Loved Me.*"

They'd added two new stages this year, he said, martini mixing and high-stakes seduction.

I ate a Belgian waffle and drank some coffee. I had no desire to snowshoe and, really, for an hour or two I wanted a break from being Buddy's audience, and from Kip who kept hitting me with snowballs when I wasn't looking, and yelling, "*Nobody* expects the Spanish Inquisition!"

By my lonesome I toured the exhibits and displays of the Olympic Village ("Welcome World, We're Ready") thinking of where I'd just been. You could hardly journey farther from equatorial Africa than this — not just the single-digit temperatures and snow and all those colorful parkas from Austria and Japan and the Netherlands and Canada, but the blizzard of money and world attention.

The Africa I lived in was away from the postcolonial power grabs, and machine-gun-toting child armies, and overcrowded relief camps you read about, and nor was it a land of verdant jungle, with me in the back of a jeep. It was spare and hot and dusty, and filled with challenges, and moments where you felt you were doing God's work. We spent our first two months in training, learning French, and acclimating ourselves, and learning to live a stripped-down existence. I should also have had a month or two to train for my return, to get used to people with first-world needs.

I bought an Olympic postcard to send to Gauthier, a teacher who'd been my comic sidekick and best Gabonese friend. It had a picture of a raccoon wearing ski goggles, with a bandanna around his neck.

Here the locals embraced their transformation. They'd "dropped off their flannel shirts and exchanged them for a little Bill Blass," one of the TV reporters said, and it was true. The stationery and hardware stores had cleared out for ones selling designer skiwear and Revillon furs. A lot of locals had rented out their homes; a Texas oil executive leased the biggest one in town for the week for $50,000.

And every fifth person it seemed was someone we knew from New York, and plenty from the TV world.

"Anton," they'd call out, and then they'd ask about Buddy, and I'd tell them how great he was doing, and how he looked forward to getting back to work.

"Late night hasn't been the same," they'd tell me in one form or another.

"It will be again," I said, feigning confidence, and making mental notes on who to call when the time came.

Elliot Kaplan, the producer who'd been testing the waters for Buddy's reemergence, was working the games for ABC Sports, and would be at the U.S.–Norway hockey game for which Kip and I had tickets. Buddy arranged for us to meet up in the second-period break.

"He wants to talk about cable, he says. I know nothing about cable," Buddy said.

"It's the future," I said. "I'll report back at 0600."

"All right, captain."

The game would take place in the old Olympic Arena, where Sonja Henie won her skating medals in 1932 and which was the size of a midwestern high school gym. A weirdly small venue to host what had become the talk of the games — hockey, and specifically the U.S. team, who with a roster of college kids had already managed to tie the Swedes and rout the powerhouse Czechs 7–3, which Buddy likened to St. John's basketball team taking down the Knicks.

As we entered the arena, chants of "USA! USA!" began all around us. People wore USA hats and scarves and T-shirts and carried flags. Quite a few had their faces painted red, white, and blue.

"Nuke the Nords," someone yelled.

"Throw 'em in the sauna," said someone else.

"What if I root for Norway?" Kip said.

"Why would you?"

"Because *someone* has to. And it's an incredibly beautiful country, Mom says. More than a thousand fjords."

"All right, but if they take the lead you have to switch back."

"Geir Myhre is the best!" he yelled.

"Yes!" a pretty Norwegian girl yelled back. She looked college-age and had a friend with her. The two of them gave Kip a thumbs-up.

"Who's that?" I asked.

"Norway's best player. Right winger, born

in Oslo."

"You read up. Dad would be proud."

The game started sloppily. Missed passes, clunky skating. The Norwegians outplayed the U.S. throughout the first period and led 1–0. Geir Myhre in fact scored the goal, their only one of the game. Kip waved over to the Norwegian girls, who were seated around five rows up, and they waved enthusiastically back.

"I want to move to Norway," he said into my ear.

"What would you do there?"

"Norwegian things."

"Reindeer racing," I said.

"They have reindeer?"

"Of course," I said. "It's where Santa goes to recruit."

Mike Eruzione scored within the first forty-five seconds of the next period, then it all caved in for the Norwegians. The U.S. scored three times in the second, then twice more in the third, and our goalie, Jim Craig, shut them down.

Between periods, I walked up to the press box to visit with Elliot. Kip ran into a friend from school and went wandering around the T-shirt stands and food vendors.

We sat in empty seats watching the Zamboni machine shine the dulled ice.

"In some ways it's better that I get to talk with you first, Anton," Elliot said. "How long were you in Ghana?"

"Gabon. A year."

He glanced at the other journalists around him, scribbling notes and filing by phone partial game reports.

"You want to take a walk?"

"Sure," I said. We walked in a loop around souvenir and refreshment stands.

We bought slices of flavorless pizza and grabbed a table. He told me of all the colleagues and friends who'd never gotten over the end of Buddy's show, how they'd all tune in the moment he reemerged, and that to make that happen, "we just need to think outside the box."

"In what sense?" I asked.

"You're courting the networks, right? Because anything else would be a step backward. Buddy Winter on cable? That's like Ali in a pro wrestling ring, right? Wrong, Anton. Cable is the new frontier, the Wild West. It's exploding."

I nodded because I had read as much.

"For instance, Bill Rasmussen, gets fired by the New England Whalers? He gets Getty Oil to kick in money and five months ago he starts a sports network he calls ESPN. This spring they're carrying the NCAA basketball tournament, and their sponsor is a little beer company named Budweiser. Ted Turner puts broadcasts of his local UHF station TBS out of Atlanta on the RCA satellites, and *bingo* — he's got the first national superstation. Now there are dozens of these — a lot of them are religious. Ever seen the PTL station? There's also the Trinity network and the Christian Broadcasting system."

"I'm mesmerized by those."

"Amazing, huh. No dressing for church anymore, the Lord comes to your bedroom via cable satellite. Turner's new venture is twenty-four-hour news. It'll launch this summer. You wake up at three in the morning and you want to know what's going on in Dubrovnik? Now you can. It won't have any competition. Eventually the networks might have their own cable companies — but for certain there'll be more programming — *a lot* more. You heard of *PopClips*? Brainchild of the Monkees' Mike Nesmith, short videos of pop songs and news about music. Soon there'll be a fashion channel, a food channel, a yoga channel for all I know. Niche programming is the wave of the future."

"And someone will make money on this?"

"Everyone will. Here's how it works. You get everything for free now but you have no choices. Cable is made up of subscriptions. A program on prime time that fetches twenty million viewers you call a failure. It gets you canceled, but on cable if you have, say, five million subscribers paying two dollars apiece for a show, that's ten million dollars in revenue right there."

He threw some more numbers and stories at me, and told me the networks were yesterday's news, and not to worry if the big three froze us out.

"You think they'll freeze us out?"

"I don't actually. But you might be better off without them."

His optimism was infectious, and I thought of the shows Robert Klein had done on HBO, which were hilarious and uncensored.

"I have to get back to hockey now, Anton, but look around and talk to people, and I will too, and we'll meet up in a month or so when I have less on my plate and see where we are. Sound good?"

"It does."

"Is that your brother?"

Kip was walking our way with what looked like a rolled-up poster.

"What have you been feeding him? He was a little guy like yesterday, and now he's my height for chrissakes."

"I bought a U.S. bobsled poster," Kip said.

"Seriously? That's too cool," Elliot said. "I'll give you ten bucks for it."

"No way," Kip said. "It's going up on my wall."

I called Rachel that afternoon from the room, to razz her about not being up here with us. Rachel taught tenth-grade English at Coolidge, an all-boys school, and was spending the weekend grading papers. She asked how much money we'd spent.

"Not an exorbitant amount," I said.

"You're lying."

"I might be."

"How much are the rooms?"

"A hundred and fifty I think."

"For both?"

"Each."

Silence on her end.

"And I bet you're not eating Big Macs either."

"Nope," I said, and then quoting Buddy, "but how many times will we have the Olympians on our doorstep? At least we didn't spend anything on airfare."

"Classic Dad. At least I didn't buy a *mountain.*"

"So listen. I agree with you, but the point was for all of us to be together and have some fun, and you're the one who isn't here. You'd get it if you were here."

"I'm sorry," she said.

"We miss you."

"Did you see Eric Heiden?"

"We did."

"Total babe."

"He's four years younger than you."

"I'm taken, Anton."

"By who?"

"Randy."

"The cop? I thought he had a girlfriend."

About a month before, Rachel's neighbor on her floor had been burglarized and Rachel developed a crush on one of the officers investigating the break-in. He was smart and "soulful," she said, had gone to NYU, and was taking a screenwriting course at night.

Twice he'd gone back to ask her follow-up questions and the conversation had gone off topic for at least an hour both times. Then he'd actually caught the thief and returned most of the missing items to Rachel's neighbor.

"That ended."

"Well, look at you." And then because I couldn't resist, I asked, "Has he handcuffed you yet?"

"No, and nor have I touched his gun."

"Yuck," I said.

"Anton?"

"Yes."

"Don't get sucked in again."

"What do you mean?"

"You know exactly what I mean. Shall I quote you on all the reasons you needed to get the hell out of Dodge?"

"That's all right."

As a girl Rachel loved a movie from the 1940s, *National Velvet,* in part because the story revolved around the daughter, Velvet, and *her* dream above all others. The father was a kind and watchful butcher, whose worst act of irresponsibility was to bet on a horse race.

"If you leave right now, you can still make the end of the party we're going to," I said.

"Have fun," she said.

"Oh, we will," I said. "You'll read about us in the paper."

8

That night, the well-heeled and well-connected (aka the Winters) attended a black-tie party thrown at the Lake Placid Resort Hotel by an East Side socialite named Marylou Whitney. We arrived there by horse and carriage; other guests came by dogsled. I borrowed a tux from Buddy. I tried talking Kip into coming along but he met up instead with some high school friends, one of whom claimed he could get them into the athletes' village.

Buddy and my mother polished off a round or two of vodka gimlets in the room, and on the way over were holding hands and singing dirty limericks, a weakness of theirs. It was around 8 degrees out and snowing.

"Therrrre was a young man named Mc-Nair," Buddy sang.

"—Who was bonking a girl on the stairs," my mother chimed in.

"He petted and stroked and the bannister broke."

"— So he finished her off in the aaa*air*," she sang.

Then to my regret they sang a chorus, "Roll your leg o-o-over, roll your leg o-o-over, roll your leg over the girl in your bed!"

My father sniffed at my mother's neck as though it were a rose. She kissed him.

I don't know how many parents acted like this, but I was glad mine did. On good nights they were like characters in *The Thin Man* movies they both loved. When, once in a blue moon, they fought, it was scary, in the way arguments can be between smart people who know exactly how to hurt each other.

In the Lake Room at the resort there were fortune-tellers in Styrofoam igloos, and the room was festooned with silver snowflakes and cellophane icicles. An athletic-looking Santa Claus handed out gifts, Olympic necklaces for the women, and Olympic cuff links for the men.

The Lester Lanin orchestra played big band numbers like "It's De-Lovely" and "My Funny Valentine." Among the guests were princes and princesses, the Spanish ambassador to the Soviet Union, the French ambassador to the United States, the Italian ambassador to Germany, Canada's governor-general, Edward Schreyer, and his bejeweled wife, Lily.

I know all this because the hostess made a point of introducing Buddy and my mother to everyone.

They served what she heralded as a typical American buffet, with Virginia ham, roast beef, potato salad, coleslaw, and ice cream. Behind the table, servers dressed as Winter Warlock and the Abominable Snowman filled our glasses with champagne "direct from the Finger Lakes," they informed us.

"A blend of the sophisticated and the prepubescent," Buddy whispered to me.

I talked a while to a woman named Astrid, who was a Swedish Olympic attaché, while her husband danced with a woman I was told was a distant cousin of Teddy Roosevelt.

We talked about skiing. She told me about a resort in her country called Åre (pronounced "Aura"), which lacked the crowds of the Alps but was "just as nice." The summit could only be reached by snowmobile.

I tried as hard as I could not to look down her dress. I think I succeeded.

It was that kind of night.

Buddy was speaking with a man from Austria who'd won a bronze in the giant slalom at Grenoble about Ingemar Stenmark, and whether he was the best skier ever. Buddy made his case for Jean-Claude Killy.

"Let's float," my mother said, and we walked around together. I worried she might be searching the room for a young woman for me to talk to and was relieved to realize she just wanted to people-watch.

Terry Bradshaw cavorted alongside his figure skater wife, JoJo Starbuck, one of the glamour couples of the Olympics. He was weeks from winning the Super Bowl. I'd seen them earlier at the hockey game.

"My problem is I'm a hayseed. I don't get ballet. I get square dancing," he said. "We're like the *Green Acres* couple."

"He wants me to quit skating," she said. "And I won't."

"I admit it. I'm a male chauvinist pig. Cooshawn. Is that how you say it?"

He tried to feed her an hors d'oeuvre. She took it from his hand and placed it on the table behind her.

"I love your skating, sweetheart. That's why we're here."

They kissed.

"Aw, *lovebirds*," the woman who'd been

talking to them said.

"A couple in deep trouble," my mother said when we were out of earshot.

We worked the crowd some, allowing Buddy to do the same, talking with various luminaries about the competitions we'd seen. My mother was pleased to find one of the event organizers with a Kennedy pin on his jacket. At one point she caught Buddy's eye and he raised his glass to us, and then we did the same to him.

"You guys seem good," I said.

"What a thing to say to one's mother. Of course we're *'good.'*"

"I'm saying you look happy."

"We're at the Olympics. Everyone's happy."

I told her of my conversations with Elliot Kaplan, his prediction that we'd soon get a shot at a new show, and my sense that Buddy was ready to work again.

She didn't answer.

"You disagree?"

"It depends on what *ready* means," she said. She tilted her head and looked away from my eyes to form her thought. "Here's the thing, Anton. . . . I love the way our home has felt lately."

"Me too."

"It's been different, *homier.* We watch TV

together, play Scrabble, read books, and the time he's spent with Kip has been transformative for both of them."

"He needs to work," I said. "He can't just retire and sit on his ass."

I was pushing too hard, I knew, but I needed her aboard on this.

"He's much better, yes, but he hasn't had the stress of preparing for a show every day, of having to be *on* for an hour straight. Who's to say we won't go through the same thing all over again?"

"We won't," I said.

"You know for certain."

"I know he'll go crazy staying at home."

She didn't answer.

"Poor word choice," I said.

"He's still figuring himself out, Anton. He *does* need to work, and lord knows we need the money, but if it doesn't happen immediately, we'll live."

She was trying to temper our expectations, and maybe her own.

On cue, Buddy made his way toward us from across the room.

"*Damn,* that man's handsome," she said.

"What are you two plotting?" he asked.

"I've decided you're too sexy for TV," she said.

"How many men has she said this to

tonight?"

"You're the third," I said.

"Could be worse. Dance? Or shall we have our fortunes read?"

"Fortune-tellers disturb me," my mother said.

"Then let's dance," Buddy said, and off they went.

The party's younger set gathered outside one of the fortune-telling igloos, drinking cocktails and smoking French cigarettes. I recognized a few of them, sons and daughters of people my parents knew, one guy I recognized from a sailing camp on Block Island when I was twelve.

"Your parents?" a girl my age asked.

"How could you tell?"

She wore a press lanyard around her neck.

"Because of how you're looking at them."

"How am I looking at them?"

"With concern, and affection, like you're praying they get home safe."

"You're British."

"How could you tell?"

"A hunch."

"Wasn't the accent?"

Her name was Olive Diop. I guessed one of her parents was from West Africa.

"BBC, huh?"

"Afraid so. Don't hold it against me."

"I've actually been following two of your athletes," I said.

"*My* athletes — have you."

"There's Konrad Bartelski."

"Born in the Netherlands, but yes, our greatest Alpine skier."

"And then Robin Cousins of course."

"You fancy a man in gold, do you?"

Cousins won gold in the men's figure skating competition.

"Did you cover it?"

"I'm not a sports reporter. I'm doing sidebar bits," she said. "I'm actually supposed to do a piece on this party," she said.

"I don't see a notebook."

"I already did my interviews," she said.

The igloo line had thinned. A woman in a gold evening gown walked out with a serene smile on her face.

"Good news?" I asked.

"The best," the woman answered. "I'm so relieved."

The fortune-teller poked her head out and caught my eye. "Enter the mystical igloo," she said.

She must have been in her late fifties and yet she had one of those unscathed faces that allowed you to see what she must have

111

looked like at seven. Like an aged child actress.

"You're going in there, aren't you?" Olive said.

"Did you?"

"Yes of course."

"What did she say?"

"Nothing really. She missed her mark a few times, so she just said 'This year will be better than last.' But other people said she was freakishly on target."

"All right then," I said.

The igloo carried the scent of incense, rich lady perfume, and some sort of plant, sage maybe.

"You watched the hockey game today," she said.

"That was an easy one."

"Lucky you. They're an exciting bunch."

I nodded.

"But there's more on your mind these days than hockey."

"Probably."

She studied the cards in front of her and breathed deeply.

"You are about to embark on a great adventure," she said.

"I think you have that backward," I said.

She paused and then closed her eyes as if

searching inward for a vision.

"No. I see something arriving soon. Something big. You have been very sick, is that correct?"

"You talked to my father."

"I've never met your father. Have you been sick?"

"Yes."

"And you nearly died."

"This is ridiculous."

"Your father has been sick as well."

"Yes," I said.

"With the same thing you were sick with."

Now I had her.

"No."

"Your father is very proud of you," she said.

"And me him," I said.

She tried to read my face.

"I believe it," she said.

"But I *am* proud of him."

"I'm seeing a storm of some sort."

"Here at the games?"

"Where you live. You live in . . . Chicago, is that right?"

"No," I said.

"Boston."

"No."

"New York."

"Yes."

"This year will be better than last year," she said.

"Here's hoping."

"Enjoy the Olympics," she said and then led me out of the igloo.

"Learn anything?" Olive Diop asked me.

"Can't say."

Just then a man also with a BBC lanyard came by and told Olive he was leaving.

I assumed that was my cue to head back to the hotel, but Olive stayed and the man left.

"Are you turning in?" she asked.

"I was."

"I've got something better," she said. She had dark brown eyes, and sexy creases around her mouth. Her hair was cut in a bob with side-swept bangs.

"What's that?"

"You like boxing? Heavyweights?"

"I love Muhammad Ali."

"Close," she said.

"What do you mean close?"

"You'll see."

We sat in the back lounge of the Whiteface Inn. Olive ordered us martinis, and beers, and a big bowl of mixed nuts.

I told her I'd been fortunate enough to attend the Ali–Frazier fight when Ali came out of retirement and Joe Frazier won in a decision. I was fourteen, and it was the most amazing thing I have ever witnessed before or since. We sat within shouting distance of Woody Allen, Frank Sinatra, and Norman Mailer, all of whom we knew.

In round 15, Frazier pounded Ali mercilessly, but couldn't manage to knock him out.

Ali never acknowledged he'd lost, even years later when he regained the title. But he lost that night. Frazier got destroyed two years later by George Foreman and lost two more spectacular fights with Ali. But I saw him at his greatest, and now here he was serenading the nightcap crowd at the Whiteface Inn.

The MC exclaimed, "Settle in, folks. In just a few minutes, straight from the streets of Beaufort, South Carolina, with a sweet voice to match his hellacious left hook, Smokin' Joe and the Knockouts will be taking the stage!"

"He won a gold medal in 1964, and now he's back and better than ever," Olive said.

"This is the best thing at the Olympics," I said.

"They're the only other brown faces in Lake Placid," she said, "besides your bob-sledder."

"So you live in London?"

"Guess again."

"Somewhere outside London."

"I live in New York."

"You cover the city."

"Lots of things."

"How long have you lived in New York?"

"Around three years. I went to Columbia for graduate school. My background — I'm half Irish, half Senegalese. I'm not in touch much with my Senegalese past. My father pretty much disappeared. My mum moved when I was four to London, and I was raised there."

"I lived in Gabon for a year."

"Peace Corps?"

"How'd you guess?"

"I have a confession to make. I knew who you were. And I know who your father is. I watched the show the last year it was on."

"So you saw what happened."

"I did."

"What did you think?"

"In all honesty? I thought A) it was incredible television. I mean great theater really. But B) I also thought how painful that must have been for him, for you, for your mum and your brother and sister."

"It was pretty messed up."

"I'm sorry. I'm getting too personal," she said.

"No problem," I said. "So you like the city."

"My mum is worried. You saw what's been happening? Six people have been pushed in front of trains. We did a segment on what they call stranger killings. There's been an epidemic. Someone called them Clockwork Orange Killings, but that's the wrong image. There's no fun in this stuff."

"When I was a kid I used to have my bus pass stolen every time it came out. And I carried at least ten dollars in my wallet in case I got mugged."

"They mugged the little white boy."

"They mugged black boys too I'm sure."

"Have you ever dated a black girl?"

"Yes."

"In Gabon."

"Yes. I'm not sure we officially dated. It was all pretty awkward. She liked me, I learned. I liked her. We had lunch together. Nothing came of it other than some giggling and awkwardness. I felt like that if I did anything I'd probably have to marry her."

"Why? Maybe she just wanted a good roll?"

"Maybe. Then I guess I missed my

chance."

"Indeed. Better not let that happen again."

Just then Joe Frazier came out to do a mic check. He wore a black silk jacket and a beautiful teal-colored tie.

Olive leaned in and loudly whispered, "In case you were wondering whether or not there were second acts in American life."

The former champ played his own version of "Mustang Sally," "Proud Mary," and then a killer version of "My Way."

His backup singers sang, "He's gonna do it his way. He's gonna do it his way. Go get 'em, Joe!"

Then Smokin' Joe took over:

"Prepare . . . to take the dare . . . it's time
    to climb . . . right through them ropes
    now.
"You face a man . . . who has a plan and
    stakes that plan . . . not in a shy way.
"Well that's his right . . . but come the
    fight . . . I'll fight him my way."

"He's good."

"Of course. He's a champion. What do you expect?"

On our way out, Olive said, "Anton. Isn't that your father over at the bar?"

It was, in fact, and with a small crowd around him, one of his impromptu Buddy Winter Shows.

"Anton, come over here," Buddy said.

Once I got over to the bar, he continued, "This is Terrance."

We shook hands.

"Terrance makes snow. He works those machines we were talking about. Without Terrance there are no games."

"I wouldn't go that far," Terrance said.

"No. What are the Winter Games without snow? I'll tell you what they are. They are the fall games, and no one will pay to watch Alpine events at the fall games."

"Snow is crucial," I said.

"I guess so," he said.

"Buddy, this is Olive Diop. She's from London."

"My regards to the queen," Terrance said.

"Pleasure," Buddy said.

"An honor," Olive said.

"And this is Willem. Willem is a rep for Rossignol skis. He says Oswald didn't shoot Kennedy. That he was shot from the grassy knoll."

Assassinations was one of our topics at home. Buddy knew a great deal about them and had held shows with ballistic discussions after both the Robert Kennedy and

MLK killings.

"Mom wanted to sit this one out?" I said.

"*Exhausted,* she said. I made the mistake of having an Irish coffee."

"They had the president's body altered to look like he was shot from behind, not from up front," Willem said.

"Of course," Buddy said.

"I just read an excellent article about it. They faked the autopsy photos and substituted them for real ones."

"When did they take the body?" I asked.

"The body, or the casket?" Willem asked.

"I suppose the body in the casket?"

"I'll head home then," Olive said.

"Shall I walk you?" I asked.

"No, stay," she said and flashed a lovely smile first toward me and then toward Buddy. "I think your father could use your assistance here."

"You listening?" Willem said.

"Yes," I said, and Olive left the bar.

"So here's the deal, the body was stolen from the casket right about the time they were swearing Johnson in as president in the front cabin of Air Force One. When they landed they rushed the body to Walter Reed, where it was altered surgically and they put the bogus X-rays together. And then they got it to Bethesda Naval Hospital and returned it to the original casket."

In the dark days Buddy would have lost his stack, not here. He smiled and simply said, "Is that really *plausible*?"

"Certainly. There were a lot of people in on this, not just one nouveau Muscovite in a hotel room."

"How could they possibly steal the body with Jackie and Lyndon Johnson and everyone else on the plane?"

"They had other things on their mind."

"Well, it's something to think about," Buddy said.

"Question," Terrance said. "You had Kennedy on your show, didn't you?"

"I had Bobby on during my first year."

"Sitting as close as me."

"Yes."

"Don't you miss it?"

"I'll be back," Buddy said. "I'm just on sabbatical."

We walked the frozen mile together back to our hotel, Buddy reveling in the clear mountain air and the view above of a thousand stars, and me unhappily realizing I'd failed to secure Olive Diop's phone number.

"You know if I had my druthers . . . ," Buddy said.

"Dad?" I asked. "What's a druther?"

We did this from time to time.

"No one knows," he said, smiling. "But you've got to have them. They're the secret to happiness. You could sell them. Come get your druthers!"

"Could I trade you a qualm for a druther?" I said.

"Bad deal. Druthers get you further than qualms."

"True."

"And you shouldn't have any qualms, Anton."

"I wouldn't," I said, "if I had my druthers."

When we got back to the Mountain Home Inn, Buddy came into the room with me. Kip was fast asleep with the TV on. Buddy moved Kip's hair aside and kissed him on the forehead, like he did to Rachel and me when we were little and pretending to be asleep, and I thought of my mother's concerns.

"He's snoring," I whispered.

"Said the boy who talks in his sleep," Buddy whispered back.

9

I moved up to the ninth floor the night we returned from Lake Placid. Robert Fielding left behind his pillows and linens, and all his glasses and dishes, and a liquor cabinet stocked with sophisticated booze: cognac, Pernod, ouzo, French aperitifs, Italian vermouth. He was a former *Esquire* writer (in the fifties) and had lived the sort of bachelor life the magazine scripted. There were photos of him interviewing famous subjects and off on exotic trips.

In the sitting room he had a nice braided rug from somewhere in Southeast Asia, a bronze and wood wall clock, and a couple of African masks, a lumpy couch, twin bookshelves lined with everything from *The Sun Also Rises* to *Fear of Flying,* a tiny stove and a mini-refrigerator, and oddly enough a bathtub near the window so you could lie back in sudsy water and look out at a slice of New York sky. It felt like the kind of place maintained by someone who traveled most of the year.

The ninth-floor hallways snaked around the four corners that comprised the building. One of my neighbors described the Dakota to me once as a square doughnut, the courtyard being the center. There were four separate elevator banks and separate lobbies on the corner of each floor. The people who lived up here traditionally were maids and cooks and other domestics, and the rumor was that several illustrious tenants kept mistresses in apartments like Fielding's, and I'm pretty sure the heart of the beautiful young woman who slipped in and out of the room up the hall from me belonged to someone in the lower seven.

A writer who a year earlier had published a history of our building called the residents on our floors the Leftovers — people who'd been left behind when the owners had moved away.

In the old days, men from the theater world lived up there, singers and actors. A guy named Jimmy Martin, who had sung and danced on Broadway (and whose eye was destroyed by an errant piece of scenery), worked as a valet for a downstairs tenant and stayed on "living in his armpit of an apartment," according to Fielding, out of the building's largesse, next door to a sick and elderly woman who decades ago had been a mistress to a famous opera star.

I really did feel far away from my family up there, though if I wanted I could be back at the breakfast table in five minutes.

Here's a line from Fielding's memoir, the pages of which I found on the bottom shelf of his desk: "I believe today I am a humble man because I have seen a hyena eat a lion carcass, and I have seen the buzzards eat the hyena that ate the lion."

It was about his trip to Tanganyika, which he said was going to a place of serenity, where he understood "what a small ant I was in the hill of life."

Or a line about his peripatetic existence: "I have been sick in more strange hotels than Ernie Pyle ever was."

When I began looking into the array of options Elliot described, it seemed that without an agent, I was fumbling in the dark.

So I rolled the dice and called Harry Abrams and told him what I'd heard.

"Well, sure," he said. "Someone'll take a chance on him. We're talking about Buddy Winter. A lot of important people watched that show religiously."

The very sound of his voice made me

nostalgic.

"So what's your plan?" he asked.

"We don't really have one. We need you back, Harry," I said. Then I fibbed, "Buddy really misses you."

"Has he actually said that?"

"Many times. We all miss you."

The line went silent.

"We were brothers."

"I know," I said. "He wants you back."

"You sure about that? He said some pretty strong things to me."

"And to all of us. He knows he's been a prick and he's sorry."

"I washed my hands of him, Anton."

"So you won't work with us."

"I can't."

I didn't know what to say, but I knew without Harry we were fucked.

"Goodbye then," I said.

Before either of us hung up, he said, "Claudia told me that you wanted to make amends. That's *his* job, Anton."

"He knows."

"Do *you*?"

"Yes."

I heard a lot of sighing, and I imagined he was shaking his head at the weakening of his resistance.

"Oh geez," he said. "A lot of water under

the bridge, a *whole lot* . . . but if he wants to talk, I guess I'll listen. He and I need a night out, a round or three of drinks at the Lion's Head, and then we'll see whether we can pick this up again."

"Pick a night and he'll be there."

"All right, so in the meantime . . ."

"Should I write this down."

"The last visual people have of Buddy is his meltdown on stage," he said.

"A given."

"So then the first thing you do is erase that image."

"How?"

"Through what we in the business call a *charm offensive.* We get him on air in non-controversial settings, whatever we can get so long as he can show he's back to his charming self. I can put out some feelers I suppose."

"You're a good friend."

"Yeah, well. I'll tell you now, there'll be some resistance. Buddy let down a lot of people."

"Understood."

"Okay then. I'm hereby dipping a toe back in the water."

My mother and I drove up that weekend to Manchester, New Hampshire, to canvass for Ted Kennedy and for her to reconnect with Joan Kennedy before another day they had planned to spend together in New York next month. We traveled door to door for a few hours in the crisp sunny day trying to persuade on-the-fence voters to come out for Teddy, drawing from a script the campaign had cobbled together on the economy, Afghanistan, and the hostages.

Most people we met were friendly enough, but quite a few expressed disgust with Teddy still over Chappaquiddick. There had been a front-page story in the *New York Times*, using tide reports and other scientific data, contradicting his account of his swim from the submerged car.

The campaign assembled a team of admiralty lawyers and oceanographers to rebut the article, to which Buddy said, "It's never a good sign when you're calling in the oceanographers."

As I walked down Main Street, I passed parked cars with bumper stickers reading IF KENNEDY WINS, YOU LOSE and TEDDY FOR LIFEGUARD.

"How do you feel about the president's refusal to debate Teddy?" we'd ask on our rounds.

"He's a coward," the likely Kennedy voters all said, and the Carter supporters told us the president had more important things on his mind than campaigning.

"Like what?" I asked.

"Bringing the hostages home."

"How's he doing on that front?" I said.

And they'd glare at me like I'd just spat on the flag.

At a birthday party for the senator at a Manchester social club, Ted and Joan danced cheek to cheek for the cameras. Seated at the main table were eighty-nine-year-old Rose Kennedy in a wide-brimmed hat, Ted's blond-haired daughter, Kara, on leave from Trinity College, and his twelve-year-old son, Patrick. A local campaign head, a tense-looking woman named Patricia Finn, told us in a hushed voice, "She's much better about Chappaquiddick than he is. She speaks from the heart."

"She does," my mother said.

"Imagine, pregnant with a house full of kids and friends and he calls his girlfriend. Poor Joan picked up the other line in the house and heard Ted weeping to her."

She then waddled off to the buffet.

"Now you see the problem," my mother said. "When your own campaign staff bathes in it you're toast."

"So Teddy's toast?"

My mother liked dinner and cocktail parties, and dissecting them afterward with Buddy, or us kids, as though they were character studies, and her observations were cheerfully unforgiving. "I'm just stating the obvious," she liked to say, though it was only after she said it that it became obvious to the rest of us. She saw through artifice and could always tell, she claimed, when people were lying. Buddy liked to say that my mother was perceptive but overly confident about her perceptions.

On this night she'd had two generous glasses of wine, and wasn't holding back.

The senator, flushed and broad shouldered, dropped by our table for ten minutes or so.

"Happy *birth*day, Mr. *Pres*ident," my mother sang, aping Marilyn.

A risky thing to do in front of JFK's brother, but she got away with it.

"You want to get up there and sing it, Emily?" Teddy said.

"I'm wearing the wrong outfit," my mother said.

He scanned the room then and breathed deeply. "New Hampshire in February," he said.

"Carter's afraid of the cold," I offered.

"You betcha," Teddy said.

"I'm sensing a big win here," my mother said.

"Me too. The polls are up and down, but the people are tired of a shit economy. They're tired of runaway inflation, and they want our men and women back from Iran."

"How exhausting is all this?" I asked him.

"Not at all, my boy. If being out on the road and spreading the gospel gets you tired, you're in the wrong line of work."

My mother looked at him skeptically.

Teddy leaned in. "I'm ready to sleep for a month. But not just yet. In November maybe."

"But you'll be busy with your transition then," the man across from us said.

"That I will," Teddy said. "Are you two hitting the pavement again tomorrow?"

"Morning till night," my mother said.

"Fantastic. Oh, here comes Joanie," Teddy said.

She placed a hand on my mother's shoulder. "Hi, beautiful Emily. Hello, handsome Anton."

"So caught up in appearances," my mother said.

"With you two. Buddy's another story."

"He is at that."

"How is your husband?" Teddy asked.

"Very well. We were just at the Olympics."

"Big hockey game with the Russians tonight," he said.

"We saw them smoke the Norwegians," I said.

"Fantastic," Teddy said. "Well, listen, I'm going to shake some hands and kiss some babies."

"So long as you don't kiss some hands and shake some babies," my mother said.

"Go, darling," Joan said.

The candidate leaned over to Joan and demonstrably kissed her on the mouth.

"Love you!" he said.

And she said, "Love *you*."

"Good thing we got that out of the way," grouchy Patricia Finn whispered to us.

"Promise me one thing," Joan said to my mother.

"What's that?"

"That you won't tell me how strong I am, how well I'm holding up, and how great Teddy and I look together."

"Okay then, you look terrible," my mother said.

"Thank you," Joan Kennedy said.

"I lied," my mother said.

"You know what gets me?" Joan said. "That after all these years of begging him to enter the race, of telling him he has to come and save the country, and he'll be the best president since his brother, and maybe better, and then Teddy says, 'Fine, I'll do it,' and they say, '*Not* so fast.' Do you know what I mean?"

"I do indeed," my mother said, thinking of Buddy I'm certain.

We watched the U.S.–Soviet hockey game that night in the packed lounge of the Manchester Inn. Volunteers from the Bush, Baker, Reagan, and Carter campaigns filled the seats and the bar area, along with a few Kennedy cohorts. No one talked politics, only sports. The U.S. fell behind 1–0, and then 2–1. And then the tide turned just before the end of the first period. Dave Christian fired a slap shot that the immortal Vladislav Tretiak fumbled away, and there was Mark Johnson slipping between two defenders and firing the puck into the net as the horn went off.

"They won't count it," a man in a Bruins hat near us said. "It's gonna be like the basketball game against the Russians in '72. They'll screw us on the time."

In 1972, the Soviets were awarded a second chance to win the game in the final seconds because of a clock malfunction. It was the first time the U.S. ever lost an Olympic basketball game.

To our beery glee the judges ruled it counted.

"Take that, Ruskies!" the man said.

When the U.S. won, the players rushed the ice, and the whole hotel rocked with the joy.

"I fear a rush of irrational patriotism," my mother said, "that'll push Carter over the finish line."

"Or maybe we'll all come to our senses," I said.

On our way out, my valiant mother called out to the folks heading to their cars, "Vote for Ted Kennedy on Tuesday for a better America!"

10

The Rose family's apartment was a source of envy even in the Dakota. It featured an enormous colonnaded salon with fireplaces on either side of the room (eight fireplaces, and fourteen rooms altogether in the apartment). The salon had been used in the old days as a ballroom. On the walls was a mix of modern — a Warhol and a Kandinsky, and pieces collected from their travels to Peru, Malaysia, India, and Egypt. They had a screening room, where Rowan showed movies, and in the parlor room there was a Steinway piano, and in a back wing, a small sunken swimming pool.

Rowan Rose's parties — on holidays and whenever he was in the mood, like for the Tony Awards, or St. Patrick's Day, or the Super Bowl, or the birthday of an opera or ballet star he admired, or the first day of spring, or the last day of summer, or New Year's Eve — were famous. The food was

135

from one of the two restaurants he owned, the Park Tavern and a notorious East Side pickup spot, the Rosy Thorn.

Buddy wore a tweed sports jacket and jeans. Our whole family came for this one, my mother in a gray cashmere V-neck sweater Buddy had bought for her years ago.

There were actors and artists, a few bankers, some writers, a circus acrobat. Lauren Bacall was there, Rex Reed, Rudolph Nureyev, who rumor had it was buying an apartment in the building, Nastassia Kinski, who'd been in Polanski's *Tess* and who I'd have liked to meet but was far too intimidated. Also there was Leo Larson, holding forth about real estate values. And then I watched Buddy walk over to where John Lennon was standing by himself placing a book back on the shelves.

He wore his long hair tied back in a ponytail and his face was covered in a somewhat scraggly beard. He wore a blue collared shirt and a thin black necktie and looked like he'd been vacationing somewhere warm. His nose was peeling.

"You're suntanned," Buddy said.

"Negroid," John said.

"Florida?"

"God's waiting room. Palm Beach. Went down there with the Peter Boyles for Yoko's

136

birthday."

"That's right," Buddy said. "Tell her happy birthday."

"Tell her yourself, she's in the kitchen."

"I will."

"Anyways, we were having a grand old time, hanging around the pool. I played some songs, Peter danced around like a spastic bear for Sean. So we headed out for dinner at a *fancy*-pants French restaurant, Le Petite Marmite, which in Australian translates roughly to the Little Sticky Brown Food Paste. It's Peter's choice, but what he hasn't in*formed* us is that it's where everyone in town goes to be seen."

Peter Boyle had been on Buddy's show when he'd played the monster in *Young Frankenstein*. He was smart and political and "a solid guest," Buddy said after.

"There were photographers," Buddy said.

"Fuck a pig there were."

"Of course there were."

" 'Over here, Mr. Lennon, is that a mouthful of peas?' " John said.

A server brought over a tray of pork dumplings. Buddy and I each took one. In the next room was a long mahogany table with selections from the Park Tavern. There were cod cakes, scallops wrapped in bacon, baby lamb chops, pillows of beef tenderloin, cold asparagus wrapped in roasted red peppers, spinach and feta in phyllo tarts, all of it incredibly good.

"So, acting like the prick I'm apt to be on these occasions, I take it out on poor *Peter* when we get back to the house."

"Oh no."

"Oh yes, I'm afraid. I accused him of choosing the place so he could have his picture taken with us, and I called him a lamebrain, which if you know anything of Peter's insecurities was a lancing blow. So I followed up by asking him how he could have been so *stupid,* not meaning it, I just wanted to get under his skin a little, and then you could see the steam and flames rise from his head. 'Don't you call me *stupid.* I'll tear your fucking head off.' "

I pictured him as the Frankenstein monster, grabbing John by the neck and shaking him until he went limp and lifeless.

"Then I laughed and he realized I was teasing. And we sort of made up. And then the next morning they took us out to brunch at a place that was exactly like the restaurant the night before, only with more people staring and more people taking pictures."

A malady shared by a lot of the building was that of being famous. John described it as a form of imprisonment, albeit a pam-

138

pered one, and he told Buddy once he'd give a few years of his life to be able to walk around wherever he wanted and be ignored.

I once heard Buddy himself say this, but being ignored would drive my father crazy.

There was an unwritten code in the Dakota that you made nothing of people's celebrity and you treated everyone simply as neighbors, and for the most part we did.

But it was hard not to feel the electric current of the Beatles.

Buddy's occupation invited attention from those who wanted to be celebrities; everyone it seemed wanted to get on *The Buddy Winter Show*. Waiters and cabdrivers and strangers on the street would break into song, or a string of jokes, or an impromptu magic trick, and Buddy would wince, then smile and say they could call his assistant and send over a cassette tape but that he was out with his family and trying to enjoy the day.

"So the beard hasn't worked as a disguise?" Buddy said.

"Now it's a famous beard. Did you ever grow one, Buddy Boy? I'm trying to see you with one and I just can't."

John Lennon was the only one other than my grandfather who'd ever called my father Buddy Boy.

"I had one a few months ago on my trip."

"*Ah yes,* the grand Winter voyage. I wish you'd have taken me with you."

"That would have been a sight," my mother said. "The two of you surfing off the coast of Bali."

"I'm seeing a beach chair and a nice young masseuse," John Lennon said.

A stout bearded man sat down at the piano and began to play classic Ella Fitzgerald songs like "Dream a Little Dream of Me" and "It Don't Mean a Thing (If It Ain't Got That Swing)." A woman in a long flowing blue dress was singing and people were gathering around. A few were dancing. People had walked over to the windows and were looking at the view.

"Did you do any sailing?" I asked John.

This was our topic when we saw each other. John was determined to learn this year how to sail, and I'd spent summers since I was ten out on the water.

"Funny you should ask. I'm driving around with Fred one morning and we pass by a dock with a boat in it named *Imagine.* So he looks up the captain's number and asks if we can take it out for the afternoon. So he books it without telling them who for and then *we* show up."

Fred was John's assistant and the nephew

140

of Sean's caretaker.

"They must have died," my mother said.

"Here's the beautiful part. They tell us they were huge Beatles fans, and one night when they were out of their heads on acid, they flipped on *The Buddy Winter Show* and there I am in my living room in England playing "Imagine" on a white grand piano."

"You're kidding," Buddy said.

"They decided right then to get a boat and name it *Imagine.*"

A little later, an actress named Lucretia who'd been on my father's show was explaining to my mother Buckminster Fuller's theory of electromagnetic conversations, which happened all the time without our knowing.

She said, "Ninety-nine percent of reality could only be comprehended by our metaphysical minds."

"Hunh," my mother said, as though accepting a truth.

A server came by with a tray of stuffed mushrooms. My mother took one, placed it in her mouth, then closed her eyes in pleasure. "These are *amazing,*" she told the server. "Is that a hint of basil?"

Lucretia continued, "The brain is just a place to store information. It can get overloaded, corroded, fried. But you can communicate outside of it through these electro-magnetic waves."

"Okay," my mother said.

"*You* can do that?" I asked.

"My brain's not at that level yet."

She kept talking and my thoughts wandered. At some point Lucretia was talking about trance channeling, and she was throwing names at me of people who believed fervently in reincarnation: Mark Twain, Walt Whitman, Pearl Buck, Henry Ford, Robert Frost, Rilke.

My mother said, "It's preposterous. We have one life and this is it."

"Now that's even more preposterous when you think about it."

Yoko said, "Don't you think everyone has something happen they can't explain. And there are people you meet, and you feel a karmic connection, as though you knew them, only you've never met before."

"I guess so," I said, because it was true; there had been people I felt like I knew.

"You have the sense there's stuff still to work out," Yoko said.

I thought of the stories I'd heard about them relying for financial decisions on the advice of numerologists and card readers, and how one of them had told them to buy the dairy farm in upstate New York that Kip and Alex and I had visited once.

"The spirit world is everywhere around us," Lucretia said, and she gestured around the room and beyond. "Our consciousness is too dense to see it but it's there. But you can *feel it,* can't you? I mean, take your father. Where do you think all those ideas and inspirations come from? Don't you get a sense that he — that all of us, really, are guided by an invisible force?"

"Not especially."

"How do you explain child prodigies then? How do you explain Mozart, or Chopin, or Franz Liszt?"

"Or Michael Jackson," said my brother, who'd wandered over.

"Exactly. They play perfect music because they *remember* how."

Throughout the party Rowan, who was wearing a garish plaid custom-made suit, was throwing his arm around someone, refilling a drink, or making introductions. As the city floundered, his businesses were thriving, and his parties were where everyone wanted to be.

He came from a moviemaking family, but his restaurants were his life, that and *making people happy,* he liked to say, though he rubbed some people the wrong way, and too often spoke his mind, damn the consequences, in the way the very rich can do.

He was close with John, and friendly with Buddy.

"I got a couple propositions for you," he said to me. "For one, you can bus at the Tavern if you want. I can't get you a waiter job just yet because the rest of my crew would string me up. But you'll share in the tips and you can make around a hundred dollars a shift."

"I'd like that."

"A few of the waitresses are sexy as hell. You're gonna love it. The ass you'll get might top the pay."

That actually sounded promising to me. I could use a little ass, I thought, though I doubted I'd have much luck.

We looked over at Buddy holding forth, then listening, having a pretty good time from the look of it. My mother came by and held his hand.

"I gotta ask you this, Anton."

"What's that?"

He pulled me into one of the side rooms, which looked like a library with floor-to-ceiling books, and one of those rolling ladders that we'd been thinking of getting.

He lowered his voice to a loud whisper.

"Is he crazy?"

"What? No, not at all."

"I love your father, you know that."

"He's not crazy," I said, probably loud enough for a few people to hear.

"Cause it's fine if he is. I'm crazy for chrissakes, just ask anyone here."

"He's better than ever," I said.

"Then let's see if we can get him back on the air, don't you think?"

"I would like that," I said.

"Good. Well, I know people, as you can imagine. Let me see what I can set up."

Rowan's presenting himself as more connected than us in the media world put me off, but given all that had happened it wasn't out of bounds.

"I think we'll be okay," I said.

"Well, if I hear of something I'll let you know."

"Sounds good."

"Okay then, now go out there and drink a little, and eat some too. Did you try the cod cakes? They're out of this fucking world."

In 1971, John and Yoko went on *The Buddy Winter Show.* Half the country watched it. Buddy was gracious and a little nervous really, and afterward my mother would say he should have been a little tougher on them. I was fourteen then. They talked about Jerry Rubin's blowup on *The David Frost Show,* and then the issue arose of the Beatles breakup and Yoko's role in it.

Yoko's outfit was amazing, really: hot-pant shorts and a low-cut top, in a matching peach/orange color. John was fit, and wearing a form-fitting army-style shirt, his hair still short a month after he'd cut it all off. I've seen the recording of this a dozen times and I'm still struck by how lively and funny John is, and how great Buddy is with him, enthralled without being intimidated. They both fawn over Yoko, and John plugs a list of her ongoing projects: a new film, a book of poems called *Grapefruit,* and her museum exhibit up in Syracuse. He talks directly to the camera like he's selling knives or encyclopedias, and Yoko seems pleased with the attention. Then they dim the lights to show Yoko's film, which is of a naked woman's body with a fly walking up and back and what I took to be Yoko's voice approximating a fly's.

That it was weirdly brilliant was beside the point. Buddy was going to like it no matter what. A kinship rose then between the men, because Buddy was buying the version of themselves they were selling.

They could say whatever they wanted, and

he would get it, and his audience would as well.

11

My grandfather Roland Winter taught me to sail off the coast of Maine, and for years we took sailing trips every June to Penobscot Bay, or Bar Harbor, or up to Campobello Island, where Franklin Roosevelt spent summers as a kid. We had a long-keel Cutlass, and then a masthead sloop named *Happy Hours.* And I loved especially the stories my grandfather read to us the nights before a voyage, ones by Melville and Poe and my favorite, by Ray Bradbury, "The Fog Horn," about the Loch Ness Monster, the old salt McDunn empathizing with the monster as it slipped into the sea, "It's gone back to the Deeps. It's learned you can't love anything too much in the world."

I was recalling how dreamlike those stories were the night Kip and I went to see *The Fog,* by John Carpenter, the guy who directed *Halloween.* The ads, with the haunting blurry image of silhouetted ghosts

148

marching through fog, red dots for eyes, covered subway walls and bus kiosks with the tagline "It is night. It is cold. It is coming."

The Fog opens with kids, faces orange lit, seated around a campfire, and John Houseman in a captain's hat and scraggly white beard, telling them of a clipper ship that drifted into a fog a hundred years back and then — guided by a light on shore — crashed into the rocks, drowning all its passengers. The town's people had used the light to induce the crash and then steal the ship's gold.

Now the fog has returned and with it a tribe of drowned and vengeful passengers, angry ghosts with hooks and spikes. The movie is beautifully shot, somewhere in northern California, and super-scary. Kip closed his eyes through the bloodiest scene and asked me on our walk home to describe it in detail, and when I did he winced as though it was happening around us.

We argued over what was the scariest movie we'd seen.

Kip said *The Exorcist,* which he'd seen when I was away. I said *The Hills Have Eyes.* Just the title freaked me out. And so did the drowned passengers in *The Fog.*

"What were they doing the last hundred

years?" I asked him.

"The *ghosts*?"

"Yeah, I mean before returning?"

"Lying dead I think, like at the bottom of the sea."

"Nursing their grievances."

"Whatever dead people do," he said.

What I thought of were all the people on the ninth floor slipping quietly in and out of their one-room dwellings, unnoticed by the rest of the building.

"Do you still believe in ghosts?" I asked him.

"Not with hooks and spikes, but yes, I guess I do."

"Why?"

"I've heard things. Haven't you?"

"Not really," I said.

Quite a few of our neighbors swore they'd seen or felt the presence of ghosts, including John and Yoko, who after moving in to the old Ryan apartment held a séance to reach Jessie Ryan, who'd died there, and convince her spirit to leave. Our parents split on the matter, my mother a nonbeliever, and Buddy filling our heads with tales of ghosts who'd haunted the hallways, some made up, others passed down from Dakotan to Dakotan, a porter who witnessed a shovel flying through the air, elevators moving of their own volition, a little girl seen by several accounts bouncing a ball by herself in the middle of the night (though no little girl who fit her description existed among the tenants).

Then there was *Rosemary's Baby,* which did for the Dakota what *Jaws* did for the ocean. Your kindly old neighbors were secret Satanists ready to impregnate you with the devil's spawn. It felt like we lived in a haunted castle, which on the whole I liked because I thought it kept the prim and timid away.

It had snowed while we were in the movies and on the street afterward there were kids in the midst of a massive snowball fight. We'd made our way to the corner when Kip reached down to make a snowball and then fired it up the street, nailing one of the fighters on the shoulder of his throwing arm.

"Hey!" he yelled and then threw snow our way.

Kip yelled out, "Our chief weapon is surprise. Surprise and fear! Fear and surprise! Our two weapons are fear and surprise!"

One of our many Monty Python routines.

"And ruthless efficiency," I said.

"Our three weapons are fear, surprise, and

ruthless efficiency."

"And an almost fanatical devotion to the Pope," I said.

He started throwing snowballs high in the air into the street so they'd land on passing cars.

"Really fucking smart," I said.

"Try it."

I shook my head.

"You know you want to. Pick a car you want to hit, pussy."

"Who are you calling 'pussy'?"

I waited for a limo and then hurled a snowball, which landed with a loud thud on the car's roof. The limo pulled over and the tree-sized driver stepped out.

"Hey, douchebags!" he yelled.

Kip rifled off another snowball, hitting him on the shoulder.

We ran.

"Not good, not good, not good," I intoned.

"It's just snow," Kip said. "It's not like we're throwing rocks, or even ice."

Kip had a vandalistic streak, and he had been caught and then suspended for a day in the fall for writing graffiti on a playground wall. He liked pointing out his favorite taggers to me like bands I should know — Quik, Bil Rock, and Zephyr — and in an empty lot on Amsterdam he showed me a cartoon drawing of Uncle Sam smoking a joint, beside a skeleton in a top hat and tuxedo below the message People Who Live in Glass Houses Should Be Stoned.

As we made our way down Broadway Kip asked me, "Will you come watch my match on Saturday?"

Kip had tournaments most weekends, so many my parents had stopped going to them except on special occasions. The matches were held as far away as the northern stretches of Long Island and southern New Jersey. This one would be out in Long Island, he said.

"Absolutely."

"I'm not going to win."

"Not with that attitude."

"I won't," he said. "You'll see. The guy I'm playing hits about a thousand miles an hour."

"Well, I have to see *that*."

"It won't be pretty. He could actually kill me."

"Should we pick out caskets tomorrow? Cherry or mahogany?"

"Cherry," Kip said, "but don't go overboard."

"Rachel wouldn't let us."

It was around eleven when we arrived back

at the Dakota and there were still around a dozen Beatles fans (the zombies, Rachel called them) hanging out for the one-in-a-hundred chance they might see John.

"He's away skiing," I told a pretty blonde girl in a puffy blue down jacket.

"Oh my god, *where*? Hunter Mountain?" she said, as though she might jump on a bus that night to get there. She had a beauty mark on her right cheek and blue-green sparkles on her eyelids.

"He doesn't ski," another girl said. "The Beatles don't *ski*."

"Why wouldn't he ski?" the first girl said.

"They ski in the movie *Help!*," said a skinny teenager who wore a Beatles shirt over a red sweatshirt.

"That's right, the 'Ticket to Ride' scene."

"He's out to dinner," said someone carrying several cameras.

"Where?" someone else asked.

"Mamma Leone's, I don't know."

"I saw Mick Jagger last week walking in to go to a party," said one of the girls who'd been arguing about skiing.

"Bullshit," said the guy with the cameras. "I happen to know he's in France right now."

On the elevator up, Kip asked, "don't they

154

ever get bored?"

"You would think, wouldn't you?"

"What happens if they see him? They can say they saw John Lennon?"

"It's like the people who travel to the Vatican or to Mecca. They feel like they're closer to God."

"Did Buddy say that?"

I felt affronted.

"No, I just did."

"Okay then."

I shook my head.

"You do like to quote him."

"I'll try and do it less."

And then we were silent.

"I didn't say it was a bad thing."

In truth I sometimes lost track of where Buddy's thoughts ended and mine began. For years I couldn't tell if I liked a movie or a book or a *New Yorker* short story without consulting him first. Then later I disagreed for the sake of disagreeing, failing to see how much I was still in his sway. In later years on the show I learned to write lines for his monologues in his voice and to come up with the sort of questions he'd be likely to ask in his interviews. He told me once that I'd become the other half of him, which he meant as a compliment but made me feel weird, like his soul had subsumed mine.

One reason I left New York for the Peace Corps was a desire to silence his voice within my thoughts.

Kip and I foraged in the refrigerator, then ate ice cream sandwiches at the kitchen table. Kip as always licked around the edges before taking a real bite.

My mother was in the den poring over bills. I'd heard some conversations last week between my parents over how much we'd spent in Lake Placid, and how maxed out they were on their credit cards.

"How was your movie?" she asked.

"Super-scary. You would have liked it."

"I'll come along next time," she said.

"Everything good?"

"Good enough," she said.

"Bills," I said.

"They pile up, don't they. We may have to cut down a little on all the fun we have."

"I promise not to have any," I said.

"Just not for the next month," she said and smiled wearily.

12

"He's where again? A nudist retreat?" Harry Abrams asked.

"It's a four-day meditation retreat in Nyack, New York."

"What do you do at a meditation retreat? Sit and space out?"

"More or less. It's silent, for one thing. You get up every day at four thirty. There are no radios or TVs or books. It makes him more mindful, he says. By focusing on his slightest movement and quietest thoughts he becomes more aware and insightful."

"Aw Jesus, Anton. Tell me he isn't chanting."

"He *might* be," I said. "He hasn't joined a cult if that's what you're wondering."

Harry and I were in the lobby bar at the Algonquin with the velvet wing chairs and the bronze floor lamps, where the famous Algonquin Round Table used to meet. Harry was drinking a Tanqueray and tonic, and had ordered me a gin rickey, which he said was F. Scott Fitzgerald's favorite drink.

"What was Hemingway's?" I asked.

"Easy. A mojito."

"Dorothy Parker."

"Let's ask the waitress."

When she came back, she told us, "A whiskey sour."

Harry began then filling me in on his legwork, which included meetings with the networks and PBS and two of the local stations and a few industry insiders. Some excitement, followed by questions about Buddy's health and state of mind.

"It all gets flipped, doesn't it?" he said. "Those things they loved about you are suddenly your disqualifiers. In Buddy's case it's his 'unpredictability.' "

"Buddy has a line about that: 'It's genius until you break.' "

"Well, based on our night out it's still genius. He really seemed at ease, like the Buddy we all love, though you've more to go on than me."

Buddy and Harry had buried the hatchet in a libertine night of drinking at their favorite watering hole, the Lion's Head on Christopher Street. Buddy called me from a pay phone outside the bar at one A.M. and said at a soused volume, "The cold war is over! I've got my best friend back."

Harry's initial goal he said was to return Buddy to TV and have it feel as though he never left.

" 'Buddy Winter circa 1975 is what we want,' said one of the executives I spoke to."

"He might be better in some ways," I said.

"I agree. He's edgier, cooler. But still damn funny. So I say we amend our approach."

"How so?"

"When we were out the other night I started to think that where Buddy was most appealing, most *alive,* was talking about his journey, after the meltdown. His sitting alone in a strange motel room, or driving a rental car in the middle of nowhere and running out of gas and having to hitchhike with that crazy guy with the angry dog in his truck, and he ends up staying at the *guy's house.*"

"The guy's brother's trailer I think?"

"And then they stayed up talking about religion? That's pure gold."

"It's weird."

I'd always resented how real Buddy got with strangers over the years, that he'd tell something none of us knew about him to someone he just met. His stock-in-trade was

159

indiscriminate familiarity.

"I'm saying, rather than run from what happened we *use* it. You watched the Winter Olympics. You know the background segments they do on the athletes."

"The back story. That's our favorite part."

"And what are they about, smooth sailing to the medal stand? Who'd watch that? They're all about hardship, and times of self-doubt. We root for them because of what they've been through. Our struggles make us human."

"And so . . ."

"So after we establish he'll show up and be professional —"

"And never ever walk out again."

"Yes, exactly, after that we use to our advantage the fact that Buddy has journeyed life's hills and valleys. He's had his *Razor's Edge* trip. He's seen rock bottom and soared to the mountaintop, and unlike the other hosts nothing he says will ever be repackaged, or preapproved."

"And how do we get that message out?"

"We find the right venue, the right moment. The message is what happened to Buddy happens to a lot of people who on the surface are living the lives everyone wishes they could live. What matters isn't that it happened, it's that you're not done in by it."

"He was done in by it."

"He was knocked down, and now he's back in the ring."

"With his eye and lip bleeding, and a pain in his gut."

"With a bounce in his step."

"All he needs are some smelling salts."

"Exactly. Now on another front, how's it going with money?"

I wondered if Buddy had said anything about this.

"Not so good. It's been a while since Buddy's last paycheck."

"And he still spends money like a television star."

"Pretty much."

"He's always spent money."

"He's sold off a bunch of our savings bonds."

"That's not good."

"Do you have any suggestions?"

"I could get him a local commercial, but I think that smacks too much of ex-celebrity desperation," he said. "What I could get him in the next few weeks are a couple of stand-up slots in Atlantic City. A thousand a pop but he won't do it."

"What's stopping him?"

"He thinks it's for the Shecky Greene crowd."

"Is it?"

"I sure hope so. It's good money, and I think he'll be great."

"He's been doing a lot of writing, figuring out his angle. A few of the new jokes are really good."

Harry ran his finger over the rim of his cocktail glass.

"The thing I worry . . . ," he said, and then stopped himself.

"Go ahead."

"Okay," he said. "He's nearly fifty, and he's been out of the game for a while, and well, he's not the new kid on the block. It's a different market out there now." He then slapped the table with his palm. "But if anyone in this big beautiful world can do it . . ."

"I'll drink to that," I said, draining my second cocktail.

"How's your lovely mom?"

"Stressed, to be honest. She's thinking of going back to work."

"*Interesting.* Are we talking movies, theater, commercials?"

"Anything."

"I can help with that."

"I hoped you'd say that. I'll tell her."

I told him then about the Kennedy celebrity fund-raiser she was throwing at a lavish Park Avenue apartment.

"Will there be any press?"

"The *Times,* the *News,* the *Post.*"

"Perfect. The more people see Buddy out there, having a good time, the better."

Buddy's reemergence into the limelight meant being seen at the right events, dressing sharp, spending money we had less of these days, turning up at the occasional Knicks game. Shirts needed pressing, jackets needed tailoring, because as Harry said, "your slip shouldn't show." He should seem as always, congenial and charming, not at risk, not *desperate* — with the options a beloved TV star might have in his prime, all this publicly, while privately we took on water, and scaled back on the fun, as my mother put it. Fewer nights at the theater, opera, and ballet; fewer impulse purchases, like coffee table books and flowers and cheesecakes from Mrs. Grimbles. My parents placed a ten-dollar cap on birthday gifts for each other and began talk of dropping club memberships and selling the old Mercedes, which made sense but made me sad.

There was an accepted truth that above

your job, your salary, the organizations you belonged to, the clothes you wore, and the car you drove, the biggest indicator of status in New York was your address. For as long as we lived in the Dakota, we were fine, by appearances if not in truth.

Harry was adamant the breaks would come our way. He also said that if worse came to worst we could all move in with him, which seemed like a genuine offer and filled me with vertigo.

On my way home I stopped by the Park Tavern and I found Rowan Rose in his office readying to leave for the night.

"Anton, my boy. Come in! Come in!"

We talked some about my mother's fundraiser, which he said he was hoping to attend, then with a warm smile he asked what had brought me in.

"I'm ready to work," I said, "if the offer still stands."

"Of course it does," he said. "Bussing, not waiting tables, you understand."

"Bussing tables," I said.

Oh, how the Winters had fallen.

"Then come in a week from Monday at four P.M. Glenn'll show you the ropes. It's a lot of grunt work, but you'll love it."

"I'll be there grunting," I said daftly.

"How's your search going?" he asked.

"For a new show?"

"No, for Gina Lollobrigida. Of course for a show."

"We're getting close," I lied.

"I can't wait. Let me know when you strike gold. We'll have ourselves a little party."

13

With Buddy still at his retreat, Kip and I rode the Oyster Bay train out to Glen Cove for his round-of-16 match against the sixth seed, Eric Steiner. We shared my Walkman on the way, listening to Talking Heads, Madness, and the Jam, who we both loved.

Kip wore a dark blue Adidas warm-up top over blue jeans.

He packed with him a blue paperback copy of *Zen and the Art of Motorcycle Maintenance,* which he was reading for class.

He pointed to my book, *The Executioner's Song,* which I took from my parents' bedroom.

"Is that like about the guy who was executed."

"Yes."

"Is it good?"

"It's pretty amazing."

"Dad said Norman Mailer shot his wife."

"He stabbed her."

"And he didn't go to jail?"

"Probation I think. She never pressed charges."

"Why did he stab her?"

I actually knew this. "They had a party, and Mailer got drunk and high, and he was supposedly out on the street punching people, strangers. When he got back inside his wife called him a faggot and said his mistress was ugly and so he stabbed her with a little penknife."

"What the hell?"

"He was crazy."

"Dad was crazy, and he didn't stab anyone."

"They're different people. And Dad wasn't crazy, just messed up for a while."

"Kids in my school think he's like crazy."

"Who does?"

"This kid Leonard told everyone he was in the loony bin. It actually got me some sympathy. I had a teacher take me aside and tell me she was so proud of what I did 'in such terrible circumstances.' "

"What did you say to her?"

"I said I didn't know what she was talking about. She said, 'You're a brave young man.' "

He opened the book and read the first page.

"Can I read this when you're finished?" he said.

"Of course."

I thought about the fact that Mailer had done the indefensible back in 1960, and then gone on to his greatest celebrity. He'd made it back. John Lennon went nuts in a club in Hollywood, punching a bodyguard and yelling incoherently, and it was part of his lore, not an epitaph he had to stage a campaign to reverse.

"What's the guy like who you're gonna play?"

"He hits the hell out of the ball. He'll either wipe me off the court, or I'll beat him in three sets."

"How will you do that?"

"He's kind of a head case, and I'm not."

"You're cool and collected."

"Pretty much."

I hadn't seen Kip play a match since he got really good, and it was startling to see the change in his strokes, his footwork, and his demeanor. I even heard one of the tournament officials whisper to another as Kip went out to the court, "This could be interesting." Eric Steiner carried five rackets and wore a red and white striped headband over his shoulder-length dark brown hair.

He had a huge serve and big ground strokes and he took the first set in around fifteen minutes 6–1. Then Kip broke him to start the second set, which appeared to shock Steiner (as though a small dog bit his ankle and drew blood), and that shock expanded when Kip held serve and then broke again. Kip took the second set 6–2.

A crowd of other players and parents gathered at the window to watch.

Eric Steiner's tanned and designer-jean-clad mother said several times, "He *never* misses that shot," and "Come *on,* Eric. You're *better* than this!"

Steiner was outraged after every point he lost, as though Kip was stealing bites of a dessert Steiner had saved for himself. *"No more!"* he said when Kip passed him, but there was more.

Self-flogging works as a tonic for your opponent's confidence. The more Steiner berated himself, the more gears Kip could drop into. Steiner was up 3–1 in the third set and then Kip hit an absurdly perfect lob to break his serve. In response Steiner smashed his Wilson Jack Kramer Autograph racket on the clay court, then picked up another Kramer and smashed it, then a third, and left it resembling a broken butterfly net.

Kip glanced up at me, and I mouthed, "You got this."

He calmly closed it out. Steiner purposely slammed the last two returns past the baseline, past Kip, into the fence, a protest against his wayward strokes. *"You suck,"* he yelled. *"You suck worse than anyone who ever played."*

The Zen master who worked with Buddy and Kip spoke about the two selves within each of us and silencing that part of you, your nasty twin, who kept yelling things at you like *How bad are you?* Or *Move your feet!* Or *How can you be losing to this loser?* Imagine, he said, having that guy in your kitchen in the morning. *You suck at making eggs! That's not a pancake, it's a flour-based abomination!* You'd kick him out before you cooked anything, right?

Steiner was savaged by his nasty twin, the same one, Kip's coach would say, who'd praised him for all his victories, for his high ranking, for the free rackets he received from Wilson, for the girls who let him feel them up at high school parties. The ego-mind sees within each compliment the seeds of an insult. "We think, *If he likes one shot, he will dislike the other.*" The practice of a good/bad standard leads to divided concentration and ego interference.

Compliments, he said, are criticisms in drag.

"Ending judgment doesn't add or subtract from the facts before your eyes. You see things as they are," said the Zen coach.

"Then how do you explain John McEnroe?" I once asked Buddy.

"Watch him," Buddy said. "I mean when he's *playing,* not when he's complaining. He's all instincts and no ego. The kid plays like he was born with an elongated arm that has a racket head and strings at the end of it. There's no internal critic when McEnroe's playing. If there was, he'd likely change those messed-up-looking strokes."

I called Buddy at the retreat to tell him how Kip had beat the sixth seed.

"How did he do it?"

"Like you told him, one shot at a time."

"And the other kid went nuts."

"Smashed three rackets."

"When's the next match?" he asked.

"In an hour."

"It's good you're there. He so missed having you around."

Almost two hours later, in the quarters, Kip played a kid named Jamie Wallace who had a face full of pimples and never missed a shot. He beat Kip 6–3, 6–4 in the feature match of the afternoon. It seemed a little unjust that Kip had to play a second match after playing a three-setter already, and with Wallace having won his match the night before. But Kip never complained and played his heart out. The other kid was just better.

Compounding the challenge, Wallace was a sweet kid, and complimented Kip whenever he hit a winner. "Too good!" he'd yell. He was easily as Zen as Kip, and would ultimately win the tournament.

On this day Wallace won all the big points and never once got rattled the way Steiner had earlier.

"Amazing match," I heard him tell his father within earshot of us. "I just got lucky."

I figured Kip was spent but he asked if we could take a later train so we could drill for a while.

"You can wear my warm-ups," he said.

"You've been on the court for five hours."

"Please. Just for a half hour or so," he said. "If they've got an open court."

I changed into his warm-ups and drilled him for a half hour using one of his Dunlop Maxplys. I tried my best to destroy my little brother, side to side, up and back. I had played the junior circuit too until I was Kip's age. I had some decent wins and some embarrassing losses. I remember a coach telling me *You've got to want it more than anyone else out there.*

I never wanted it like this. I thought, as I watched Kip dig in for a shot deep in the corner then sprint to the other side, that I should try and find something in my life I wanted as badly as Kip wanted everything.

When I'd pushed him as far as his legs could take him, he pulled up with a leg cramp.

"I'm done," he said. "Thanks. Let's go home."

On the train back to Penn Station I thought of something Rachel said, that Kip's determination came from being abandoned. Buddy was gone, and I was gone, and she was preoccupied, and no one was watching over him and so he worked hard as hell to become special.

He read his book on the way back and I read mine.

"You were a demon out there," I said. "Your ranking just went up ten places, I bet."

"I doubt it," he said, but he knew it would.

I told him that I spoke to Buddy and how

proud he was.

We both spaced out for a while and watched the world go by in the window.

At one point my brother asked, "Did you know John Lennon has a son my age he never sees?"

"Julian, yes."

"Have you met him?"

"No."

"Why doesn't he live in the building?"

"He lives with his mother in England."

"The whole time? Don't most kids split time with each parent?"

"I guess he doesn't."

"It's weird. It's like he doesn't exist."

"Pretty much."

"I would hate that."

"I heard they spent a week together last year in Palm Beach," I said.

"If he ever stays over in our building I want to meet him," Kip said.

We had a mother's helper named Jenny who grew up outside Liverpool and told us stories she'd heard about John. His father left home when John was two.

When John was six, his father kidnapped him and took him to a seaside resort called Blackpool, where John spent three weeks with his father around the clock, going to shows and on rides, and eating sweets, and hearing stories I would imagine of his father's trips at sea, things he had to imagine when his father was away.

Buddy's disappearance had been the hardest on Kip, but I never once heard my brother complain. He just asked when his father was coming home. And now weekly he asked me whether or not I thought he was better. He's a better parent than when he worked all the time, I said.

Kip, Buddy told me once since my return, was his chance "to finally get it right," which I thought was a strange thing to say, like he'd gotten it wrong with us.

Kip told me something later, about the kid Steiner who'd had the epic meltdown. Steiner's parents were getting a divorce and his father had run off with his secretary, Kip heard, which was why his mother dressed like a teenager.

"I bet he was thinking of his dad when he smashed all his rackets," Kip said.

Kip skipped a lot of classes the year Buddy disappeared and a few times whole days and he had to be transferred to a special school with less structure, Calhoun on West End Avenue, where the curriculum is built loosely and organically around particular themes. The students had all struggled at other places. He thrived there.

He went regularly to a therapist, a man who bore a remarkable resemblance to Gabe Kaplan in *Welcome Back, Kotter.* We went with him as a family a few times, and at these sessions Rachel and I tore into my father, and Kip and Buddy stayed mostly silent. When asked, Kip said he couldn't remember Buddy being around. The therapist pressed him to come up with a fond memory, and he said when Buddy would do his show after dinner and interview us as his guests, which I'd forgotten about and was pretty cool.

"That must have been something," the therapist said.

And then Buddy told him about those nights in hilarious detail, and Kip and my mother were in stitches, and the therapist was rapt, and I remember Rachel saying later how angry it made her that instead of facing the music, he'd managed again to win over the room.

14

Harry arranged a series of casual lunches and meetings with whomever he could get at the networks, mostly second-tier folks who would then report to the higher-ups. The discussions were a mixed bag of talk on how exciting it was to see Buddy "back in the game," and understandable hesitation to build a new show around someone who'd so publicly brought his previous one down. One young executive told us, as his hearts-of-palm salad arrived, that he'd "grown up watching the show," and if it were up to him "I'd do this in a heartbeat." But in order to get a new show, Buddy would need to prove himself reliable and healthy and on top of his game again.

"It can happen fast. A good appearance on someone else's show might open some doors. Let him guest-host for Mike Douglas or David Susskind."

"How about *The Tonight Show*?" Harry said.

"Yeah, sure, but is that likely?"

"He's done it in the past," Harry said.

Buddy guest-hosted for Johnny twice, before he had his own show, and Johnny had made the suggestion that Buddy could come back and then never got back to us with a date.

"He's got enough drama to deal with in his own life," Buddy explained when I asked once if he'd heard from Carson.

Another executive had an idea about a participatory story, like the kind George Plimpton conceived where he'd play football for the Detroit Lions, or box against Archie Moore. Buddy had such a fluid mind he could, say, conduct an orchestra, play drums in a punk band, ride around the city in a squad car.

At a lunch at the Four Seasons, as a waitress served our entrees, a midlevel executive suggested that Buddy could star in a movie of the week about a man who has a nervous breakdown.

"You can draw from your own experience. I think it would be extremely powerful."

Buddy winced.

"And what would his job be?" Harry asked.

"He'd be a talk-show host."

Buddy raised his eyebrows.

"I mean he wouldn't be *you*. Not exactly you, but someone with your wry sense of humor."

"Or maybe something a little different — say he's a sports announcer, and he loses his shit while he's calling a game," said the other executive, who appeared to have blond highlights in his hair.

"Or when he's interviewing an athlete," the first one said.

"Perfect. The athlete ticks him off, and the sports announcer walks off the set."

This went on for a while, and Buddy and Harry went with it, to see how absurd it would get.

"He shoots the quarterback!" Buddy said.

"Yes, and then he moons his audience," Harry said.

No one got the joke.

"That might be too over the top," said the blond highlights guy.

"You fucking *think*?" Buddy said.

"You don't have to be rude," he said.

"I actually do," Buddy said. "That's where you're wrong, sonny boy."

"Maybe this is a bad idea."

I bumped Buddy's leg and put a finger over my lips.

"Listen," Harry said, "I think we have some things to work with here."

"Absolutely," the blond guy said, gathering himself.

On our way out of the restaurant, Harry pulled us aside.

"They're in over their heads," he said. "But you can't do things like this and expect me to get you a goddamned job."

On our way home from one of these dispiriting lunches, Buddy was dejected in a way that concerned me and made me worry he might spiral.

"I'm not used to this, having to fucking sit there and say the right things to the little dingleberries fifteen years younger, who don't know anything about me, or about TV, or about anything other than ratings. It's beyond depressing."

"You did well there until the end."

"I'm like a band that used to play stadiums and now has to round up gigs at county fairs," Buddy said.

"You're Three Dog Night," I said, and he smiled.

"Maybe it's irrational, but I thought that because I was better and felt like myself it would all fall quickly together," he said.

"It will," I said. "You'll get another shot."

"On what? *Hollywood Squares*."

"Sure. Or *That's Incredible!* Or *Fantasy Island*. We'll get a beach vacation out of it."

"I'll be the next Robert Goulet."

"Who's that?"

"Exactly," he said.

We passed the Paris Theater where Truffaut's *Day for Night* and *The 400 Blows* were playing.

"When the going gets tough," he said.

"The tough go to the movies," I said.

It was a line Buddy used when the world felt dark.

We got a large popcorn and two Cokes, and we leaned back in our seats and waited for the film to start.

I had an image of him in that instant taking me on the subway to see the Mets, in their third year of existence, play the Pirates at Shea Stadium. He's in a straw hat and his Ray-Bans, and I wear a Mets T-shirt, blue shorts, and Keds. He had a Mets yearbook with him he kept in his jacket pocket. He pulled it out when we sat down and he told stories about each of the players. He read a line from their bios and then made up fantastical things about each of these guys who played for the worst team ever assembled.

People on seats nearby glanced our way

and then craned to hear the stories of wooden elbows, acrobat mothers, a curve that broke so heavily batters ended up in traction. Every once in a while, he'd raise his eyebrows at a particularly ludicrous moment, as if to say to his Queens-bound audience, But this is *true, all of it.*

"I had an intense desire to pour my drink on that asshole," he said now.

"I'm sure glad you didn't."

"I'll tell you this, I couldn't do this alone," Buddy whispered to me just before the picture rolled.

"Luckily you won't have to," I whispered back.

Then we lost ourselves in the stories. At the end of *The 400 Blows,* the boy, Jean-Pierre Léaud, has escaped juvie and is on the run along the sea. He turns toward us, the camera abruptly freezes, and the word *"Fin"* appears across the image. Buddy said, "You know what happens to him, don't you?"

"Jail?" I said.

"No," he said with a pained smile, "he becomes a talk-show host."

As we said our good-nights at home later, Buddy said it was time I got paid for my efforts on his behalf, like in the old days.

"What I propose is that we make this a real job. You put in twenty hours a week and I pay you three hundred dollars. If you work more, or if you have to travel with me, it goes up from there. I should pay you a helluva lot more, but that'll certainly happen when we get a show."

I had a panicked feeling, like I'd walked into a movie I'd seen several times and it was too late to switch my ticket.

"Not that you'll have to work on the new show," he said, having read my thoughts. "That'll be up to you. You're not my prisoner."

"I accept then."

"I'm pleased," he said. "So I've made a list of things we need to look into. I want to keep us to a schedule. Harry will work with us on all this. Part of your job will be to call him every day with questions and ideas, and to find out what he has cooking. You'll be the one who talks to him, and you can take some of the meetings. And if something else opens up for you, you can quit, no questions asked."

"Sounds good."

"Doesn't it?"

He'd picked the right moment to ask because just then I felt tied to his quest. It was those lunches, how deflated they left us, but also how persuasive Buddy could be, the way he could convince you the worthiest thing to do with your life was to align your fate with his. I know Harry felt that, and my mother from the night they met. And it was on me not to disappear again under his star.

15

That next Monday I launched my storied career as a busboy at the Park Tavern. The headwaiter, Glenn, a tall russet-haired man from Tennessee, introduced me around to the rest of the staff, the dishwashers, and then the line cooks, who weren't as scary, he said, as they looked. He toured me through the various stations and themed rooms, and told me how best to earn respect and avoid the doghouse.

"Ask your waiter or waitress every so often if they need something, but don't overdo it. Meaning don't kiss our asses. We're busy. *Read* our faces. We'll let you know when we need you."

He told me when and how to talk to the lead chefs, or to customers who try to place orders with you instead of their waiter, how to deal with broken glass, or someone choking, or spilling wine into their dinner plate or their lap. How to help out the dishwashers, and restock the napkins and glasses and silverware, and handle wine and water glasses from the bottom ("no grubby fingers in the glass to carry them away"), and how you should never — on punishment of death — clear one or two dishes away before others are finished eating.

A waitress with streaky blond hair named Janet, who'd been listening in, said, "When that happens they usually drop their tip by thirty percent."

"Which you'll cover," Glenn said. Waiters decide how much the busboys get at the end of the night.

"You want major points?"

"I do," I said.

"Then do the crap work. Grab those bus pans and bring them back to the kitchen and empty them for the dishwashing crew. They'll love you for it. Learn how to expertly crumb a table."

I nodded.

"Lastly, hang out with us, get to know everyone. When your shift's done don't be in a hurry to leave."

"I won't," I said, and I had the feeling I might actually like this.

On my first two nights I made rookie mistakes, including spilling wine and clearing a plate too soon, for which Janet, who adopted me as her busboy, glared at me, and told me, not in a sweet or flirtatious way, that next time she'd have to give me a spanking.

Otherwise I was like any other Ivy League–educated busboy. It was in some ways like the set of a talk show, I decided. The waiter is your set designer, the tabletop holds your props, and your dinner companion provides the drama, *not* your busser, who should be as invisible as stagehands who slip out between scenes to rearrange the furniture and remove evidence of what's transpired.

The second night a girl from my high school class walked in with a man a good twenty years older. She wasn't in my station, which was a relief for both of us, I'm sure.

Janet caught my eye and mouthed, "Table five. Clear the dinner plates and set up for dessert."

I nodded and headed to table five.

"Could you tell the chef the chicken Kiev was superb," said a woman with long fake eyelashes and sparkly dangling earrings.

Her dining companion studied my face and said, "You look familiar. Have you ever been on TV?"

"Not recently," I said.

187

"You definitely look like someone," she said.

"You're right, he does," the woman with the dangling earrings said. "Who *is* that?"

They wanted me to tell them who I might be.

"I'm not who you think I am," I said. It came out sounding like I had lied to them.

"You sure fooled us," said the woman with the earrings, with a trace of disgust.

My classmate, Elena (Swiss father I think), was now holding hands with the older guy. He said something to her and she looked shyly down at the table then returned his gaze.

Janet was standing next to me. "Do you know them?" she asked.

"She was in my high school class."

"I had a one-nighter with him a while back."

"That guy?"

"Yes. He works on Wall Street. I'll bet he doesn't even remember me."

"Where did you meet?"

"Here. I waited on him."

"I'll bet he remembers you."

"It's a big city for guys like him."

For no good reason I asked, "How was he?"

"He was very complimentary. Then he

tried to put his finger in my ass."

"A bridge too far."

"You said it. Table six. Refill the waters and clear the appetizer plates," she said, and we were off to our separate tasks.

I made seventy-two dollars that night. Buddy would pay me my three hundred.

At this rate I might make more than five hundred a week, which was a good start, and might make me for the moment, I considered, the biggest breadwinner in the family.

I ran into Elena on her way out.

"Hi, Anton," she said.

She introduced me to her date and as I shook his hand I tried not to think of the places his finger had been.

"You're a waiter," she said.

"A busboy. I had to do something with my Ivy League education."

"I thought you'd be working in TV somewhere."

"Not for now."

She turned then to her boyfriend.

"Buddy Winter is Anton's father," she said.

"Shit. I used to love *The Buddy Winter Show*."

I instantly liked him. It was that easy to win me over.

Then he handed me his business card.

"Give me a call if you ever want to widen your horizons," he said.

I looked at the card. He thought this was my horizon.

"I'm gonna run this place someday," I said, because those words came out.

He looked at me quizzically. "Well, good for you then," he said.

And they slipped off together into the night.

That night I went to meet Alex at the Dublin House on Broadway. I ran into the girl with the light blue jacket and the blue-green sparkles on her eyelids who hung out outside the Dakota all the time; Katrina, she said her name was.

"I know *you*," she said.

"And me you," I said, though we didn't know each other at all. She was with some friends, having a good time, and it surprised me a little that someone who spent so much time hanging around our building had an actual life in the broader world.

"John's out of town," she said.

"I wouldn't know," I said.

Actually, the night before John and Buddy had spent an hour in side-by-side isolation tanks at a place in the Village. I'd done it once with Buddy. You climb into a tank where the water is your exact body temperature and the same salt level as the Dead Sea. So you float, and you wear earplugs, so you see nothing, hear nothing, feel yourself floating in the ether, or in my head across a wide ocean, and whatever you'd been worrying about drains right out of you. At least it did for me. Rachel says it's unsanitary, but I guess that's only if you think of all the people who went before you, which I refused to do.

"I saw you with him once, leaving the building."

"We're neighbors."

"I'm not like the others out there, you know," she said.

"How so?"

"You won't laugh."

"I can't promise that."

"He's going to fall in love with me."

I waited for a smile, but none came.

"You know he's got someone already," I said.

"Yes, but he had someone when he met Yoko. You know how Yoko got him? She wouldn't leave him alone. He's in a limousine with his wife and this crazy dragonlady artist jumps in the car with them. And then he left his wife for her."

"So you figure it'll happen again."

191

"The third time's the charm."

"With you."

"Look at me." She looked down and appraised herself. "I'm a *fox*. And unlike Yoko I know everything about him, his childhood, his half sister. How he misses his dead mother. Yoko's his *mother* now, you know. It's all about the mother with those two. I heard he calls her mother."

"I think it's a long shot," I said.

"All the best love stories are long shots. Tony and Maria, Romeo and Juliet."

I was struck by how normal she seemed one moment and how delusional the next.

Of course girls who fixated on famous men sometimes got to sleep with them. It must feel like they'd jumped into a movie screen, I thought.

"Those all ended badly," I said.

"*Ours* won't. Anyway, I have to work out what I'm going to say when I meet him. I figure I've got about fifteen seconds to make my case."

"That's a lot of pressure."

"If it's meant to be it'll happen," she said.

Alex walked over as the girl went back to her friends.

"Who was that?" he asked.

I replayed our conversation for him.

"I think this shit is getting dangerous. Not

192

her necessarily, but all these people outside your building waiting for John."

"I've stopped paying attention."

"But they're always there, right? And didn't some guys get into the building somehow?"

"One of them's working for him I think, doing errands."

"See, that's like feeding pigeons. Now all his friends will be out there waiting."

I shrugged.

"I got mugged last night."

"Shit, where?"

"A block from my house. I was coming home late from that party I tried to get you to go to. It blew by the way. Anyway, three guys walked over and asked me if I had five dollars they could borrow. And I said, no they couldn't 'borrow' five dollars, and so one of them hit me in the face."

"Fuck."

He showed me a bruise on his right cheekbone.

"One of the other guys had a knife. Not that big, and I didn't think he'd use it, but I gave them my wallet. They took the money out of it and my cards and dropped it on the sidewalk. One of the other guys punched me in the stomach for good measure."

"They could have killed you."

"I guess. Time to start packing heat."

"Like Charles Bronson."

"They were junkies I'm pretty sure."

"You heard about Chris Frankel," I said. Chris Frankel was a guy from the class two years ahead of us in high school who'd been killed trying to help a woman who was being attacked outside a grocery store on West Fourth.

A guy who'd been standing behind our bar stools said, "Eight people so far this year pushed in front of subway trains by strangers."

" 'I *love* New York,' " Alex sang the state's tourism theme song.

"What are the odds that some Travis Bickle out there tries to take a shot at Kennedy this weekend?" our eavesdropper said.

I'd watched a panel discussion on the Susskind show about the campaigns of the other Kennedys, how Bobby crazily rode through town in a slow-moving convertible allowing people — none of whom had been searched for weapons — to touch him or even pull him out of the car. A journalist said when he told colleagues he was skipping a late handshaking reception to get some sleep, they warned him he was "risking the possibility of missing it," meaning the assassination.

Alex asked me, "Isn't your mom doing some kind of event with Joan?"

"She's spending the whole day with her."

"Tell her to keep safe."

There was a fight outside the bar as we left to head home. One guy was trying to escape and the other caught up to him and started hitting him in the back and then in the face, breaking his nose from the sound of it, and then they both were throwing punches. The police showed up then and we took off.

Not every night was like this, not even close. Still, sometimes it felt like we were living through the end of the world.

16

"This is the most I've done since Teddy's first Senate run," Joan Kennedy said when we joined her for the ride uptown in a chauffeur-driven black Lincoln sedan. My mother explained where we were heading: to a construction project in Harlem, a rehab of a four-story brownstone, done by ex-felon women learning the construction trade.

"It sounds like an incredible project," Joan said.

"The best part is that the women get to live in it," my mother said.

It was too bad Joan wasn't the one running, my mother had said at breakfast that morning. She'd been far better on the campaign trail than anyone expected, headlining rallies and charming the press, and staying sober; though the more voters liked her, a columnist wrote, the worse it was for Ted, who drove her to drink in the first place.

"Did you know either of these two?" Joan asked.

Splashed within the *Daily News* she'd been reading was the story of the girls' prep school headmistress, Jean Harris, who'd shot dead her longtime boyfriend, the Scarsdale Diet Doctor, Herman Tarnower, for displacing her in favor of his twenty-nine-year-old nurse.

"We actually met Jean when we were looking at boarding schools for Rachel."

"Old Herman's no dreamboat," Joan said. "Maybe he's a tiger in bed."

"A tiger no longer," my mother said.

Of the Kennedy wives, Joan was considered the most fetching and *human;* she was nicknamed "the Dish," though she was known to occasionally step in it, saying the wrong thing to the wrong person, like telling a reporter she'd once borrowed one of Jackie's wigs ("What? The First Lady wears *wigs?*"), or wearing a miniskirt to a White House party and drawing stares from Pat Nixon ("Who *is* that? Oh, Joan Kennedy, of course").

She was, my mother said, unpretentious and unrehearsed, which is why they'd been friends so long.

"What was Jean Harris like when you met

197

her?" Joan asked.

"Pleasant, professional. She said she watched Buddy, but didn't say whether she liked it. You know those people. 'I *watched* your show,' they say."

"That's what people say all the time about Ted's speeches. 'I *watched* Ted's speech.' And you're supposed to ask them what they thought, but I really don't want to know unless they want to tell me they loved it, because I really can't do anything about their being disappointed with him. What can I say, 'He disappoints me too sometimes'?"

"Where did you two meet anyhow?" my mother asked.

"You know this story, don't you? I was at Manhattanville College, about twenty minutes from here," she said, smiling now in memory. "We were fixed up by his sister Jean."

My mother had a gift for pulling friends out of gloomy ditches and onto sunnier topics.

"He called me a bunch of times before we went on our actual first date. He wanted to get to know me, he said."

"Without being distracted by your beauty."

"It was the essay part of the test."

"You know I couldn't do what you've been

doing for Ted, for Buddy or anyone. I wouldn't last ten minutes."

"The campaign fishbowl."

"Exactly."

"Did you see the story on me in the *Herald*?"

"I heard about it," my mother said.

The *Boston Herald* had run a front-page story — with supposed before and after photographs — suggesting that Joan Kennedy had undergone a face-lift.

"They couldn't just say I looked nice."

"Not and boost their circulation I guess."

"It's depressing. It feels like they hate us sometimes."

She took a deep breath and pursed her lips.

"Don't you think that strong feelings — I mean really passionate ones for public figures — are fake?" I said.

It was something I'd been thinking about.

"What do you mean?" Joan said.

"It's fake when you love them, because if you've never met them what are you loving? A *role* they played in a movie, or on stage. And when you loathe a public figure it's the same. Every great man in history was hated by someone, and most villains inspired devotion. Hitler had women who gave up their lives for him."

"And then Jack and Bobby had men hating them so much they killed them," she said.

"Exactly," I said.

My mother shot me a disapproving look about where I'd steered the conversation.

We passed by Columbia, where I'd gone to college. I saw one of my old professors on the sidewalk eating a bagel on his way to class.

"Sometimes," Joan said then, "I'm relieved that Teddy's campaign is nothing like Bobby's. None of the leaping into the car to touch his hair, or grab at his shirtsleeves, none of the physical contact of that campaign. That was scary to me, even before what happened."

I remember Buddy telling me once that charisma could be a dangerous thing. Maybe Teddy would be saved by his lack of it, I thought.

Up at Project New Life, we sat in on a workshop and toured the building, where there was lots of sawing and hammering and energetic activity. It was inspiring. It made me want to build something, to use my hands again like I'd done in the Peace Corps.

As we walked around the site, the supervisor filled us in on the crimes each of the women had committed, some of them pretty grisly.

"The woman putting that shower together over there, Mara. Used to assault old people for drug money. Now look at her. I'd hire her tomorrow if I could."

"Why don't you?" Joan asked.

"That's the tricky part. They're not in the union."

"Is it hard to get into the union?"

"Big-time, but we're trying to change that."

When I asked New Life's director, a short frizzy-haired woman named Gail, about the women who rehabbed the house being able to live in it, she said there was some pushback from a neighborhood group about having ex-felons living near working families.

"That seems both shortsighted and unkind," my mother said.

"Teddy should really see this," Joan said.

"The senator is welcome anytime," Gail said. "We might just put him to work."

"Not with his back," Joan said, and then said to my mother, "I need to keep my mouth shut."

"What's wrong with saying he has a bad back?"

"I mentioned it once and he was furious with me."

"Why?"

"He said it made him sound weak."

"It was from a plane crash that he survived, wasn't it?"

"Yes."

"Hiding it is what sounds weak."

"You're right. I'm going to tell him that."

I raised my eyebrows at my brazen mother, and she nodded back to say, *I know, I know.*

They went back to Joan's hotel to work on her "Women's Talk" and I went for a half-assed run in the park by myself listening on my Walkman to Gang of Four's *Entertainment!*, then went home for a shower. On my machine was a message from Harry with the news that Phil Donahue wanted Buddy to come on for a full hour on his show. It would be a tribute to Buddy, he said, and then they would talk about Buddy's external and internal journeys.

I called Harry's office.

"I like this, Anton. I like it a lot. And they're filming that week in New York, so we don't have to travel."

I pictured the women in the audience with teary-eyed faces of sympathy.

"It sounds potentially disastrous," I said.

"Like any bet with a big payoff," Harry said.

At the Acorn Room at the Park Tavern, my parents were among those latecomers standing in the back of the room, which was filled to capacity, all two hundred seats taken by supporters. Signs nearby read WOMEN FOR TEDDY and TEDDY CARES ABOUT US.

After a rousing introduction by the president of the League of Women Voters, Joan stepped onto the stage, her blond hair flowing, in an orange, stylishly cut dress. ("She loves orange," my mother whispered.)

She tested the microphone a couple of times, and said, "Can everyone hear me all right?"

She began by praising what she admired about Teddy as a man and as a father, and what this campaign meant for the country at large. I thought of the speech my mother might write on behalf of Buddy, and I imagined it being like one of those bits at a Don Rickles roast ("When he said 'Let's be unpredictable,' I didn't realize it meant he'd leave us high and dry. But seriously now, Buddy has a lot to give. To those he barely knows."); Dean Martin and Sammy Davis Jr. and Angie Dickinson would all wince, and take a sip from their drinks, and finally my mother would blow a real kiss my father's way, and they'd affectionately lock eyes, and my sister would say, "What a fucking train wreck," but in a loving way. Joan talked of her own efforts on the campaign trail and the people she'd met in places like Iowa, Wisconsin, Florida, "and right here in New York!"

Then she pivoted to the material she'd been fine-tuning for the last week.

"I'd like to say something here about the women's movement which I find very exciting. I'm new to it," she said. "My husband's record on women's issues makes him the man for the women of America."

"Oh yeah. You *know* it," said a crazy-eyed man in a Star Wars T-shirt.

"Sshhh," my mother said.

"Christ, he's balled half the women of New York and New England."

Joan paused for only a moment and then continued, "My dream is that through our struggle we can bring women into full and equal participation in American life. And the end result won't just be equal participation in the old man's world of power, work, and competition, but the chance to change the world, to make a new and better, and more humane, world."

The heckler called out, "In which a powerful man can leave a girl drowning and not call anyone about it for twelve hours."

"Will you please pipe down?" my mother said. He was around ten feet from us.

"It's a free country, isn't it?" the heckler said.

"What are you *doing* here?" my mother asked.

"Listening to the candidate's wife, like everyone else."

"Then *listen* like everyone else," Buddy said, his face tensing.

"You want to do something about it?" the heckler said.

Buddy looked ready to fight, which was beyond a terrible idea.

"He doesn't," I said. "Come on, Dad."

"Don't I know you?" the heckler asked.

"Unlikely," I said, standing between Buddy and the heckler.

Joan took the microphone from the lectern and walked with it toward her audience, like a rock star or a televangelist.

"Let's address the elephant in the room," she said into her mic, her voice resounding through the room. "As many of you know I have suffered from alcohol addiction, an illness that has affected my family, my health, and my self-esteem."

Silence now. The room was hers.

"You're all drunks. *Every one* of you," the heckler said, and then two security guards appeared at his side.

"We're going to have to ask you to leave," one of them, a burly guard with a mustache, said.

"I'm going to have to ask *you* to leave," the heckler answered.

Joan narrowed her eyes. "You must have some sort of a perfect life to take potshots at us."

"I loved your brothers-in-law," the man said.

"Come on," the guards said.

"I did too!" Joan said. "And if they were alive, they would be here tonight talking about what a *magnificent* man their younger brother is. There isn't a man alive more perfectly suited to address the country's illnesses than Ted Kennedy," Joan said.

There was silence for a moment and then tepid applause across the room.

She was just revving up and had more to say. She spoke for another ten minutes about moments of kindness for which Teddy was responsible — real ones, worthy of praise — and then she walked offstage to loud and respectful applause.

I walked home thinking of that heckler, of

Buddy treating him like a blowhard at a neighborhood association meeting when he could easily have been a lunatic with a Glock strapped to his leg, and I thought of Alex getting jumped, and the subway riders pushed in front of trains, two more in the last week. What made you want to end the life of a stranger? And did you plan your crime, or did the desire seize you out of nowhere, like the impulse to key the side of a car? A week ago Kip had climbed two flights of subway stairs on his way home from practice and when he reached the top a gold-toothed behemoth of a man grabbed his tennis rackets and threw them down the full stairs, because he felt like it. He even smiled, and he said, *"What?"* as though Kip hadn't the right to object.

Something mean was building out there.

As I made my way up the unlit side of Central Park West, I felt my heart quicken with fear. It's nothing, I thought — Joan won the night, and I'd kept Buddy from trouble. Still I flinched when a bus pulled by with that ad for *The Fog* again: "It is night. It is cold. It is coming."

17

And still . . . a mere five days later, Joan's husband won the New York primary going away. He'd trailed by thirty points the night of her speech, and he somehow won by twenty, and took Connecticut too, and for two full days, his was a winning campaign. My steadfast mother with her husband and oldest son in tow got to celebrate in style at Teddy's victory party at the Halloran House Hotel on Lexington and Forty-Ninth; six hundred supporters squeezed into a ball-room on the second floor, where the music pounded and the drinks flowed, and Teddy said unrealistically that the race had just turned in his favor.

A woman in a sparkly blue dress and wearing a red, white, and blue Kennedy skimmer hat kissed me forcefully on the mouth. She was tipsy and in the darkened room it was clear she thought she was kissing someone else. After a few seconds she said, "I'm sorry. I thought . . . ," and then she said, "Oh, fuck it, who cares," and went on kissing me.

She instructed me to wait while she retrieved her coat, that we could share a cab together, and then on her way to the coat check she found the guy for whom the kiss was intended, a man in a white oxford shirt like my own and around my height, but ten years older and with a more muscular build. She waved to me and shrugged, as though she'd just as soon have been with me, an outlier, on this outlier night.

I found my parents celebrating on the other side of the room, my mother wearing a Kennedy hat and Buddy serenading the room with a red and silver noisemaker. They raised their champagne flutes. In a season of discouragement finally a nice surprise.

"Call off the vultures," Buddy said.

My father had his own rise-from-the-ashes victory a week later on *The Phil Donahue Show*. It was mostly the candid and soul-baring conversation, but it was also the signature moments from Buddy's career that Donahue's producers wove in before each commercial break: the night Nixon resigned, the night Norman Mailer and Jimmy Breslin launched their fifty-first state campaign, Joe Namath a week after the Super Bowl, Joan Didion and Pete Hamill after the bombing of Cambodia, Jim Bouton aping Mickey Mantle playing on a hangover.

Donahue, who usually filmed in Chicago, had scheduled a week of shows in New York, at a studio on West Fifty-Second and Broadway. He and Buddy had breakfast together at the Café des Artistes and caught up. Donahue was excited about his upcoming marriage to the actress Marlo Thomas, whom he'd met when she was a guest on his show.

"Must have been some interview," Buddy said, between bites of his omelet.

"You know it really was," Donahue said.

"I almost did that once," Buddy said, straight-faced.

"Fall in love with a guest and later propose?"

"Yes. With Groucho Marx, but my mother disapproved."

"Why?" Donahue said.

"There was just something funny about him, she said."

Donahue, in his adulatory intro, recast Buddy's nervous breakdown as a midlife crisis and suggested we all have them, or *should* have them, that it was our spiritual obligation to at some point step outside our driven paths and investigate the wider world around us with our paperback copies of Carlos Castaneda and our peyote. He referred several times to Buddy's *Razor's Edge* journey, and showed short clips of Tyrone Power in the film climbing in the Himalayas.

"So when you walked off that stage, did you think it was a one-night thing, you'd be back the next day?"

"I knew it was more than that."

"But you hadn't planned anything in advance."

"No. It just happened. It felt like I was watching from the front row of the audience. I remember thinking, What in hell are you doing? I left the theater and got a cab right away. How often does that happen? I told my driver to head out of the city and so he got on the West Side Highway, and kept going."

"You had money."

"A hundred bucks. I'd gone to the bank that day and that's what I took out whenever I went to the bank. I had my credit cards too."

"No clothes."

"The ones I was wearing."

"So where'd you end up?"

"Poughkeepsie that first night. I stayed in

a motel room that had a painting of a swan."

"It's funny what we remember."

"There were two Bibles. I remember that too. And a purple comforter."

"Did you watch the news? You were on it that night."

"Then I'm glad I didn't."

"And you called your family."

"I did, to tell my wife I was okay. And then to say I *wasn't* okay, and that I'd be gone for a while."

"How did she take it?"

"Not well, as you can imagine."

"You drove west after that, and you told me yesterday about stepping out of your car on a Wyoming road, with the bison patties and the tumbling sagebrush and the scraps of snow, and no cars or people around for miles."

"It felt like one of those *Twilight Zone* episodes where the world ended and no one told you. I'd never been so isolated, and yet I felt more connected to who I was and what things meant than I had in months."

The audience was rapt.

"Then the sun dipped, and the sky went red and a herd of elk passed in the distance, and I lifted outside myself into the sound of the wind, and that heartbreaking light."

"It sounds like dying," Donahue said.

"Or living."

I thought he might be putting everyone on, that he'd stop there and break into a smile. But then he told a story I hadn't heard before.

"That night I went to a country bar and I met a cowboy, six feet three, real cowboy hat, mustache, and we got to talking. He'd been born Jewish in Crown Heights, moved out west ten years ago, stayed, got a job on a ranch, and then converted to Buddhism. He said to me, 'Bet you never met a Jewish Buddhist cowboy before.' I told him no, and certainly not one with a New York accent. He bought me a beer. 'The best in the world,' he said, 'Miller High Life.'

" 'You want to start living,' he said, 'then stop living in the future. Stop making plans. People who live in the present have no use for making plans. The ones making plans all the time never enjoy anything because by the time they get there they're making new ones, like a dog chasing after a bone that hangs in front of their face from a stick attached to their collar.' He got very close to me then. I could count the whiskers in his mustache. He said, 'You're never *here*. You never *get there*. You're always thinking about the future when something different'll happen, and then when it doesn't, when today is like last week, or last year, then you want more time, *more time please*! But what you're really afraid of is death, and why? Because death stops the future.' "

"So what's the answer?" Donahue asked.

"I asked him that, and he said, 'Live in the present. Be here.' "

"And . . . ?"

"And that was it. And then the song 'Mammas Don't Let Your Babies Grow Up to Be Cowboys' came on. And my Jewish Buddhist cowboy friend yelled out, 'It's too fricking late for that!' "

"But he didn't say 'frick.' "

"That's correct."

"But that was never my issue. I live in the moment. I just have trouble sometimes figuring out what all the moments add up to. And at some point it occurred to me that I wasn't going at the answers in the right way."

"What's the right way to go at the answers."

"It's to learn how to listen, and not just to what's said."

"To the truth beneath," Donahue said.

"Yes," Buddy said, reveling in his role as talk-show sage.

Before the commercial break they showed another clip of the misty-eyed tuxedoed

Tyrone Power in *The Razor's Edge,* this time explaining his restlessness to a worried Gene Tierney by telling her of a soldier he saw killed in the war. "The dead look so terribly dead when they're dead," he says.

When they resumed, Donahue said, "So now you're at peace."

"Which poses a whole new set of issues."

"How so?"

"You make this realization that the peace and serenity, and even the comprehension, is at odds with ambition, the fuel of which is rage and dissatisfaction not only with the world but with yourself. That's your drive. Once you have bliss, peace, you want to sit back, and sleep, or take a walk, or go for a swim, all good for your soul, but maybe not your career. The drive itself is about filling a hole inside you, and once it's filled what the hell do you write about."

Donahue nodded thoughtfully.

They talked then about how Jack Paar had also walked off his show over a battle with the censors over an innocuous joke. His *Tonight Show* audience had liked it. But NBC replaced it with five minutes of news. Paar steamed off his show the next night and in his words "wound up in Hong Kong."

"He returned after three weeks, and they

gave him his show back," Buddy said.

"And then he quit two years later," Donahue said. "Passed it on to some guy named Carson."

It was catharsis as entertainment, and the audience ate it up.

At the show's conclusion the camera settled on Donahue's charitable face.

"A few weeks ago it dawned on me why so many of us have felt lost in these turbulent times. Maybe it's *this:* that the night Buddy Winter left the stage was the night we lost our guiding spirit; that at the end of a bewildering, mad-as-hell day we always felt sane again watching you." He turned and faced Buddy, seated alone on stage. "So please come back, Buddy. Wherever you turn up, we'll tune in, so you can once again decipher this upside-down world for us, and make us laugh and think along the way."

After the taping, I stood with Harry Abrams, as we waited for Buddy.

"Remember what I said about our Olympic back story," Harry said.

"This was it?"

"Now we go for the gold."

18

I too once vanished.

I remembered this as we left the studio. I was ten, and Alex and I decided not to head home after school as we always did. We would occasionally go to one or the other's apartment, and then call home to check in. This day, without telling anyone, we went to Loew's 83rd and watched a double feature, and then we made the poor decision to watch the first movie a second time. Meanwhile our mothers had called each other, and then some other mothers and then the school and then the police.

I think we didn't call because we knew they'd be pissed at us, and we'd be punished, and the adventure would be over. So instead we watched three movies and then we went to a pizza place and had slices, and when we walked out a police car spotted us and put its siren on. They pulled over and took us in.

We'd been gone seven hours, a shitty thing for me to do to my mother. I thought of that day when Buddy was missing in silence for fifteen hours, and then when he chose to stay away for weeks. I was less worried than angry once we heard from him, because I didn't understand why he couldn't just come home. Buddy's breakdown had to do with his brain being a radio antenna tuned to all the best stations, and to too many stations, and then to none at all. He wasn't Larry Darrell in *The Razor's Edge*, as Donahue intimated. His demons weren't from a war or from the things he never did, because he married well, picked the right job, and had the right kids, or at least he always said so. Buddy had new and hard-earned things to say about the mind and the human spirit, which made for watchable television, but a part of me feared his comeback would consist now of public sessions of amateur psychoanalysis, Band-Aids of "meaning" to follow a recounting of his blue moods and sleepless hauntings (*"It began a period of darkness in Buddy's life . . ."*), which I'd rather not see. Not on TV. Not across from the cloying Barbara Walters or the noxious Tom Snyder, or that smug David Frost. I wanted to move on to whatever came next.

218

But it wasn't my call. He'd gone out there and had fun of all things. People applauded, and Harry was thrilled. All in all, I was too.

While I'm confessing things I should add here that I found four journals Buddy had stashed away, with his diary notes from his travels. I'd opened one up, read a page, and then backed off, out of respect for his privacy and fear of what I'd find.

After my shift I felt wired still from the Donahue taping, and from my hours at the Tavern, and so rather than go home I went to the park with Ricky, a bartender, and Manuel, a pantry cook, and two waitresses, Bronwen and Janet.

We drank pints of Guinness (nicked from the bar) on the benches around Bethesda Fountain, where a dozen or so people were hanging about, among them a man playing Arlo Guthrie songs on the guitar, seated on a blanket with a long-haired kid playing bongo drums, and a couple in matching gold jackets and shorts roller-boogieing around a transistor radio.

Ricky was recalling the birthday party Yoko Ono threw John and Sean — they shared the same birthday — at the Tavern last fall in the glass-enclosed atrium, a party my parents had attended, a fact I didn't share. I'd seen photos at the restaurant, John dressed in black and wearing plastic yellow sunglasses, and the rest of the guests in T-shirts Yoko had printed up with their names under a huge red heart.

"He's a really cute kid. Sweet too," Janet said.

"He's got a life ahead of him, doesn't he?" Bronwen said.

" 'Boy, you're gonna carry that weight, carry that weight a long time,' " Ricky sang.

"Remember that letter they wrote?"

The Lennons took out a full page of the *New York Times* explaining their years away from the limelight and that it didn't mean they didn't love their public — they just needed some respectful distance.

Not everyone liked the letter.

"You know what she said once?" Janet said. "She said that if she was a Jewish girl during the Holocaust she would find a way to be Hitler's girlfriend, and after ten days of sleeping with her he'd do whatever she said."

"Hitler cums, then succumbs," I said.

I made her laugh. It was a crazy boast, Yoko's, but I bought it, that she'd believe in her power through sex over famous men.

"I love that it's ten days of fucking, don't you?" Ricky said.

"I'd really like to fuck John Lennon," Bronwen said.

"Who wouldn't?" Manuel said.

"You want to fuck him."

"I would," Manuel said.

"I thought you liked young guys," Ricky said.

"I do, but for a Beatle I'd make an exception."

"I don't think he goes that way."

"I heard he did a few times. Did you hear that, Anton?"

"I didn't," I said.

"Are we making you uncomfortable? We make everyone uncomfortable."

I took a long draw of a joint that was going around. It felt like they were performing for me, as if to say, Aren't we crazy? Can you handle us?

"Are you high yet?" Bronwen said.

"Getting there."

She took what sounded like an enormous hit.

"Come here, Anton," she said. "Open your mouth."

I did; she blew smoke in.

"She's a tease, dude," said Ricky.

"I'm more than that," Bronwen said. "But work is work and pleasure is pleasure and the two don't mix. Just ask Ricky."

Manuel said, "Ricky fucked one of the managers."

"Which one?"

"Who do you think? Becca."

"You're kidding me," I said. Becca looked like Stevie Nicks from Fleetwood Mac and had supposedly dropped out of Barnard. Her father was friends with Rowan.

"One time."

"And."

"She's a mess, my friend. I mean she's an animal, but a very complex human being. You don't want to go there, believe me."

"Anyone ever fuck a customer?" Manuel asked.

"I did once," Janet said. "I mean we dated for a while."

"And you liked him."

"Well, yeah. We dated for three months."

Someone other than Elena's boyfriend, I thought.

"Who ended it?" Ricky asked.

"None of your business."

"He did," Bronwen said.

"No, *I* did," Janet said.

"You cheated on him."

"Well, yes. But it was with someone I used to go out with so it wasn't like I started something new."

"Did he catch you together?"

"Can we get off this subject?"

"Holy shit, I'm right," Ricky said.

"Anton, spill the beans. What do you have going?" Bronwen asked.

"Boys or girls?" Manuel asked.

"Those are my only choices?"

"You're single I'm guessing," Bronwen said.

"Decidedly so."

"Good for you. That won't last long. Not in this city and not working nights. It gets crazy," Ricky said.

Manuel blew out smoke and said, "Hell yeah, motherfucker."

Bronwen and I left the park together and I got more of her story. She was a nightclub singer, she said, but for now she was auditioning for commercial jingles. She'd gotten two small radio spots and had just missed getting a national TV commercial, for L'eggs panty hose. Like everything else in the world, she said, around twenty-five people sang 90 percent of the jingles and if you were one of that prized group you made a good living.

I asked what they looked for in a jingle singer and she said good diction, a good ear, an ability to make even the most ridiculous lyrics sound real. I asked her to sing one.

"Airline or beer?"

"Airline."

She closed her eyes, and then like Lena Horne sings "Stormy Weather" she sang, "Pan Am makes the going great, Pan Am makes the going great."

"Fucking brilliant," I said.

"Thank you."

I then said, "Beer please," and she sang, "It's refreshing not sweet, it's the extra dry treat, why don't you try extra dry Rheingold beeeer."

"I'd listen to you sing a parking ticket," I said.

We walked to her subway station at Seventy-Second and Broadway, and along the way stopped to buy hot dogs at the Papaya King. I told her beyond jingles she should be singing in a Broadway show. She said it was a hard world to crack, that all the best things were within closed circles. She asked me with all my connections why I was bussing tables, and I said because I didn't know what else to do, and that it was as good a job as any, and that I was Rowan's neighbor and he asked me. She said Rowan would probably move me quickly to waiter, that I'd have her job soon, that there were a lot of people at the restaurant gunning for her.

I wondered if she saw in me exactly what she was up against, that there were people like her with talent and ones like me who knew people, and if it was someone like me against someone like her, the ones like me usually won, which was unfair, but how the world worked. I wanted to find something of my own that had nothing to do with Buddy, where I sailed on my own merits and nothing more.

"If it's your job, I wouldn't take it," I said.

"It's nice to think that," she said. She kissed me on the cheek and slipped down the stairs toward her train.

19

I received my first check from Buddy the next day in Fielding's mailbox, three hundred dollars, with the subject line Project Renaissance. I was to log in my hours each week, and include overtime, which I wouldn't do because we were, in Rachel's words, hemorrhaging money. My mother said we were okay until summer, we had some rainy-day accounts we could cash in, that I shouldn't worry, which made me worry more.

Buddy spent hours in his study, writing jokes and his thoughts on a yellow legal pad. He'd begin with the things he felt in a broad sense; then he'd free-associate until he landed on something funny. At his best he was stupefying to watch. It drove Harry crazy, he told me once. He'd have an essay to write, a few jokes, or a skit, and he could bang it out in around ten minutes and it would be letter perfect. "Something that

226

would take a human two hours to write."
I saw these things on his notebook —

No tired truths.
Sharp humor needs fresh modes of see-
ing.
Figure out what it is you have to say.
To do: write a new monologue every day,
no ifs or buts.

When we weren't working on the show, we'd pretend to be Parisians or Germans touring the city. We'd go to places like the Frick, the Museum of Natural History, the planetarium, the Paley Center for Media, and on a warm day in early April to one of our favorite spots: the Explorers Club for a talk on the *Kon-Tiki*, presided over by two of the participants.

"Someone is meeting us there. I'll leave it a surprise."

"Who?"

"Would it be a surprise if I told you?"

The city's transit workers were on strike, which meant no buses or subways, and the city was transformed, bikes everywhere, and people on roller skates or skateboards, or just walking long distances in running shoes. There was something unifying about things like this — and blizzards and heat

227

waves and blackouts — that made it feel like we all lived in the same glorious and flawed small town.

"Everyone's smiling today, but let's see what happens when this goes on for three weeks."

The worst unifier by far we all lived through together was the garbage strike, when the city was a dreamscape of garbage, ten thousand pounds a day of rotting food and bottles and cans and fast-food packages, and moldy, bruised fruit in overflowing paper bags, and rats everywhere, and no clear spot on the sidewalk on which to walk, and the streets themselves covered in refuse, cars rolling through to the crunch of breaking glass. The day they cleaned it all up felt like a miracle, and I remember my mother stopping in the street to hug a sanitation worker.

As we strolled around the Explorers Club looking at the photos, a man in sunglasses and a baseball cap descended on us.

"Did you come by skateboard?" he asked.

John sometimes, with his hair tied back and that downsloping nose, looked to me like someone doing an amazing John Lennon impersonation.

"Roller skates," Buddy said. "We raced, and I shamed my poor son. I think it's the malaria."

"Keep your kids sick if you want to stay on top."

Until recently the Explorers Club had been located on our block.

"This is my favorite ocean voyage story," John said. "Casting out to sea in a balsawood raft with five men and a parrot. Eating the flying fish that topple aboard and waving at the sharks. Fuck being a rock star."

We circled around the exhibit.

There were photographs of them chopping down trees in the Ecuadorian jungle for the balsa logs, and another of them lashing the logs together with hemp ropes.

"No nails or metal allowed," John said.

There was an enticing photograph of them out in the currents with the sails billowing, two of them posed at the top of the masthead.

"Look at that. That could be you and me, Buddy Boy. . . ."

More pictures of them sailing through high seas. They covered as much as seventy-one miles in a day, and averaged more than forty.

"That's the life. At the mercy of the winds for five thousand miles."

On the same wall was a great shot of Thor

Heyerdahl at the steering oar with a rising mountain of water behind him. Another of Torstein Raaby holding up a three-foot snake mackerel that had leapt onto the boat and somehow wriggled into his sleeping bag.

"Not the type of nighttime visitor you'd want on a lonely night at sea," Buddy said.

"Too skinny," John said. "Give me a shapely dolphin and I'd be happy."

In the next room were scenes of them hanging out in the bamboo cabin under a roof of plaited bamboo and banana leaves, which made them feel, Heyerdahl said in the label copy, like they were in a virgin forest; then scenes of food preparation, and of all the fish they caught, which Heyerdahl wrote could have fed a flotilla of boats.

We sat for the lecture. Thor had pitched a story to *National Geographic*, but they passed, saying it was a suicide mission, that they would surely drown at sea.

"This is my next life," John said after.

"You want to sail around the world."

"Not all the way, but a small bit of it, yes. I'm buying a sailboat you know."

"You said you might."

"What kind are you getting?" I asked.

"I don't know. A Sunfish, I think. Something small."

"Get something a little bigger than that,"

I said. "A Sunfish is a toy. You'll spend the whole day soaked. At least get a Mercury, or a Bullseye. You may even want a little cuddy up front to stash a sleeping bag in case you want to sleep out on the water."

"He knows his stuff," John said.

"This is your sailing guru," Buddy said.

"I need one," John said.

"He'll get you shipshape in a week."

"Well then, get yourself out to the house, and we'll start the lessons. I want to be seaworthy by June."

"We can do that," I said.

"Not next week, though. Yoko's got me on a vow of silence."

"Seriously."

"Ten days. Like the Tibetan monks. No TV, no books or newspapers or magazines."

"What's the point?"

"It cleans everything out."

"I've done it for a few days. More than that I'd go crazy," Buddy said.

"No you wouldn't. You sit there, and then you withdraw. And then at some point you start to see these different parts of yourself. Like spirits passing through a temple, and you're the temple."

Buddy nodded. "And then you go mad."

"Maybe. We'll see. It's not a year. It's only ten days."

I'd heard Yoko had sent John around the globe for a spiritual realignment.

"Best to move slowly right now, Yoko says. It's Mercury Retrograde."

"I know something about this," Buddy said. "It means . . . what does it mean?"

"It's a bad time to make any decisions, to begin new endeavors."

Mercury rules reading, editing, researching, negotiating, he said. The theory is that the planet Mercury was resting, so it couldn't supervise the tasks it was best at overseeing. It's like leaving the kids alone in the house. While it naps, there's no well-functioning planet supervising things.

"Venus and Mars are in retrograde too," John said, "which means it's a particularly bad time to have any plastic surgery done. Venus rules beauty and Mars rules surgery."

"I'm canceling my boob job immediately," Buddy said.

At a café down the street from the explorer's club, John asked about Buddy's quest for a new show and Buddy told him about his lunchtime humiliations.

"They're trying to see if I'm crazy. I had to make sure I wasn't dribbling my soup or screaming at the busboys. One of them said he wanted to be sure I was 'good to go.' "

"Fuck them. They're always poking at you, prodding you, seeing if you're daft, or if you're too stoned, or if you've been coerced by a Japanese temptress, or if you're under the spell of the maharishi and his tantric LSD."

"I *was* on acid at the lunch meeting. Was that a mistake?"

"Not with those fucks."

"I don't think they trust me not to go mad again."

"You might have to do a primal."

"I've actually thought about it."

"Primal scream," I said.

"Powerful stuff," John said.

"Did it work?"

"Maybe. You got to some dark stuff, that's for sure. What kind of material do you need to get to? I had a dad who ran off, and a mum who got run over by a drunken policeman."

"My childhood was too normal to explain my troubles."

"You haven't dug around enough. They'll get you in a room and poke around your emotional cavities until you reach the scream. When you hit it, they tell you to *go with it* and then you make a cosmic, mental, and physical alignment with it, a break-through."

"And you learn something."

"That's the idea. But it's more that you crack the seal on the shite you didn't want to face."

"Did that happen with you?"

"More or less. Yoko thinks Janov was a daddy for me, that I have a father complex and am always searching for my daddy."

"Are you?"

"Sure. Janov in a sense was a daddy, and the maharishi. There's lots of daddies around. But they all let you down now, don't they?"

He was looking at me then.

"Don't answer, Anton," Buddy said.

"They do. You did, because you weren't the fuckin' paragon of goodness and cleverness that people wanted you to be," John said. "You snapped and then Daddy died, but you weren't their fuckin' daddy, and nor was I. You're Anton's daddy, and I'm Sean's and Julian's for all my mistakes."

"I've been a shitty daddy," Buddy said.

It was like that possibility was dawning on him for the first time.

"You're not now," I said.

"He's the best fuckin' dad in the world so far as I can see. Who does what you two do? You bloody work together. I wish Buddy was my dad."

"Maybe I can adopt you."

"Too late. I'm already out of my nappies."

We walked home, the three of us, through the Central Park Zoo, which was like walking through an animal concentration camp, Buddy said.

"The seals are the only ones with any life to them."

The polar bear cage was the saddest, with these huge beautiful bears pressing their noses against the bars.

"We're our own particular animal, ex-stars. They deprive us of space, hound us, and then we want to escape to do our thing, and if we peek our faces out, they stare at us, prod us, judge us, and who are they to judge, what the fuck did they ever do?"

"Fucking nothing," Buddy said.

"They want to *meet* us, why? They don't want to even bloody listen to us, they want our autograph, our signature, or photograph, or an item of clothing, the dregs of our wine. They want our souls."

He looked at the polar bears again.

"I know what you're thinking, big boy. You want a couple of nice juicy Winterburgers."

One of the bears grumbled and then began pacing.

"He says he wants the rock star," Buddy said.

"I'm not gonna go quietly," John said.

"His mother was hit by a car?" I asked when we got back to the building.

"When he was seventeen and in art school. Terrible story. She'd been over at her sister's house, John's aunt Mimi."

"Where was John?"

"I'm not sure. Out somewhere. Anyway, his mother stepped between two hedges and then started crossing the street and she was hit by an off-duty police officer who was drunk, it turned out."

"How did John find out?"

"You know, I think he was at his mother's, with her boyfriend, who John didn't like. And another cop came by and told him."

"And what about his father?"

"Don't you remember? He talked about this on the show."

"He left to work on a tourist boat, right?"

"His father was a character. Was up until he died from what I gather. He worked on merchant ships during the war as a saloon steward. He did skits for the passengers and sang."

"How old was John when he left?"

"Three I think. And he was gone a lot

before that. But when John was three he took off for around a year and a half. He worked in New York at Macy's while he was on shore leave, was thrown in jail for a couple of weeks for desertion and later for stealing a bottle of whiskey. John said they didn't know if he was dead or alive."

"So when did he take John away to Blackpool?"

"That part's a bit murky. His mother was carrying on with a man named Bobby Dykins who no one liked. Alf had fought him on the front porch of the house. So from what John said, Alf decided to take him away. He convinced Mimi he was taking him shopping for clothes, and then they took a tram to Blackpool."

"And his mother showed up three weeks later."

"That part is so poignant. This five-year-old kid is told right there to choose which of his imperfect parents he'll live with and which one he might not ever see again."

"So he didn't see his father again."

"He'll tell you if you ask him. His father showed up when John was performing with the Beatles. He came to the theater with a nineteen-year-old girl who would end up being his wife."

"John's stepmother."

"Which is all to say he had plenty of things to scream about."

I felt hearing this lucky, that I'd had such a relatively ordinary if extraordinary childhood. No parent stealing me away, neither of them being run over by a drunken cop, not yet anyhow.

Our period of misadventure was what we were now living within.

20

"You sat on the edge of the bed *didn't ya?*" Alex said. "You put your fingers between your toes, you picked your feet, *didn't ya!*"

"Nice," Randy said.

"He's an actor," Rachel said.

It was Oscar night and my mother ordered ten large pizzas and Buddy mixed cocktails and we had a small awards party with Harry Abrams and his wife, Judith, a dozen or so neighbors, Alex, and my sister's new boyfriend, Randy the cop.

The subject at hand was our favorite movie cops and Alex's was Popeye Doyle in *The French Connection.*

Randy said his was Steve McQueen in *Bullitt.*

"Look, you work your side of the street, and I'll work mine," Alex said, squinting McQueen-style.

"Not as good," Rachel told him.

"He lives in the building," I said.

"Steve McQueen?" asked Randy.

"No, Peter Yates, the guy who directed *Bullitt.* He's up for an Oscar tonight."

"For what?"

"*Breaking Away,* the bike-racing movie."

Rachel's favorite was *Serpico,* which she'd seen four times and was, she joked, a big part of why she was dating Randy.

"Is the police department as corrupt as people think?" Alex asked.

"Yes and no. We've got problems for sure. But there are a lot of good cops out there."

He said it was easy to slip into bad habits.

"Such as."

"Taking free stuff, free meals at restaurants, tickets to the Knicks, and then you start looking the other way when you're supposed to be handing out citations."

"You do stuff like that?" Alex said.

"I don't actually."

"Have you done any big drug busts?" Kip asked him.

"I think those days are over, the big shipments arriving in the panels of cars. Most of the heroin these days comes in by mail, in letter-sized envelopes if you can believe it."

"Seriously?" Alex said.

"They send out dealers on bikes to make drops at scattered mailboxes to throw us off. And it isn't coming from Marseilles. They closed down those refineries. It's coming from Burma and Thailand, Laos. The Golden Triangle."

"And they're using mules. Do you know what a mule is, Anton?" Rachel asked me.

"*Yes*, Rachel, I know what a mule is."

"Middle-class families," Rachel said, "and kids from Choate and Exeter are paying for their three-week vacations to Thailand with drug money from smuggling."

"Your friends and neighbors," Randy said.

"I so admire you guys," said our fourth-floor neighbor Geoffrey Knudsen, a tax attorney who wore a shiny blue ascot under a starched white dress shirt. "You're really undermanned out there, aren't you?"

It was a relief to have the conversation revolve around something other than Buddy's fortunes. Nights like this were particularly hard, because six years ago Buddy had *hosted* the Emmys and was talked about as a potential Oscars host. He might be hosting them tonight instead if he hadn't screwed the pooch, he told me as we shopped for party provisions that afternoon. "Now here I am making sure Geoffrey Knudsen has enough brie to spread on his Wheat Thins."

Nothing had gone our way, and whatever

bump up we thought we'd get from Dona-hue hadn't yet materialized.

"At least they have the vests now," said Carol Overton, a frizzy-haired Broadway set designer.

"Yes, finally," Rachel said.

The city had only recently announced funds for bulletproof vests.

"Are you wearing one now?" Carol Over-ton asked.

"No. Should I?"

"Sure," Buddy said. "It's the West Side after all."

"It's red carpet time!" my mother called out.

Harry Abrams walked over with a bottle of Moët and refilled our glasses.

"Make sure you watch the intro," he said.

Carson was hosting for the second straight year.

"Did you send him any jokes?" Alex asked Buddy, though I'd told Alex he had.

"I might have," Buddy said.

"Should we just guess which one?"

"A hint," my mother said. "It's not the one about all of Mickey Rooney's mar-riages."

"On the list of exiles watching the Oscars in detached locales around the world, I told him to include the president."

"That's good," Alex said.

"He won't use it."

Johnny looked characteristically dapper in his white tie tuxedo. That world seemed light-years away from us right then. And I remembered times when Buddy and my mother were there in the red seats (they attended twice), and others where they went to swanky parties whose guest lists were a who's who of theater and TV people in Manhattan. It felt in that instant like we'd lost all that, and I was understanding I'd lost it too. I'd grown accustomed to having that world all around us, and now I saw how fast it could evaporate.

I'd gone to a couple of clubs with Alex where I used to be comped and they'd passed me over. I thought I didn't care, and now I realized that maybe I did. I always figured I'd go to the Oscars one day. Now the stage looked like Oz, and we were lost in Munchkinland.

I glanced over at Buddy as he watched his friend settle into his intro like he watched Kip play tennis, thinking, How did a guy I used to beat easily so entirely pass me by?

Johnny made some jokes about the *National Enquirer,* then about ash-spewing Mount St. Helens (a bad place on which to buy a summer home), then about a citywide sale in Beverly Hills where prices had been "slashed down to retail."

Who wrote this drivel? I wondered.

He then said, "You realize this show is being watched right now in some secluded, isolated areas where people have lost all human contact. And *President Carter,*" he said, into the camera, directly into our party, "I hope you enjoy the show too."

"Well, I'll be," Buddy said, beaming.

"You'd have told it better," I said.

"You're officially back," Harry said.

"You knew, didn't you," I said to Harry, in the kitchen after.

"I had advance word."

"Buddy looked pleased."

"He might soon be a good deal more pleased," Harry said.

"How so?"

"I got a call this morning. Next month Johnny heads off to Europe for a couple weeks of R and R. London and Saint-Tropez. Then Monte Carlo for a car race."

"And . . ."

"Guess who's on the list of potential guest hosts?"

"Holy shit."

"Don't say anything, because I don't know for certain if it'll come through."

"Mum's the word," I said.

"Four nights hosting *The Tonight Show*. It's Buddy or David Brenner. Stay tuned."

"Fuck David Brenner," I said.

"If it'd make a difference," he said.

It felt like that moment in Monopoly when you're nearly out of money and you land on Free Parking. My heart swelled. After months of clouds, a sliver of blue.

Around the TV, the talk was about *Kramer vs. Kramer* sweeping Best Picture, Best Director, and Best Actor; Dustin Hoffman, who might or might not have kissed Jack Lemmon on the lips on his way up the aisle; *Apocalypse Now* being robbed; and my mother winning the Oscar pool.

"Divorce wins over war this year," she said.

She walked over to the cash bowl and began luxuriously stacking her bills.

"No gloating," Buddy told her.

To which she answered, "I love the smell of napalm in the evening."

We all stayed late, finishing the rest of the champagne, and playing charades. (Randy was a revelation.) My mind was out in Burbank. It was the shot we needed, and Buddy was ready, or would be when the day came, I believed.

If I had to break David Brenner's legs myself, this would happen.

Because good things arrive in twos, that night an envelope was slipped under my door. Inside was a note from John's assistant, Fred. It said I should plan to come out to Cold Spring Harbor on Thursday late morning and I would stay through the weekend in one of the guest rooms. I should travel by train and they'd pick me up at the Huntington station. John requested I bring seaworthy stories to read by the fire, and clothes and gear for long days out on the Sound.

I tried to make this feel normal, no big deal, a few days away at the weekend house of a neighbor.

But I kept thinking of Charlie Bucket and the golden ticket.

I'd pulled a golden ticket to the house of Lennon.

I sat in the armchair by the window reading to a single light, *Early Man and the Ocean,* which John had talked of so effusively at the Explorers Club. I then set the book aside and slid into bed, my mind racing with images of Beatles on sailboats, Buddy stepping out on the *Tonight Show* stage. Our fates had shifted.

Breathe, I told myself.

21

"Your sail is like an airplane's wings," I said, repeating the first of several lessons my grandfather pressed on me when I was ten and sailing off the coast of Campobello. "They're there to maximize lift and minimize drag. You let the sail out" — he did so — "and then you slowly bring it in, that's it, that's *excellent,* you're trimming your sail."

"Bloody right, we don't need a paunchy sail now, do we?"

It was a performance. I was the young salt teaching my student the tricks of the sea, *what was your name again?* I taught him how to keep the rudder of his new sailboat, the *Isis,* from stalling, to wet the back of your neck so on a downwind run you can feel a soft wind.

In my desire to prove my worth I was overloading him.

"Too much?" I asked.

"Give me all you got, my good captain."

After an unsteady first hour, John found a rhythm. We made our way around the light tower at Fort Hill toward faster seas, and a wide smile spread across his face.

"You're doing it!" I said.

"You're fuckin' right."

The spray streaked his sunglasses.

"When you see it luff again, flap that is, then bring the sail back in."

He did so like he'd grown up on a boat, as coolly content as the guy in the bubble bath in *A Hard Day's Night.*

A wave smacked the boat hard then, sending buckets of spray across our faces.

John yelled out, "A doubloon to the first lad who spots Moby-Dick!"

I was only a few hours into my stay at the Lennons' country home, a century-old three-story stone house in Cold Spring Harbor on the north shore of Long Island, with an oak-shaded swimming pool, and a small beach with a creaky wooden dock. They'd been careful not to leak the place's whereabouts even to their friends so that they could be left alone. Fred joked that they'd considered blindfolding me on the drive from the train station so I wouldn't know the route. It was a chance for John to live near the water, as he had as a boy, only without the rats and drunken stevedores. Two weeks ago, he'd purchased a new fourteen-foot sailboat, which is where I came in.

"Give me *more!*" he said on our journey back, and so I taught him about deep sails and flat sails, how you kept a deep sail through high waves, a flat sail when the sea is glass.

"You know when you're in low gear on a bike. That's what a deep sail does. A flat sail is like being in high gear."

Another of my grandfather's images. John took in all of it, along with the points of sail, which he'd been laboring each night to memorize.

I instructed him with the wind behind to move from a broad reach to running, both sails out, and how when you pull the sail in to close haul and the boat starts to tip it's actually pretty fun and doesn't mean you'll capsize. Then I told him what to do if we did capsize.

I grew tired of hearing my own voice, but he kept firing questions.

So I taught him how to tack against the wind, and then trim the sail again, waiting each time for the sail to luff, then bringing it in until the flapping stops.

I heard him singing under his breath, "All you need is *luff,* dadadadada."

We arrived back at the house with our faces red from the sun and wind, and our eyes tired from all the glare. And I swear I saw a new light shining within him.

In the evening we drove in John and Yoko's Mercedes turbo station wagon to a seafood restaurant in Huntington. On the ride over, I heard the story of Fred, on John's insistence, buying a thousand gardenias for Yoko's birthday.

"I thought they were her favorite," John said.

"And they weren't?"

"Turns out they're a funeral flower. The flower of death."

"Who knew," said Fred, who was driving.

They seated us in a back dining room. John still had his beard, with his long hair tied back under a Panama hat.

We ordered two-pound lobsters and hush puppies and buttery corn on the cob. The waitress did a double take and then tried to act normal. She asked us if we were locals, and I said we were.

"Where's your accent from?" she asked John.

"Spain," he said.

"I thought it sounded European," she said.

"Some people think it sounds British, that's because I once spent a summer in England," he said. "Funny people *Eng*landers. Such funny ways of saying things."

"My uncle lived for a while in England," she said.

"How were his gums?" John asked.

"Can't say."

"Oh, to be a dentist in England."

The family at the next table was clearly talking about us. John looked over and waved, and then went back to his drink.

"Don't come over, don't come over," he said into his corn.

The man began in fact to come over and Fred put his hand up out of John's view to say stop, and so he returned to his table and sat down.

"It's like Jesus walked in and sat down to eat," Fred said to me.

"You know the story about George's dentist, don't you," John said.

"No," Fred said.

"Ask me later," he said, and glanced toward Sean, who was drawing with crayons on a notebook Fred had brought with him. George's dentist had famously dosed the band's coffees with LSD.

They piped in Beatles music. I don't think

it was intentional and the songs drifted from the Who's "My Generation" to Chicago's "If You Leave Me Now" to the Beatles' "It's Only Love."

"Is it strange to hear yourself in a place like this?"

"Awful," he said.

"You wrote this one, right?"

"One of my least favorite," John said.

"Why?"

"Because it doesn't mean anything."

"It's a fantastic melody," I said.

"Now it's Muzak for lobster aficionados."

A Stones song came on and John talked a while about Mick, then came "Don't Be Cruel," and John's eyes lit up.

"We met Elvis you know. In Bel Air, at his house."

"I think I knew that," I said. "What was that like?"

"You know, growing up we were *obsessed* with him. We listened to him constantly. We dressed like him, oiled our hair like him," he said. "So Brian arranged with the Colonel that we'd drop in on him in his California palace. We get to his house and there's Elvis, you know, in his swanky parlor room in a red shirt, and skintight black pants, playing bass to Charlie Rich's 'Mohair Sam.' I asked if I could play one of his

253

guitars, then Paul picked up one too, and we played for a while."

"Is there a recording of that anywhere?"

"I wish there was. *Elvis and His Trusty Beatles.* He had a blackjack table and a roulette wheel. Ringo played roulette, I think, with the Colonel. George had a smoke with the Memphis Mafia guys. We had a blast. But it was a bit like visiting someone in prison."

"How so?"

"He seemed trapped. He was shooting a movie, one of those Hawaii beach things, and when we asked him about it he said, 'Same old crap. I beat up the bad guys, get the girl, and sing ten lousy songs.' The Colonel had him doing three movies a year. It ruined him. That and the army."

"Was he drafted?"

"Poor sod enlisted. They stationed him in Germany. And when he got out, the Colonel put him back on the same schedule like he owned him."

"He made him rich," Fred said.

"Most rich people I know are suicidal."

"Seriously?"

"Yes, because they sold their souls. People don't realize Elvis had a good brain. He was searching just like us. He had stacks of books on philosophy, psychology, the mystics. He was meditating before we were. A talented actor too. Go watch *Jailhouse Rock* for fuck's sake. Real directors wanted to work with him, but the Colonel kept them from him."

"Did you ever feel like that could be you?" I asked.

"Shit yes. I didn't want to be Fat Elvis in Vegas, popping pills to get up in the morning, and having visions of angels and UFOs, and standing on my couch preaching sermons to my bodyguards."

"Do you have bodyguards?" I asked.

"Sshhh," he said. "There at the next table." He pointed over to an elderly couple, working on their lobster claws, wearing matching bibs.

John continued, "The difference always was that we had each other. We grew up together. We talked about what was happening to us. Elvis was always alone."

As you are now, I thought, but didn't say.

For dessert Sean and I ordered ice cream, which John said, as we dug in, was like eating cyanide. "Once upon a time, ice cream was healthy, like. These days it's all laced with emulsifiers, bactericides, 'agents,' and Christ knows. Pure toxic shite. You've got paint thinner and antifreeze slugging it out in your large intestine as we speak. I'm not joking."

Since my arrival, John had educated me on the horrors of chickens ("loaded up with antibiotics, additives, and drugs, including tranquilizers to keep them from scratching at their cages"), store-bought fruits and vegetables ("coated with pesticides"), and the can of Fresca I'd bought at the train station ("the alum from the can leaches into the soda").

I took another spoonful.

"If you die tonight, I think we still might have some gardenias for your funeral," he said.

Around the fire that night we'd read aloud some of the stories I'd brought along as requested. John read to us Melville's "Rounding Cape Horn," Mad Jack throwing the ship into the wind, close-reefing the topsails within a hurricane, slanting sleet and hail, the main topsail shattering. The writing was so intense you could feel the raging sea around you, until the storm broke and the seas calmed ("Gray-beards! Thank God it is passed!").

Fred read Stevenson's "The Man with the Belt of Gold" — not nearly as exciting — and then I read a story called "The Cruise of the *Torch,*" which also has a ton of shipwrecking storms and begins with a passage to Bermuda through waters splashing and foaming and white with breakers.

Then John played "Blue Suede Shoes" and "Love Me Tender" in tribute to Elvis. I got chills listening, and it felt like one of those dreams I didn't want to wake up from, not now, not for a long long while.

With John expertly at the helm on our sail the next morning, I described for Sean the *Kon-Tiki* crew's daily rituals, which included gathering the flying fish that leapt aboard and frying them up with a little salt and pepper for breakfast.

"Then if there were no sharks around they'd leap in the ocean for a swim."

The raft was made of logs draped in seaweed and barnacles, and looked like a bearded sea god tumbling in the waves, I said.

"They ate that stuff," John said. "Picked the seaweed as salad, and the barnacles for soup."

"At night the sea was lit with phosphorescent creatures," I said, on a roll now, "tiny shrimp with little green flashlights, and on some nights Thor, hearing ripples in the water, would crawl over to the side of the raft and peer out and he'd see two huge round shining eyes rising from the sea and staring right at him."

"What *was* it?" Sean said.

"It was an enormous squid, like the kind you and your dad probably know from the Natural History Museum."

"It wasn't technically a *giant* squid," John said.

"A near giant," I said, "but they weren't predators. They were happy squids with their devilish green eyes shining in the dark."

"Can we find one?" Sean asked.

"Quite possibly," I said, and raised my eyebrows.

And then John wrapped an arm like a tentacle around his startled son's leg.

Watching these two took me back to Buddy teaching us to swim by a system he called the Toss and Bubble. He would wade into the ocean holding one of us terrified in the air, and then hurl us as far as he could. We were commanded to swim back blowing bubbles through our noses. It was harrowing, salt water in my four-year-old lungs, my arms grasping, legs kicking. But it worked, and all of us became strong swimmers.

It was like that doing stand-up your first few times, he told me years later. They tossed you on stage and told you to blow bubbles, and if you didn't drown, you owned the room.

We passed a few impressive homes on our route, including the mansion owned by Billy Joel, who had become notorious as a party host, like Gatsby, someone had told John. "Shall we invite ourselves over?" he asked.

"I think he'd be thrilled," I said.

"He might hurl a few of his gold records at us."

"Feeling competitive?"

"Paul's the only one who can make me feel competitive."

Earlier we'd heard Paul's "Coming Up" for the tenth time since I arrived.

"Hey, *Billy!*" he yelled.

"I don't think anyone's home," I said.

"Either that or they're inside committing crimes."

"Does he know you live here?"

"I imagine he might have heard. Things get around. He tried to buy an apartment in the Dakota, you know."

"They didn't let him in?"

"No. They didn't want another rock star."

There was still a little of the art school dropout in him. I felt like he was capable of breaking in to Billy Joel's house and making

259

an afternoon of it. As we traveled out of view, he yelled, "Biiiilllly! We love you. We're your biggest, horniest fans!"

We watched *Mutiny on the Bounty* that night, the Clark Gable/Charles Laughton version, which I'd seen maybe six times over the years. On my suggestion Fred had found it on videocassette and John had seen it twice since they'd been there.

I loved the opening when Fletcher Christian bursts into the pub and gathers up the men. Or when Byam's father answers his son's questions about what Captain Bligh is like: "He's a seagoing disaster. His hair is rope yarn. His teeth are marlinespikes."

John longed, he said, to be a stowaway on his father's ship, and when boats pulled in he wondered if his father might be aboard.

The acts of cruelty multiply. They flog a dead man. Chase Byam up the masthead and make him stay up there during a storm. The storm lashes him nearly to death before he's pulled down to safety.

"It's like Liddy in the bloody electrical storm," John said after that scene and retrieved G. Gordon Liddy's recently published memoir from his room. "You have to read it."

"I will then."

Then we went back to watching.

Later, when Bligh's cruelty reaches its apex, John said, "Christ, you know who Bligh is, Fred."

"Who?"

"It's Paul, drunk with power, pushing us all around."

"And you're Fletcher Christian."

"Exactly, and with a foreigner for a wife. George is Byam, his own man, not on either one's side."

When the *Bounty* got to Tahiti, John rubbed his hands together. "This is my favorite part," he said. "They get their reward. Nice plump Tahitian girls lining up to meet the men. How many fat Tahitian girls would you like, young Winter?"

"Just one," I said.

"And we'll leave your other five to Fred."

Liddy's book, which I unwisely imbibed before sleep, read as if the demon child in *The Omen* had written a memoir. Young Gordon at five apparently found his uncle's gun in a suitcase, and managed to get the hammer locked and the safety off, before walking into the living room to greet the grown-ups.

At six, he listened to recordings of Hitler's speeches alongside the family's German housekeeper, who secretly worshipped the Führer. At nine, preparing for a future in the army, he killed squirrels and decapitated chickens ("until I felt nothing and could kill without thought") and he later conquered a fear of heights by jumping from rooftop to rooftop.

The section that mesmerized John was Liddy's painstaking recollection of strapping himself sixty feet high in a tree during an electrical storm with a safety belt fashioned out of clothesline rope, a D ring, and a steel snap link to overcome his fear of lightning. At first he closed his eyes to hide the blue flashes; but then he commanded himself, "Open your eyes," and did, staring that storm down for hours as he got sick, his heart nearly stopped, and his ears shook with the clapping of thunder.

The book read like a guidebook on how to be your own abusive father, though for John I suppose it was about something primeval, conquering your demons by inhabiting them, or something like that.

The next day we sprinkled lines from the movie into our speech. I started it and John and Fred went along.

"It ain't the size of the ship that counts,

youngster. It's the salt in the lad that mans
it."

Or the line the heavily drinking ship doctor keeps asking, "Have I ever told you how
I got my wooden leg?"

I called home late that night and told Buddy
about our days on the water and how much
fun it had been, how welcome I felt.

"He likes you. In part because you don't
want anything from him, and you've mas-
tered the art of making people feel normal."

"Like you."

"Yes, like me."

He caught me up on Kip's tournament
exploits, and a family dinner where Rachel
and my mother both had too much wine,
and Rachel launched into one of her lectures
on the insidiousness of gentrification.

"Any other news?"

"Hmmm . . . other news. Oh yes. I forgot
to mention, I'm hosting *The Tonight Show*
for four nights beginning a week from Monday."

"Holy shit!" I said.

"That's exactly what I said."

"I'm going with you," I said.

"Don't you have work, at the Tavern?"

"I think I can squeeze a few nights off."

"All right then. Burbank, here we come."

22

Johnny Carson sent a real live telegram that arrived downstairs with Hattie the night before we left. It read, "You've got this, kid." Then he left for Europe, *The Tonight Show* in our hands, like a father leaving a child with a sitter. We flew first class the next morning on TWA, wide seats, copious leg room and attention from the tall and graceful flight attendants who had name charts and called us both Mr. Winter. Buddy scanned a half dozen newspapers and magazines for topical material, pausing on a ten-page *Manhattan* article about the Scarsdale Diet murder. What still baffled everyone was how Tarnower, bald and beak-nosed and a week from his seventieth birthday, could have inspired a murderous passion from a woman as straight-laced and elegantly put together as Jean Harris. Or that Harris, in a nifty black jacket and a black skirt, as though dressed for a party (soaked through from the torrents outside), could have fired six shots from her .32 revolver into the doctor's pajama-clad body.

"Okay, ready?" Buddy said, setting the magazine aside.

I nodded, and closed my incredibly good book, *The Day of the Locust,* which Buddy bought me for this L.A. trip. Books, he believed, should be your second consciousness when you traveled.

"They lived in separate cities. So there must have been a little long-distance pillow talk."

"A given," I said.

"The headmistress calls the good doctor at midnight," he said in a bodice-ripper voice.

"Cue the music, a little Barry White."

"The doctor is in bed above the covers in his blue-tartan pajamas drinking sherry and watching *Columbo.* He mutes the sound, and after a few pleasantries the headmistress asks for the good stuff and the doctor as always obliges. *'Lobster à la Nage with asparagus . . . ,'* he says lustily. 'Hmmmm, yes,' she coos in response, 'you nasty crustacean you.' "

The two men in front of us and the couple behind stopped their conversations to listen.

" *'One cup cooked lobster meat,'* the doctor

265

whispers, *'one half cup chicken broth brought to a boil, add a quarter cup chopped parsley mixed with a tablespoon of dry dill . . .'* The headmistress begins moaning, so the doctor skips to the side dish. *'Season your asparagus with lemon juice instead of butter and cut 300 calories just like that,'* he says, which drives her wild, her breathing growing louder, until she moans, *'What about olives?'* and he answers, *'No more than four small ones or three jumbo ones of any type, but otherwise, yes, Yes, YES!'* "

The men in front of us were folded over laughing, and the couple behind us had big smiles.

Buddy waited for my response.

"Not bad," I said, "now keep going. You've got three hours before we land."

Buddy liked to say he got high writing jokes, that when the signals were strong they poured in from everywhere, hot and cold running jokes. And for years he could get there most times he wanted.

He appeared, as he sat next to me then, buzzed again in his own brain. His pen darted up and back across the page. Then he'd look over what he'd written and chuckle before moving on. I read from a stack of manila folders with articles about and preliminary interviews with the guests for the week.

After Buddy imploded, he and Johnny never spoke about it. I think in some sense Johnny, who gave Buddy his big break, took his quitting as a personal betrayal; that and I don't think he understood anyone so habitually poised doing something so strange.

When *The Tonight Show* filmed in New York, they talked daily by phone and played tennis once a week at the Vanderbilt Club before grabbing lunch. At night Buddy occasionally met up with Johnny's posse at Toots Shor's or the 21 Club, mostly preferring to head home to be with my mother. By contrast, Johnny's marital struggles were tabloid fodder.

Johnny once broke in to a secret apartment his second wife, Joanne, kept for an affair, his agent Henry told Buddy, and found along with men's clothing and some unfamiliar lingerie framed photos of his wife with ex–New York Giants receiver and *Monday Night Football* announcer Frank Gifford.

"Brutal," Buddy said, when he told me about it. "Johnny was supposed to steal the girl from the football star, and he got the script backward."

Buddy joked that my mother's acceptance of his marriage proposal was a youthful mistake, like a misspelled tattoo.

"In the morning," he said once in his monologue, "she saw that ring on her finger and screamed, '*Hell's bells,* what in the world was in those drinks last night?'"

They got engaged at a party on a barge on the East River, and they had indeed been buzzed on champagne and negronis. My mother escaped from the dance floor to get some air and Buddy followed after her. There was no one else out there but the moon, he said, and the strains of Billy Eckstine from the barge dance floor. My father had been carrying the ring for two weeks waiting for the right moment, and now he dropped to one knee, and then to his surprise my mother did too. She'd sensed he'd soon propose and had the idea that they both should, one after the other. They were teary-eyed and blissful after and floated back into the party and ordered new champagnes.

The observant bartender asked them, "Did something just *happen* out there?"

"You're the first to know," Buddy said.

"May I see the ring?" the bartender asked. My mother showed him.

"Truth is, he's pregnant," my mother said.

"Knocked me up a month ago," my father supposedly said.

"Thought it was time to make him an honest man."

"Pregnancy makes a man beautiful," the bartender said.

And Buddy curtsied.

Buddy slept fitfully before his first show back. His mind ran through failure scenarios: that his brain would go blank, his eye twitch, or he'd break into a sweat.

He had a dream in which he started speaking and gibberish came out.

"Martian," I said. "An untapped audience."

"They'll complain my jokes are too *earthy*."

Rather than smile, he seemed to believe it, that anything he did would be panned.

"It's what you do," I said. "You're paid to be you."

"I just have to figure out who that is."

Aw fuck, I thought. Be strong, for chrissakes. I thought of Rachel's line: Parents are meant to be fixed objects, not abstract paintings.

On one of our walks a week back, Buddy told me he couldn't be himself without me, as though I'd become the custodian of his charisma and wit. By recalling his best self, I could feed him aspects of it so that he

269

could return to form. I needed to *be* him to help him, he believed, and it had me recalling why it was I'd wanted to leave New York and hide out for a while. I forgot this on the good days when we were simply knocking around together.

"You're Buddy Winter," I said, impatiently.

When you're a kid, it's a defining experience to see your father nightly on TV, especially if he plays himself. It always looked like he'd invited friends over to a second apartment where he entertained, and for some reason the world watched. I imagined other rooms behind the stage, guest bedrooms and a game room with a Ping-Pong table and a kitchen where in the middle of the night guests met for hot chocolates or coffee, or a smoke, or a drink.

My dad was paid to be my dad, I thought, which seemed like an improbably good deal, better than being a doctor or a businessman, selling something you didn't believe in. It seemed like an inexhaustible resource, not something you could lose.

"All right then," he said. "Tell me what you know."

And so I took him through the notes I'd put together on four nights of guests.

Buddy worried now about little things,

how he looked, what he'd wear. He was two years older, after all. When he went on hiatus he was forty-seven; now he was almost fifty. Did it show? he asked.

"You look better now than the night you left," I said, which certainly was true.

In the hours before showtime, he was a bit manic and pored over my suggestions like an honor student's crib sheets for a final. I had sketched out the plan for each show, and each guest, in a notebook. And I gave him a few concepts to think about for his monologue. He spent an hour or two digesting it and practicing, and then we worked a while longer on the opening before he pronounced, "Done. I'm ready."

We sent the monologue over to the production staff so they could write up the cue cards.

And then just like that, it was two years ago.

Buddy slid into hosting *The Tonight Show* like a beloved dinner jacket that after years of neglect still fit. He stumbled on the first two jokes, but then he settled in. The subsequent jokes connected, and the interviews were lively and offbeat, signature Buddy.

The first night he had on Bob Newhart,

and Alan Lomax, the ethnomusicologist, who'd chosen the music for an album sent off to space. He got Newhart talking about his time on the set of *Catch-22,* where he played Major Major, one of my favorite characters in a movie that no one saw. Sarah Sands came last. She starred in a show called *Sunnyside Up,* about a father and his midtwenties daughters who take over a diner on Venice Beach — one daughter is a bookish English major at UCLA, the other ditzy and naïve, played by Sands, who posed over the summer for *Playboy* and was the type of guest Johnny liked to book. As it happened, Sands was a reader, and a bit of an activist, and pretty funny. She did commendable imitations of Goldie Hawn and of Cher singing "Dark Lady."

Buddy was up early each day meditating, looking bedraggled and bohemian, and then he'd swim twenty or so laps, and we'd meet either on the poolside deck chairs or later at breakfast, like in the old days, and go over the lineup and whatever news items we needed to work into the monologue. The pool reminded me of being a kid when he'd headline the resorts in the Catskills, and we'd play sharks and minnows and Marco Polo until late at night when our lips were blue and our fingertips wrinkled like raisins.

The big story for the last week had been the president's bungled rescue attempt in Iran, Operation Eagle Claw. The plan was straight out of a Hollywood script. Eight helicopters and six C-130 transport planes would fly into the eastern Iranian salt desert, where they'd refuel then fly to the mountains near Tehran to meet vehicles transported by American operatives. Delta Force soldiers would then storm the embassy, scale the walls, rescue the hostages, and fly them to Egypt or Western Europe.

It would be *Raid on Entebbe II,* the hostages would come home, American pride would be restored.

But it didn't go that way. Two of the helicopters broke down en route, and a third malfunctioned during refueling. The president canceled the mission, and then on their way out of the desert, a helicopter and one of the transport planes collided in a ball of flame, killing eight men.

"Too much death to build a joke around," I said.

He wrote down, "Don't let President Carter plan your wedding."

A story I'd pushed for and prevailed on was the father and son who came on the show the second night, the James and the

273

Giant Peach Story, Buddy called it, a book he read a dozen times to us as kids.

The father, an impassioned hot air balloonist named Maxie Anderson, set out to be the first to cross North America, alongside his twenty-three-year-old son, Kristian. The story was harrowing and exciting, beginning when storms in the Rocky Mountains sent them spiraling north; later, at night in the Midwest, when the gas cooled they had to hurl weight off the side and empty oxygen tanks and batteries, to keep from descending too fast, and then in the day when the sun heated the helium, they rose like Icarus into air so thin — nearly the height of Everest — that they needed to wear oxygen masks and got so airsick they couldn't eat for two full days.

The two of them took turns describing all this to Buddy, and then the son talked about them finally landing their tiny gondola of steel tubing in a forest just south of the St. Lawrence River.

"What did you do then?"

"We doused each other in champagne," Kristian said.

I thought of me and Buddy up in the heavens, no one around but birds and a few planes. The sky ours, like a boat on an empty sea.

Katharine Hepburn graced the stage after the balloonists. This was the one Buddy was most excited and nervous about. She'd done Buddy's show once before, and Buddy said it was hard to keep his thoughts straight he was so taken by her.

Remembering his great *Misfits* show, I told him to get her talking about *The African Queen,* which we'd seen at the Thalia a few weeks back. I had the sense she'd have a good story or two of her own about John Huston, and the challenge of filming on the Congo River.

I was right it turned out.

On the *Tonight Show* couch, she wore a dark blue turtleneck under a lighter blue shirt, and khakis, like she'd stepped out to the front porch after dinner with a cup of tea.

At its best, a talk show made you feel as though friends smarter, funnier, and better looking than you had decided to stop by for a nightcap. It wasn't the illusion of company. It *was* company.

They'd given her a *ghastly* room on the first floor of the hotel in Stanleyville, she said, and the Bogarts a lovely suite with a balcony. She complained to the manager. Eventually Hepburn moved John Huston's accountant and his wife's bags from the suite next to the Bogarts and moved herself in.

"Not very sporting of you. How did they take it?" Buddy said.

"They were lovely, and so I felt guilty, but not enough to give them their suite back."

Ed McMahon laughed heartily, Buddy too.

She described Stanleyville then in glorious detail, the curving river surrounded by jungle scrub and palm trees, the barges and tugs and native canoes cut out of a single tree, called pirogues, which carried bananas, timber, and bricks.

"The water was spectacular," she said.

"You mean the river?"

"No, the water that comes from your pipes. It's like honey. Most water when it comes from the tap dries on you, or peels the skin off as you scrub away dirt. Not in the Congo. You can't drink it, mind you. But on your skin it's sheer heaven, angel's fingers stroking you."

"But you can't drink it."

"It's poison."

They talked about how Huston pushed his actors to their breaking point, Buddy recalling Clark Gable and the wild horses in the desert heat, Hepburn with several stories of her own.

"He's a bit of a sadist, isn't he. Did you see that side of him?"

She straightened in her seat, then nodded.

"There's a scene at the start of the movie where my character's brother, Reverend Sayer, dies. John prepared me by telling me to do 'whatever comes into your head' when he dies, and so I wandered and I stood and I wept. I tricked myself into grief, I went on and on long after the scene should have ended, and I began to think, Is this old bastard ever going to *cut*? And then they were all laughing," she said, and she was enraged remembering this. "A practical joke on poor old Katie. Now is that funny?"

"No," Buddy said. "It's like no one ringing the bell at round's end in a prizefight, and the boxers are pounding each other's skulls waiting for it to sound."

Her face broke then into a smile.

"Only I was both of the boxers."

I thought of the pricks from the networks, including two who worked for NBC, and then the ones who wouldn't even meet with us. What happened when they turned on *The Tonight Show* and saw this? They'd gag on their vodka gimlets.

I got a call later that night from Elliot.

"You're not with him, are you."

277

"No, they splurged and gave us separate rooms."

"How's it going?"

"Well, I think," I said.

"I'd say so. I think it's gone extremely well. Katharine Hepburn. Everyone's going to be talking about that interview."

"Really?"

"Going particular, so it's not the *whole career*, it's a few sweaty weeks in the African bush with a crazy genius. That's the beauty of your dad. And the Andersons and their balloon? What a *story*, and I loved how Buddy teased every frightening detail out of them. I half thought they were going to die before the segment was over."

In *The Day of the Locust*, Faye, the unscrupulous starlet, describes assembling stories in her head like a pack of cards from which to choose an identity, which had me, when I went out in Hollywood the following night, seeing the lost souls around us — the punks, the rockers, and the gigolos, the platinum blonde Deborah Harrys, the pasty Joey Ramones, the cross-dressing David Bowies — as cards plucked carelessly from a deck. I was out with a friend from college, Will, who had been a surfer in high school, and was now reading scripts for a famous director and trying to peddle his own.

We went to the bars John Lennon went to when he lived out here with May Pang, the Roxy, the Whiskey, and the Troubadour, where he went bananas and yelled at the Smothers Brothers and punched a bodyguard.

"Everyone here wants to be looked at," I said.

"Worshipped," Will said. "You know that quote from Warhol, 'In L.A. *everybody's* beautiful. They're plastic, but I love plastic. I want to *be* plastic.' "

"You agree with that?"

"Fuck no. I hate it here. It's just a good place to work. And the girls are hotter."

"I don't think so."

"I know so. It's insane here. My dick needs a vacation."

"I'll keep that in mind."

It was around 80 degrees at ten at night. A shirtless green-haired guy on the corner was swallowing fire.

"What's it like having your dad back on TV?"

"It's great. Feels in some way like he never left and in other ways like all that was a long time ago."

"Right off it seemed like it was his show, like Johnny didn't exist. You know?"

In the Troubadour we sat in a booth drinking gin and tonics, talking about L.A. and New York. The difference, Will said, was that L.A. was more oriented around youth, and New York around older rich people. The older rich people in L.A. didn't go out to clubs, they stayed home and fucked each other's wives.

"He should do his new show out here."

"Why's that?"

"Because everything's happening out here. The music scene's better, the film world's close by, and the comedy clubs are insane. Much better than New York. It's younger, cooler. And it's perfect for you guys."

As we spoke three girls were clearly checking out Will and he motioned over one of them, a girl with pale blue eyes with permed black hair and a T-shirt that said Die Young Stay Pretty.

"You look so familiar," she said. "Who *are* you?"

"Did you see the movie *Breaking Away*?"

"Of course," she said.

"I was one of the frat brothers of the guy who loses the race at the end."

"That's so cool," she said. Her name was Linay, and she sold men's suits at a store in Beverly Hills.

"I've been in other things too," he said.

"I *knew* it."

"This is my comrade, Anton. He's been in a whole bunch of soaps."

"Really?"

"Mostly in Italy," I said, pointlessly.

"That's so cool," she said.

"Italians love soap operas," I said. "Their lives are soap operas."

"Do you guys wanna do some blow?" she asked.

"Does a bunny have ears?" Will said.

And then we were in the locked ladies room doing lines of cocaine with Linay and Meryl and Sabrina from Brentwood.

We leapt around to the Go-Go's after that, belted down shots of tequila. Will did some more coke. We smoked a joint. My head was swimming. I had that short jolt of arrogant cool that coke gives you followed by a tinny empty sense that all my choices had been bad ones. Then I leveled out into my usual state of dislocation. At the end of the evening I was talking to a tall pale girl named Nicole, who had dropped out of UC Riverside to become an actress and model.

"What's New York like?" she asked me.

"Different," I said. "You walk a lot; you bump into people. You buy food from street vendors. You never set foot in a car unless it's a cab."

"I want to live there someday."

"You should."

"My favorite movie of all time is *Breakfast at Tiffany's*. I want clothes like she had."

"And Mickey Rooney as your landlord."

"He was the only part of the movie I didn't like. I hate Mickey Rooney. He looks like my father."

When I caught up with Will, he was covered in sweat and leaving the dance floor with Linay.

"Back in a minute," she said and headed with a friend toward the ladies room.

"You know, Winter," Will said. "I always figured you'd end up here. You'd write or produce and we'd work together. Remember that play we all did in college, what was that?"

"Long Day's Journey into Night."

"But set on the Upper West Side of Manhattan. You're the one who had the idea, altered the script, picked the cast, picked me as director."

It was a high point of my time at Columbia.

"No one else would do it."

"You're good at that stuff. I mean you grew up in it, right?"

"That's the problem."

"I remember you telling me once just

because my father was a screenwriter didn't mean I couldn't do it too."

I gave him a puzzled look. I'd thought his father was a heart surgeon.

"I guess it was someone else, but it doesn't matter. You don't have to live your life as an act of rebellion."

"I'm clearly not," I said.

We hung out by the Beverly Wilshire pool and then the hot tub. Will disappeared for a while with Linay and then returned with three slices of cheesecake and a serving of chocolate mousse they'd purloined from a room service cart.

"I want to work with you on something, a script, a new show, something that's not his, that has nothing to do with your dad. Your own material I mean. You need to come out here and figure it out. We could do it together. I'm getting pretty connected here."

"We'll see," I said.

Someone from one of the hotel balconies was blasting "Dance the Night Away."

Sabrina bragged about being pulled backstage at a Van Halen concert, and while doing so she slid her foot beneath the hot tub bubbles to my crotch. "Just checking for signs of life," she said, smiling.

"All good," I said.

"I'll say," she said.

■ ■ ■ ■

Ted Turner was the lead guest on Buddy's final night. He was weeks away from launching his twenty-four-hour channel and changing the news business forever. He had also nearly died in a boat race off the Irish coast the summer before, which interested me, along with a story I read about his powerful father's breakdown and suicide.

Buddy asked him about a letter Turner's father had written him urging him not to major in the classics, one Turner had brought in to the Brown paper and had published.

"True," Turner said.

"Can you talk about what he said?"

"He said he nearly puked on his way home and he asked who I intended to communicate with in Greek."

"Did you listen to him?"

"Not on that. Before he gave me advice on how to avoid his mistakes."

"What was that?"

"He said he'd dreamt too small, that you needed dreams big enough that you couldn't achieve them in a lifetime. He'd always wanted a yacht someday, his own plantation, and a million dollars. He got all three and became depressed."

"Why?"

"He had nothing to strive for anymore."

I had a short conversation with Turner before he left the studio for the airport and let out how much we wanted a new show. He said we'd get one, that something good would happen. He had a sense for these things. He wrote something on a business card, his number I imagined, and handed it to me, and then left for the airport.

That night I watched the news. Miami was on fire. Riots had broken out. An all-white jury cleared four officers accused of beating to death a black man they'd chased due to a traffic violation. The man, an insurance salesman, supposedly put his hands in the air and said, "I give up!" before the cops beat his head with nightsticks, putting him into a coma he died from three days later. The jury deliberated only three hours before issuing its verdict.

Now there were people filling the streets, and cars and shops on fire in Miami Beach. The National Guard were out with rifles. It looked like the start of a war.

The victim, it turns out, left the marines in 1968, and married his high school sweetheart. In the photos he looked like one of those ads for *the Few, the Proud* . . .

I thought of the sort of show Buddy might do around the situation, who he could invite on. It was yet another pressure point. They were everywhere. It was the kind of stuff Turner's news station would cover 24/7.

I pulled Turner's card out before I went to sleep. He hadn't written his phone number. On the back it said simply, "Don't settle for small dreams."

23

Back in New York spring was out in full force. The cafés were packed with pretty people in stylish sunglasses, the park teemed with activity, trees bloomed. You forgot how many trees were planted right there within the cement, along the asphalt streets, maples and oaks, honey locusts and ginkgoes, the berries of which stuck to your shoes. People were friendlier, the days longer. I loved walking in fading daylight at 8:30 P.M., with the air sultry, and the women wearing tops and skirts that showed off their shoulders and legs.

Rowan put me on the schedule for four straight nights, which gave me a break from worrying about Buddy and some much-appreciated funds. I got into a rhythm setting up and clearing tables, pouring water, and refilling bread baskets. I ran into the principal of my high school one night, who reassured me, "We all have to start somewhere," and that he had spent a summer once cleaning toilets at a hotel on Martha's Vineyard. "Thank you," I said, "now enjoy your foie gras."

The reviews for Buddy's guest stint were positive, and effusive in some instances, a writer for the *L.A. Times* saying it was like seeing a favorite friend come from the dead. Harry said he'd had some interest from the son of an old friend of his, who'd been hired at CBS, a guy named Keith Osborne "out of Yale," he said. "He's on the hunt for something for us. He seems hungry."

"How old is this guy?"

"I don't know, twenty-seven? How old are you?"

I met up with Elliot at Trader Vic's and while talking about the week he told me that now was the time to start "reaching out and making a list of all the impossible gets who'll come on Buddy's show and no one else's. I'll help."

I let it slip that I'd been recently teaching John how to sail, and that John had said many times how fucked it was that Buddy was having trouble getting another show.

"Which is when you told him there's a surefire way to change all that."

"No, I guess I blew my chance."

"You get John to come on, or better yet,

with one of the other Beatles. Any one of them and have them play two songs. Then we're back in business. If he comes on alone we're still in good shape."

"I'll keep that in mind," I said.

To stay sharp, Buddy made steps toward doing some local stand-up. The club owners Harry called were all primed for his visit, though he conceded, an eight-minute slot in front of a boozy room of East Siders wasn't exactly a network show. It felt strange, Buddy said, to have had his old life back for a spell, before being booted out again, like a furloughed marine sent back overseas. The next move was foraging for guest spots on prime-time variety shows, game shows, talk shows, sitcoms, and Aaron Spelling productions, though with summer coming, the pickings were slim.

He passed on a soap opera, thankfully. I didn't need to see Buddy on *One Life to Live* as a vengeful mobster demanding "payback or *else*," I just didn't.

My mother's efforts on behalf of the Kennedy campaign were winding down along with the senator's presidential hopes, though he'd conceded nothing yet to Carter, and promised publicly to take his fight to the convention floor. In the GOP race, Reagan was improbably wiping up the field, while declaring that trees cause pollution, and the Civil Rights Act was "a humiliation to the South."

"He's like a really good car salesman who moonlights as a cowboy," my mother said. "He sounds like John Wayne, and with everything gone to shit, and our hostages still locked up in dark rooms, people long for John Wayne."

After work one night I went with Bronwen to a nightclub in the West Village where she was scheduled to do a set. She sang "My Funny Valentine," "The Man I Love," and "April in Paris." She was achingly good, I thought, though the room never quieted down enough for people to really hear. She was background noise, like the two less talented singers we heard before her. I was happy to see it didn't bring her down. She liked having the chance to sing, and if they ignored her, it was better than them throwing things her way.

"I'm sorry, that was terrible," she said.

"No fucking way. You were great."

"I wasn't."

"Seriously," I said. "When you sang, I heard Sarah Vaughan."

My mom's favorite. I guess it worked. She

grabbed my hand then and we slipped into the doorway of a nearby building. Her mouth tasted like cigarettes and tequila. Her tongue felt roughly textured, as though damaged somehow.

"I guess we're going to break the rules tonight," she said.

"Which ones."

"The no-sleeping-with-anyone-at-the-restaurant rule. But it's just a one-time thing, okay? And tomorrow it didn't happen."

"Scout's honor," I said.

She lived two blocks away in one of those tiny studios with a kitchenette and an airplane-sized bathroom. She had bamboo bookshelves, and a lava lamp. It had been a long time since I'd slept with anybody and I felt awkward and clumsy, though weirdly comfortable, like we were supposed to do this.

She made me a poached egg and coffee in the morning and at seven, pushed me out the door.

At work the next night it was like nothing had happened. She treated me exactly as she'd treated me before, not better or worse, and it felt like I was a tape she'd erased. When I smiled her way, she smiled back and turned quickly away.

It didn't happen, she was saying.

But I wanted it to happen again.

I got a phone call the night after from Fred. He'd been trying to get me for three days, he said.

"You're a tough man to reach."

"I work nights."

"John's got a boat."

"I know. I spent a week in it," I said.

"No, I mean he's chartered a yacht, the *Megan Jaye,* out of Newport, Rhode Island, in a few days. He's heading off to Bermuda."

"Wow. He's taking his big trip."

"You know what he's been like. It's all he's been talking about. He said it's put up or shut up."

"Why Bermuda?"

"There was a lot of deliberation on that. Yoko determined it was a safe place to travel during Mercury Retrograde."

"I hope it goes well."

"I called you, Anton, because he wants you to come along."

"On the boat?"

"No, swimming alongside. *Yes,* on the boat."

"When?"

"He leaves in four days, so you need to get yourself up to Rhode Island."

"I think I can do that."

"Here's the condition. He says you can't tell anybody about where you're going and who you're going with."

"I can't tell my parents?"

"Your choice, but John says he doesn't want to hear about it in the sodding elevator when he gets back. That's a direct quote."

24

There's a line I love in *Moby-Dick:* "Why is almost every robust healthy boy with a robust healthy soul in him at some time or another crazy to go to sea?"

There were five of us: John; our clear-eyed skipper, Captain Hank Halsted; Tyler Coneys, John's first sailing coach; and a crewman named Declan Jamison, employed because he was an excellent cook who knew how to prepare macrobiotic meals. We stocked the galley with tomatoes and tomato paste, corn and baby corn, beets, beans, brown rice, tofu and lentils, tuna, salmon, canned fruits for emergencies, and even some canned meat, Spam, what was in Spam?

Water. Jugs of it, because you can't drink salt water. Medical supplies, seasickness pills, laundry soap. Dr. Bronner's. Books. Yes, books.

The first thing John said when he saw

Cap'n Hank was "It's the Zig-Zag man," because funnily he resembled the man on the packets of rolling papers, with a black beard and a bandanna.

The oddest thing about him at first was that he seemed not to know who John was, that the John he was ferrying to Bermuda was John Lennon.

As they unpacked, John noticed a pair of chopsticks among Captain Hank's possessions.

"My girlfriend's Japanese," Hank said.

"Mine too," John said.

And still no recognition. An hour later it dawned on him, but his treating John like an amiable client had the effect of putting them at ease with each other. He wanted to head to sea unidentified; a father, a musician, an Englishman maybe, but not for this time a Beatle. It seemed that way to me anyway.

Our boat was a forty-three-foot Hinckley sloop, no balsa raft, no cruise ship; big enough that you felt sturdy sluicing through the waves, and small enough to feel the sea pitching beneath you. There was a little dinette where we ate breakfast and swapped stories, a few places that opened up into sleeping berths, a radio panel, storage drawers within which were charts, ship manuals, and items like waterproof gloves, a compass, binoculars, extra lines. A stainless steel sink and a stove with three burners.

Declan started in on the galley, putting food away and locating things he'd need to make meals. "Does it smell like rotten fish in here?" he asked. He sniffed his own armpits. "I guess it's just me."

Tyler had sold John the *Isis,* and taken him out in it the first four or five times.

"Have you done this trip before?" I asked.

"I've never been more than a mile off the coast," he said. "You?"

"No," I said. "Never been in the open sea."

"It's different out there," he said.

"Is there any truth to the stories about the Bermuda Triangle?"

"You mean the squadron of planes that plunged into the sea, and the ships mysteriously lost and the UFOs and the ghost ship."

"Yes," I said.

"It's shit mostly. But it's pretty gnarly to sail through in certain times of the year."

"Why's that?"

"The Gulf Stream can do some crazy things in a storm."

"What's our sailing forecast?" Declan asked.

"Nice and clear. Small chance of something hitting late in the week, but the storm season's still a month away."

From a porthole, I saw the waterline above, and it had you thinking of how little there was between you and a world in which you could never survive.

"You want the real mindfuck, go up and look back at where we just left from."

If you've never seen the shore disappear from the back of a small craft, it's both unsettling and magical. It feels like you've disappeared, vanished off the map, and of course you have in a sense. We were sailing southeast toward a speck in the ocean with only our wits and the stars to guide us.

We all went up, the five of us, and watched the ocean swallow the land.

The coastline got smaller, then smaller again, and then it was gone, "and so is your life before now," Captain Hank said.

Everywhere around us was the same, nothing but water and sky, no reference points, no street lamps, or road signs, no mountains or fields or buildings, no people.

"We're nowhere," Tyler said.

"Write that down," John said. He had a rueful smile as though thinking, Why did it take me so long to get here?

The next day the skies were clear, and there

was enough breeze to move at a good pace. We all took our turns on watch. Three hours on and then you could rest or hang out, or there were chores you could do. Captain Hank did our navigating by the stars and the sun using a sextant, which looked like a souped-up protractor.

He took me through the parts — the telescope and the shades used to dim the sun and the moon — and he taught me how to read it, and how to set the shades, and how on a bright day you need one on the horizon glass and two shades on the index glass to keep the sun from destroying your eye. I learned how to adjust the micrometer drum, then how to record your time and measurements. The simplest method was the noon sight. All you needed was your sextant and the nautical almanac and you could find your latitude within a mile or so by measuring the sun's zenith at noon. And if it was cloudy at noon, but the sun made an appearance later in the day you were good so long as you could get a sight. Or you could measure the angle later to the moon or particular stars, go back to your almanac and some reduction tables, and still get your line of position.

There was more to it, I knew, but there was something amazing about charting your course by staring at the sky, as though we were taking directions from the gods above.

We listened to songs on the radio, and when we lost reception, on a tape player Declan brought. I was amazed at how little John knew about the bands on the radio, like Blondie, the Jam, the Police, Talking Heads. He liked Madness and he liked the Jam. He liked the Specials.

John wrote in a journal and on blank pages drew scenes from the boat. He threw in some dolphins and an occasional shark.

We managed for a while to tune in to the BBC, and on one of the reports I heard a familiar voice reporting about a member of the Weathermen turning herself in for a bombing a decade ago. The voice signed off, "This is Olive Diop reporting for the BBC."

That second night when dark rained down the stars were crazy. "It's a Van Gogh sky," John said (he pronounced it "Van *Gog*," for some reason). If you looked closely, Declan said, you could see Venus, Jupiter, and Saturn. The moon lit the tips of the waves. I took the early night shift with Tyler, then at around one A.M. John and Hank took our place. I stayed up another hour with the two of them and listened to them talk about John's time in India and Hank's work at a drug clinic. Declan came out as well to bum a Gitane cigarette from John.

He told Hank about his father leaving home when he was two on a boat.

"What kind of boat?"

"He was a merchant seaman."

"That was a serious job in World War II."

"He was a bastard."

"He must have had some great stories."

"If he did I never heard 'em. He got into trouble in New York. And he spent a week in an Algerian prison. The Lennon bloodline. Without our women we get into trouble."

"Didn't Ringo's father run off too?" Declan said.

"When he was three. He grew up with his mum in a house with no hot water and no toilet. They used an unheated shed with a hole in the ground. There's a story for you. And at six he nearly died."

"Of what?"

"Burst appendix. Poor sod had to be rushed to the hospital for emergency surgery. They fixed him up and then he fell into a coma. For weeks he was in and out of consciousness. At school the kids called him Lazarus . . . for coming back from the dead."

"It's like something out of Dickens," I said.

"It got worse. A few years later he came down with TB and they quarantined him in a hospital ward with other infected boys. For two years, which is when he learned the drums. They had a band on the ward."

"A tubercular band!"

"Yes, and *little Richey Starkey* was the drummer. He'd bang his drums on the cabinet next to him. They had a music teacher who worked with them."

"Hard to sell tickets for that show," Declan said.

"They'd always cough up a good song or two," John deadpanned.

"Did you know that Joni Mitchell and Neil Young both had polio?" Declan asked. "They got it in the same epidemic and that's when Joni started singing. She sang Christmas carols in her hospital ward."

"Why was he called Ringo?" Tyler asked.

"Rings. On his fingers. Lots of them. Rory Storm came up with it."

"Who's that?"

"Leader of the band we stole Ringo from, Rory Storm and the Hurricanes. Played the clubs in Hamburg the same time as us. They weren't any good, except Ringo. He'd sit in the back of our shows yelling shite at us.

Fuckin' hooligan."

"But you already had a drummer."

"We did. One time Pete was out for some reason and Ringo sat in with us, and we thought, Oh dear."

"Adios, Pete," Declan said.

"It was a whole new level. We saw what we could be."

"You ever miss those days?"

"Hamburg? Sure. Touring in the big stadiums, never. Because as crazy as it was in Hamburg it was still small, still manageable. It wasn't mobs in the Philippines trying to yank you out of a car and beat you to a bloody pulp."

I was getting tired, and very stoned. I thought I saw jellyfish in the water around us. There was something phosphorescent in the water. I was picturing Ringo yelling things at John and Paul from the back of a club, and what it would have been like to be there.

At some point Hank asked him about his time with the maharishi, when they left the crush of fame for Rishikesh.

"Our little guru, tiny little voice," John said. *"'Meditation takes you to a place of bliiisss'"* — he used the maharishi's high-pitched voice — *"'a peace beyond understanding.'* He had that little giggle."

"Didn't he fuck around with some of the women?"

"He was Sexy Sadie," I said.

"What are you talking about?"

"Originally," John said, "it went something like, 'Maharishi, you little twat, who the fuck do you think you are, you little cunt.' "

"I guess you couldn't go with that."

"No. Too bad. And we learned a lot from him in the end."

There'd been a card game earlier and John had lost. Declan suggested an alternative to paying off his bet.

"What's that?"

"Inside information."

"What sort?"

"Well, while we're in India, where did 'Happiness Is a Warm Gun' come from?" Declan said. "It's heroin, right? I need a fix. Or else it's sex. Bang, bang, shoot, shoot."

"It's a masterpiece for the ages," Hank said.

"Is it interview the ex-Beatle time? If so I'll take the dinghy back to Newport."

"Not at all," Declan said. "We just need you to clear up some differences of opinion."

"Feck off," John said and sort of smiled.

"Six songs and I promise to shut my mouth."

"Get that in writing," Tyler said.

"An article I saw in a gun magazine," John offered. "I thought it was crazy. Guns are warm when you've just shot someone."

" 'I'm So Tired,' " I asked, in part because my eyes felt heavy.

"I couldn't sleep in India and came up with it. I like that one."

" 'Why Don't We Do It in the Road,' " Hank asked.

"Paul saw some monkeys fucking in the road once."

"The piano intro to 'Ob-La-Di, Ob-La-Da,' " Hank asked.

"That's two, but since you're the captain . . . I wrote it drunk and pissed off at Paul. He'd commandeered every bloody note and phrase on the whole song. So I went out, got myself stoned, and I walked back in and said, *'Now this is how the fucking song should go.'* I told you, Anton, Paul was Captain Bligh."

This went on for a while, this improbably perfect night out at sea with John and Hank and the rest. Eventually, Hank told me to get some sleep because I was on watch in six hours and I'd need to be alert.

"The song 'Good Night'?" I asked then.

"That one's for Julian. I gave it to Ringo to sing."

"My father used to sing 'Good Night' to Kip before he went to sleep," I said.

"Without the weepy string section I hope."

I heard Elliot's voice in my ear saying, "Ask him. Ask him for fuck's sake."

But I couldn't risk messing up the beautiful mood, and so I slipped down into the cabin, crawled into my sleeping bag, and went to sleep.

On the third morning a pod of dolphins appeared during breakfast, what looked like a hundred of them diving this way and that, from under the boat and all around us, as though they'd been booked for our early day enjoyment. It's a dazzling thing to see them, so fast, and beautiful, playful, and smart from what I'd read.

Before lunch we dropped anchor and swam off the side of the boat for a while. I borrowed the captain's mask and fins. I saw a barracuda and a lot of jellyfish. The radio, when I pulled myself out of the sea, played James Brown singing "Get Up Offa That Thing."

I took the late afternoon watch and, with the sun on my face and the warm breeze in my hair, felt a deep sense of contentment. I understood how someone could want to sail across the oceans, to spend months at sea, and I thought I could imagine why someone like Sir Francis Chichester might choose to do it alone. There's a rhythm to life at sea, and it doesn't sweep you up right away, but there was something about sluicing through the ocean waves with only the wind for power, and with the sun and moon as your guides, that felt right, like something every human being needed to do. I saw too what John had wanted from this, because without knowing it, it was what I'd wanted and needed.

Whatever you hoped for from meditation or drugs, the ego-demolishing escape could be had out at sea, because whoever you were before was gone out here. You could see in the distance the curve of the planet. It looked like we were in the middle of a fountain and the water was pouring over the sides.

Everything was better at sea, I thought in that moment, the food, the conversation, the beer, the weed, the air, the smells, the sleeping at night with the sound of the waves all around.

And now we moved on toward the Gulf Stream, and toward a tiny speck in the sea they called Bermuda, and the 'Mudian girls that John spoke of like plump Tahitian beauties. We would each of us find at least one of them to accompany us to the beach and back to their thatched-roof home, where they would feed us and lay with us, and take us in the morning to their favorite private lagoon where tropical birds would serenade us and where coconuts would fall nearby, and we'd crack them open and drink the cool milk straight from the shell.

When John was out of earshot, taking a piss I think, the captain said to me, "You realize who this is. This man is a *satellite*, he's a blessing, he's literally touched a hundred million lives. He's a certified genius. And he's spent those years hiding away. And now he's free of all that and you can see it. And we're blessed to be with him on this journey. This is the trip of your life, of my life." I thought a little unfairly of my father's voyages, and how significant it was that John had brought me out here and Buddy had left us all behind.

Later that afternoon, after my watch concluded uneventfully, the winds picked up and then off in the distance you could see a front coming in, the clouds blackening, the sunlight dimming, and it was at first beautiful and dramatic, and a small part of you thought, This could be tricky.

And when I looked over at Captain Hank's

face, I understood that we were in trouble. To be sure he was calm, but he stopped joking around and after a lot of serious watching, he began to bark instructions.

"Get your gear on," Hank said. Tyler put on his rain gear and sea boots. John did as well. My job, Hank said, was to go below and help Declan clear the surfaces, tie things down, double-check the ports, and make sure everything was secure.

"Aw geez. You feel that?" Tyler said.

It was the wind, and you could hear it now whistling through.

"I hate that sound," Tyler said.

"Why?"

"Because it'll really start ripping in a minute or two."

Then the sound was all around us. The sail flapping. The waves pounding the boat, the spray hitting our faces.

"Here we go," John said. "Up the masthead, Mr. Byam," he said to me.

I don't think he realized what this was any more than I did.

The sky went gray above us, soon to be black, and I thought of *The Wizard of Oz* when the twister swirls toward Dorothy.

Tyler looked out and said, "This looks bad." Just that.

The first part of you that wakes up in a storm, Hank would say later, is your ears. You hear the high pitch of the wind, and the slap of the sails, then the creaking of the masthead and of the boat itself, *moan, crack,* and the *rat-a-tat-tat* of the rain. Then there's the *ping-ping* sound of the wind through the rigging. And the *rip* of ropes sliding, and the creak of boards bending, and the violent music of the sea itself. And then your eyes brace for the sting of salt, and the sight of a sail tearing, or falling, and of the waves rising behind you to worrisome heights.

Down below Declan was locked in the lavatory puking. The floor of the *Megan Jaye* tilted and things flew around. A bottle of red wine slid from the counter onto the floor and splattered the walls and some nearby cushions. While I cleared up pieces of glass, a drawer swung open, and plates and cups flew out along with a knife that dropped an inch from my foot.

I did my best to mop it all up, but the sound of Declan blowing chow destroyed my own equilibrium, and soon I was equally sick. And I went back up to get some air and to see how high the waves had gotten.

Hank was at the wheel. John and Tyler were following his commands.

I looked behind the boat and saw a wave the size of a brownstone barreling toward us, poised to drown us all, and then it grabbed the boat and hoisted us to the heavens, and then dropped us on the other side. I willed myself to feel better, to not succumb to seasickness, to be strong and earn my stripes, but I was too far gone and threw up violently off the side of the boat and nearly fell in.

The storm raged all that day and into the night. Those who were seasick hung below, and those who weren't took turns battling the beast. Hank and Tyler took a watch, then John and Hank, then Tyler and John. Then Tyler got sick and joined us below and John came down after that to take a nap.

At some point the anchor had broken loose and was banging at the end of a chain in the bow of the boat. I wanted to go secure it, and do something heroic, but Hank went down there himself, crawling along the deck, the ocean crashing over him, at one point submerging the back of the boat. I watched him, and I saw him disappear for a bit, and we knew in that instant we would die, because no one could do what he could in a storm, and then we saw his head rise up, and he finished the job, tied the anchor down again, and slid back up our way.

"Piece of cake," he said.

"You're a god," John said. "The Zig-Zag god."

There's no way to escape a storm at sea; it hits you, and you can't hit back. You dodge the blows, then burrow into the belly. Tyler likened it to driving a bumpy road with eyes closed and knowing you'll hit a tree, or fall down an incline, but not knowing exactly when. I crawled into my damp sleeping bag and tried to sleep, and I even did for a while, maybe two hours, but then I woke, or half woke, and I was in my hospital bed in Gabon, sick with malaria, my head feverish, my dreams crazy, the room around me spinning, and then rocking, like a boat. And I thought it was so strange that a hospital room . . . was I now at the hospital? . . . was I still in Africa? And why was this hospital room rocking up and down like a cabin on a boat, and why were there waves outside, and the sounds of wind? It must be that a storm had hit in Africa, around my hospital room, but I was waterlogged, my brow sweaty, and tasting of salt. And then I closed my eyes and went somewhere warm. On a beach. Far away. And I must have slept for a while. When I woke again I felt sick. I went over to the sink and splashed water over my face. I wasn't hungry, but I felt very weak, and extremely seasick. Had I taken Dramamine? I was pretty sure I had, but I searched for my bottle and found one and ate it.

I got to my feet. Put my jacket on and stumbled up the steps and out into the wind and spray and the awful sound of everything flapping and creaking, that sound that makes you certain that the whole boat will soon split apart and we'll all be shark food, that makes you picture the shark in *Jaws* taking your body up to the stomach, and maybe you'd survive that way. As a stomach, a chest, two arms, shoulders, a neck, and a head. I'd seen Vietnam vets without their lower body, I think, though mostly they just had stumps for legs.

Hank was at the helm. He looked calm. He was with John, and they looked like a matched pair, like lifelong friends, and I wished that I hadn't been so useless, that I'd been out there with them. The sky was black now from horizon to horizon.

"Did you get anything on the radio?"

"Nothing's coming in. I got a report an hour ago about a storm, but we didn't need a report on that."

"How long will it last?"

"A day. Two. Three?"

"How long will we last is the question," John said.

"A lifetime," Hank said. "We'll beat this."

The waves in the Gulf Stream arise heedlessly and haven't traveled far over the ocean, which means the wave periods are shorter and the waves are closer together, and this is what's so different about them, it's that as your bow comes off one wave the trough is so small the bow has no time to start climbing the next wave, which is on you too soon, and it's bigger than the last, and it can knock you broadside, and then you're fucked.

Hank calls this state of things confusion. "You have this seven-hundred-mile tract of ocean and you run a river of eighty degree water through it, the waves get confused. And there's nothing more dangerous," he said, "than a confused wave."

The hope in a storm is that you keep climbing them with the bow and dropping on the other side and you never let the wave crash over the back of the boat.

Hours vanished, then a whole day. Was it Tuesday or Friday? The wind kept howling. Eating was a problem. We were sick, but you couldn't go days without eating or drinking. It was hard to keep the kettle on long enough for the water to boil, and once the water boiled, you couldn't pour it into cups without scalding yourself. Everything was impossible.

And I felt sicker and sicker. In my dreamy state, I imagined the ghosts of all the lost ships, and the lost planes, beneath us, awaiting our arrival. We would add to the legend. I imagined my parents hearing about it and finding out through a news report that I was on the boat. I'd be an afterthought at best. I had this crazy dream where I jumped off a building and then halfway down I realized I didn't want to die, and so I started to reach out for the ledges, and it's like in a cartoon, my hand grabbed and slipped, grabbed and slipped, then I did a flip, and my head hit a series of ledges. This went on for a while and then finally there was a window open and I managed to fall into it, and when I did it was a surprise party for me and everyone was waiting for me inside, like it was all planned. And in the dream I wondered how they would know, in that I had planned to die, and I asked my mother and she said, *We knew you'd come back,* and then I was eating cake and blowing out the candles and I made a wish, and my wish was that I never wake up, that I can live in this dream-world where everyone's waiting inside for me, and that whatever I do there's a window open for me to fall back through.

An hour, or a day, later, on my way to get myself something to drink, I saw what looked to be everyone below, Tyler, who'd been throwing up for hours, and Declan, who'd never recovered, and Hank, who'd at last come down to get some sleep.

Someone was up there shouting at the waves and singing.

"Who's up there?" I said.

No one answered.

"I thought *you* were up there," Tyler said.

"Think again," said Captain Hank.

My first thought was You have to be *fucking kidding* me, and I was furious with Hank for being so taken with John that he believed he could survive on his own out there, because I'd been with him, and he'd done fine on Long Island Sound, but these chaotic seas were too much for me or Tyler, or Declan or anyone but the captain, and we were dead I knew. We were as good as dead.

"Really?"

"Listen. Do you hear that? It's pure rapture. He's yelling at the sea gods. He's joyful! Joyful!"

Now here's the strange magical mystery part of this spectacular adventure, when I went up to look it was in fact John in the cockpit, harnessed in, legs on either side of the cockpit rails, hands gripping the steering wheel, singing at the top of his lungs the foulest, filthiest, manliest sea shanty, his glasses now sprayed over with the sea, his face glistening, guiding us through gale winds and dysfunctional waves. I would learn later that Captain Hank had succumbed after thirty hours to sleep, and thinking he'd get a half hour or so of rest within listening distance left the boat to an apprentice sailor who'd sailed it by himself for close to seven hours through raging seas, and wild winds, strapped in like Gordon Liddy to that stupid fucking tree. He seemed overjoyed, as though everything in his painful beautiful life had led up to this. Would that I'd been the one to save us, I'd thought, but only for a second, before realizing that people like me didn't do things like this, just as I'd never descended by helicopter into a stadium of sixty thousand, or brought a generation of girls to tears.

It made weird sense that he would save my life, our lives, and best of all his own.

25

"I heard rapture. I heard bliss. I heard a man who had been sequestered away for five years and now had broken through," Hank said. "You were overflowing."

He was behind the wheel now, and John was seated nearby wearing a plain white T-shirt and sunglasses. He was transformed and looked like he must have looked fifteen years ago.

"It was everything in my life up until now," John said. "I was Erik the Red, and the pillaging, marauding Vikings, and Liddy. It felt like when we were in Hamburg, and you'd take the stage and you'd be high on pills and everyone's yelling and jumping about, and you're at it until six in the filthy morning, you don't stop, you just ride it. That energy. That feeling of being alive. I feel so fuckin' alive."

"You were right there in the maelstrom. Singing, and shouting. What you looked like to me was a very sane madman."

We were like a sports team that just won a title.

John relished telling all the details of fighting the storm. I would have too. And I loved to hear him tell it. I pictured him telling it on Buddy's show, and then the two of them talking about mortality, and tuning in to the cosmos, and the rhythm of the universe. And then John and George breaking out the sitars on national TV. *Ask him,* I thought.

But again I punted.

One by one we all gave our versions of the night, taking turns, and letting each strand of the story get woven together.

"Why in the world did you trust me?" John asked Hank.

"I could feel myself getting so tired it was going to be dangerous."

"What did you say to him?" Declan asked.

"I said, 'Come on up here, big boy,' " Hank said.

"I said, 'I'm just the powder monkey learning the trade.' And he said, 'You're going to have to, everyone else is throwing up.' I said, 'You better keep your eye on me.' He said he would, and then in five minutes he was gone. A couple of the waves had me on my knees."

"How do you feel, Anton?" Hank asked.

"I think I threw up a month of eating."

"You looked pretty bad, mate," John said.

"I'm sorry I wasn't more helpful," I said.

"No one was," Tyler said.

The sun was out now, and we had a decent breeze, and though we were off course some, Captain Hank said we could get to Bermuda in a couple of days. "Four days late, but everyone alive."

We were like family now in some strange way, with Hank still as our leader.

"Think if we'd gone under. How long would it be before anyone knew?" Declan asked.

"Days," I said, "maybe weeks."

"Not weeks," Tyler said.

"And what would the papers say about us?" Declan asked.

"It would be the only story out there," I said, which was true, and the stories would have gone on for months and then years.

"I'm picturing one of those maudlin documentaries, with Beatles songs in the background. 'And then five men set out to sea . . . and they found at first a veritable Octopus's Garden."

"Yes!"

"But we'd be *missing* at first."

"We're still missing."

"We'll arrive in Bermuda in the late

319

afternoon in two days."

"Was there actually a Megan Jaye?"

"She was a stone-cold fox," Declan said.

"Aye, the lad's got a throbber for old Megan. Can you fuck a boat, dear captain?"

"It's technically possible."

"The ocean is your lubricant," John said.

"That's how you make dinghies," I said.

John smiled in approval.

"And how do you tell if your boat is pregnant?" Hank said.

"Easy," I said. "From the fullness of her sail."

Two days blissfully passed. Everyone smoked. Declan had brought a few hits of acid, but there were no takers. He took a quarter tab.

"I've got a joke," he said.

"All right then."

"So a chicken and an egg are lying in bed after fucking. They're all relaxed now, smoking cigarettes, smelling of sex. The chicken blows out a satisfied smoke ring and says, 'I guess we answered that question.'"

"Which question?" John asked.

"Oh, you know. The chicken or the egg?"

"Ah, fuck, that's good," John said.

As we were closing in, according to his charts, Hank alerted us to the fact that customs officials were likely to want to come aboard and search the boat, so we might want to do something about the weed we hadn't smoked.

"Oh, fuckin' fuck," John said. "Just what I need. I'll end up like Paul in Japan."

"So what do we do?"

"We honor the great god Sensimilla," Declan said.

So the five of us got to work.

"The Gulf Stream Smoke-a-thon," John said.

Declan rolled a huge fat joint and lit it, taking a puff like it was a victory cigar.

When we'd all had our fill, John put the last of it in a bottle and sent it off to Davy Jones.

"I'm seeing a stoned squid searching around for a slice of pizza," Declan said.

And then quite suddenly we saw land off in the brilliant blue distance, and I thought of all the movies I'd seen with this exact moment. I felt like we'd been away for a very long time, and like I was a different person.

As we pulled into the harbor John said, "So this must be the scene where we find our Tahitian wives."

"But they're wearing way more clothes."

"Times have changed."

"I want a nice plump one like the one Fletcher Christian took to the beach."

"I think you need to have trinkets to trade with."

"Oh, I have trinkets. You bet I do. Pearls as big as coconuts."

As we sailed toward shore on a turquoise afternoon, we saw first those magical long-tailed white birds with the black markings, and that sound *keee keee, krrt krrt krrt.* And then the lighthouse on the cliff, two seventy-foot cliffs, coral rock, and soon the harbor was all around us.

"Land ho!" I yelled.

Music, people, cafés and bars and houses of pink and blue and yellow, and calm water, and the sensation of being incredibly stoned and happy, and thinking that anyone who saw us now would have no idea what it was we'd lived through.

26

As we walked along bustling Front Street it felt like the sea was still rolling beneath us. The air was warm, and music pulsed from the bars, Gerry Rafferty's "Baker Street" from one, and Stevie Nicks purring "Dreams" from another ("Everything's two years late here," Declan said). We settled in at an Irish place; I was hungry but wary of my stomach still. I was tired of throwing up. What I did was gulp down something called a Dark and Stormy, which I gather was made with dark rum, ginger beer, and lime juice and tasted like the tonic of the seven seas. I ordered another, then excused myself and went next door to a hotel into a pay phone and called home collect.

The connection was scratchy and I felt very far away, which I guess I was.

"Anton? Is that you?" It was my mother's voice.

"Yes."

"Oh my god, Anton. Where are you?"

"Bermuda."

"Are you okay? We thought we'd hear from you days ago. I've been worried sick."

"We just got here. There was a really bad storm."

"We read about it."

"There was no way to call."

"We're just happy you're alive. Your dad's been a wreck. How bad was the storm?"

"Like the kind in a movie where the ship goes down."

"Good god. We almost lost you."

"For the second time," I said.

"That's right . . . that's *right*," she said, and there was a catch in her voice. "When are you coming home."

"I don't know. Soon."

"And where are you staying?"

"In a house they rented."

"Do you have enough money?"

"I do."

There was static on the line then.

"I love you both," I said.

"I'm so glad you're okay," she said.

We all crashed out in the same three-bedroom limestone cottage the first night, and then Declan went off to stay in an apartment with a woman he'd met last time he was in Bermuda, and who he said was a wildebeest in the sack. Hank and Tyler sailed back home with a friend of Hank's.

Hank and John had a long meaningful embrace before they parted, and John said, "The best adventure of my life, all thanks to you."

"You are a gift to the world," Hank said.

Fred and Sean and Sean's babysitter, Uda-san, were flying in the next day and John would be moving with them to another house, he said. I wasn't sure where that left me, but I figured I'd find something in town if need be.

"How long are you planning on staying, Anton?" he asked.

"Three or four days."

"Cool. You'll come with us then tomorrow."

"You're sure it's okay?"

"I'd tell you if it wasn't."

"Thank you," I said.

"Now then," he said. "Have I told you the story about how I got my wooden leg?"

27

Feeling invincible from having saved us all from a watery death, John broke through and began writing songs again. He started in the day we moved in to a two-story stucco house on Fairylands Drive in Hamilton. Fred had bought some reggae tapes and a boom box in town and John started blasting Bob Marley until the song "Hallelujah Time" came on, at which point he stopped the tape, rewound it, and then played it again. Then he stopped the tape on a phrase in the first verse, "Living on borrowed time." He started repeating it, *"Living on borrowed time . . . living on borrowed time . . . ,"* then he got his guitar and played for a while with that line. "That's it," he said, and he was off and running. For the rest of the day he played with it, added to it, sang, stopped, and sang again, and wrote things down. I left and went to the beach for a while with Fred and Sean, and when we returned he was still at it, now with the line "When I was *younger . . .*" Fred said he'd never seen him this way before, but he'd only been working for him this last year, which had been bone-dry songwise. By dinnertime he had down a rough version. He sang it to us. "Fucking hell, that's good," Fred said.

Later that night he had his first song in five years. He'd cracked the seal, broken through.

"More's coming," he said. "I'm tuned in to the cosmos."

It was like he could see off in the horizon not a storm, but songs heading his way.

Under the baking sun I toured the coastline on a rented mustard-colored moped, a different beach each day, and all of them obscenely beautiful, turquoise water, jagged rock formations, heartbreak coves, with the waves lapping the shore, like the videos they showed old people in the movie *Soylent Green* before grinding them into food. I met up with Declan and his girlfriend, who had blue-black hair and drove a motorcycle, at this place where you could jump off cliffs into the water. It was a good forty feet up, and Declan said if you'd lived through what we'd lived through it was nothing, which was true, and when I leapt I felt like I was dropping down into a wide cool dream, and I went deep down to where my ears clogged and the water was cold, and the sun above threw slanting blades of light that looked like the portals of heaven. I swam to the shore and climbed back up so I could jump in again, and I did this over and again, thinking that I was in no rush to fly back to New York, that there was a reason I was here, and it had something to do with how it felt to fall like that and live, and then fall again and live again.

Along the theme of surviving, we listened that night to Marley's "Ambush in the Night" three times through. I'd somehow missed knowing that it was based on a real event, the night six gunmen burst into Marley's house and tried to assassinate him. John had read an article about it and marveled that the god of reggae had held his ground and hadn't fled. "One of the gunmen was a sixteen-year-old boy, who ran around spraying bullets everywhere," John said.

A bullet grazed Marley's chest and passed through his arm; another hit Rita Marley as she fled the house with five kids. A surgeon pulled the bullet from her head the next day and miraculously she survived. A caution, John said, of how quickly your life could end. And here we were in Bermuda, cheaters of death ourselves, listening to that song and counting our blessings.

Over the next three days John wrote several new songs and parts of others, including "Serve Yerself" (a rip on Dylan's "Gotta Serve Somebody"), "Steppin Out" (which would be released years later as "I'm Stepping Out" on the album *Milk and Honey)*, and "Watching the Wheels."

Declan came over one night and John played them for us.

"If you did that in a year, it would be the best fucking year of your life," Declan said, when we left afterward to go out and get drunk.

For stretches of four or five hours John would move around the house writing songs. He was either at the piano or on the guitar, or he was listening to Third World or Peter Tosh or Black Uhuru and taking notes. On his breaks he'd head out to the beach with Sean to swim and build sand castles, and then into town to buy sweets. I thought of his father taking him to Blackpool when he was five, and trying in a few days to make up for years of abandonment. I imagined John forgiving him so he could go on another ride or score another box of treats. Seeing John and Sean had me thinking again of Buddy, of us all bodysurfing on vacation somewhere tropical, my father's arms windmilling a foot or two ahead of the break, his hair plastered to his forehead, and his face wearing a child's grin.

When we were out that night, the topic of Buddy came up, and John described his own very public nervous breakdown in L.A., when he ran off with their personal assistant May Pang and got fucked up every night with Harry Nilsson and Keith Moon.

"When you're famous and crack up, everyone hears about it. If Joe Blow goes nuts in a bar, it doesn't end up in the papers."

"They don't have a photo above the fold of them with a Tampax on their head."

"It was a Kotex," John said. "It was like that thing where you put a penny on your forehead and it sticks. Well, they had Kotex on the toilet. I slapped it on my forehead. And I came out with it stuck there. And everyone laughed, and if it wasn't me no one would have written about it or known about it, but it was me and now it's a story that will follow me around forever."

"I think it's funny."

"That's because you have a sodding sense of humor."

He explained the whole Smothers Brothers yelling thing, that he'd been yelling at Dickie, not Tommy, that Tommy was the likable Smothers, but there was something he didn't like about Dickie. "And so I told him."

"Why did you feel the need to tell him?"

"Because I'd had around twelve brandy Alexanders for fuck's sake. Have you had them? They're bloody milk shakes. You just keep drinking them and then all of a sudden you're blind drunk."

Hamburg was a better place to go nuts, he said, because they weren't famous yet.

"You'd have loved it. The Kaiserkeller in the Reeperbahn, vice capital of Europe."

"How so?" Declan asked.

"Whatever you wanted, it was there. Transvestites, homosexuals, pimps, and whores. With playing, drinking, and all the birds, there was no time to sleep. We were up on Benzedrine half the night, that and Preludin. They gave us free salad and beer at night and cornflakes in the morning. But that's where we got good, because we played eight hours a night. We did a lot of covers, but we came up with a lot of originals too. We learned to live and work together. We developed a style. We had to, to survive."

I told him Buddy talked about his early days doing stand-up in the clubs similarly as where he found his voice.

"It's so much scarier having to go out there and make people larf," he said. "That'd make anyone crazy. Me anyway."

Unwisely, because of the risk of losing it at sea, I had taken one of Buddy's journals with me on the trip. I started reading it out at sea, then stopped because it felt wrong, like I was eavesdropping on his thoughts. And now far away from everything in Bermuda, I felt like I could dip in and see what was there.

A lot of it was a funny and well-written travelogue filled with thoughts and vignettes, memories, and portraits of people he met, places he'd stumbled on, but there was also a darker side of him I didn't know that came alive here. He described deliberately putting himself in trouble at different times in his life, taking a train to a distant part of the Bronx with no money to get back so he'd walk for long stretches, and jump the turnstile later, or get into a cab and then sprint out without paying the fare. This was mostly before we were born. Or he'd order a sandwich, this time paying for it, an elaborate assortment of meats and cheeses and condiments, and then he'd go sit by the East River, throw his sandwich in, and watch the birds pick at it.

He wrote that being busy kept him out of trouble, but that sometimes he'd overload the system, and it was like a switch had turned off.

He wrote about those last weeks before he quit. He said one time he forgot who it was he was talking to, and asked a question meant for someone else.

I remembered this.

And he explained another odd moment I'd witnessed.

At least twice he said he asked a question he'd asked just a minute before, and on one occasion the guest took it as comedy and so he started answering Buddy in the exact words he'd used before. And then Buddy stopped and said, "Didn't you just say that?" and the audience lost it, laughing heartily thinking they were laughing *with* him, and Buddy went along with it, though the whole thing spooked him.

I decided I'd read enough, closed the journal, and put it at the bottom of my backpack.

I remember being with Buddy after the show where he'd seemed so lost. We went and got a drink together at Hanratty's on Broadway and talked about other things, the week ahead probably, and when we stepped out onto the street, he said he'd see me sometime tomorrow.

"You're not coming along," I said.

"I don't feel right," he said.

"What do you mean by right?"

"I don't feel right. I can't explain it," he said. "I'll catch you later."

And he went walking up the street. I put it out of my mind rather than doing anything, or trying then to help, because it was easier to think it was nothing than to acknowledge that something was clearly wrong.

28

Declan said seeing John write again, and making songs that sounded in their larval form like classics, was like watching a holy man speaking in tongues.

"It's like watching fucking Matisse at his canvas," he said.

We were on the beach collecting shells for Declan's girlfriend.

Declan said John had rid himself of all his pent-up resentment and rage, which was why he'd broken through.

I told him how I'd been resisting asking John to come on Buddy's show.

"Now's the time to get the whole shebang," he said.

"What do you mean?"

"When he says yes, which of course he will, then you say, 'And there's no way in a thousand years you'd come on with Paul. That feud's too deep.' And he'll say — I swear to you he'll say — 'You'll have to ask

Paul.' Because he won't want to be the one still carrying the grudge. It won't be his fault, it'll be Paul's. But Paul will come on."

"All right then."

"What you should really do is bring the whole band on."

"The Beatles."

"Is that their name? *Catchy.* Yes, you tell him it'll just be the second half of the Abbey Road rooftop concert the cops made them stop in '69. Shouldn't have happened, should have been finished, and now it will be, on your pop's show. How fucking *perfect* would that be?"

"Very perfect, and absurd."

"Who knows after what you two have been through, he just might bite."

"Yes, absolutely."

"They're four separate human beings, fused into a single musical being. Playing music together is as natural as breathing. It's not like you're asking him to eat a bus. He wants to get right with the world now, just like his song. He's on borrowed time, and loving his brothers again is exactly what he needs to do."

"I just want him to come on really."

"Fuck that, don't leave without Paul. Okay? It's the least you can do for your poor old dad."

Fred had bought some recording equipment in town so John could record some of the new songs he was playing, including one, "I'm Losing You," written when for several days he couldn't reach Yoko at any hour by phone, and another written for Sean, which opened with him calming his boy after a nightmare the way Buddy used to for us (Buddy would chase the monster out of my room and out the front door of our apartment, where he'd walk the hallways of the Dakota, he told us, until he found the monster party on the roof).

John had Fred play the bongos and I played the tambourine, and for a few sublime seconds I was a talentless Beatle, as were a belching family of bullfrogs below us.

When the others turned in for the night, John asked me what it was I did for Buddy when I worked for him, what was my job? I told him I was a sidekick/muse/writer/talent coordinator, that I prepped him for his interviews, and helped him with his monologues.

"You're his sodding Cyrano de Bergerac."

"I never wanted to be the one on stage."

I told him when asked which Beatle I would be if I could choose, I'd said none of the fab four.

"You said Brian."

"I did. I'd be Brian Epstein or George Martin."

"And you are in a sense, but for your dear ole daddy, bless his soul."

"I wash his psychic laundry."

"Whatever you do, don't be his shrink."

"I'm not actually."

"My father was a child," he said.

"Mine isn't," I said.

We sat for a while listening to the bullfrogs making their mating calls.

Now or never, I thought. I blurted out, "Will you come be on his show?"

"Yes, of course," he said without a pause.

"And . . ."

"And what?"

"There's no way in a thousand years you'd ever come on with Paul," I asked recklessly.

He smiled slyly.

"I guess you'd have to ask Paul, now wouldn't you?"

I called Buddy that night because it was Father's Day, and because I felt bad about being away, and about reading his journal.

He wanted a more detailed account of the storm. I told him all about it, how sick I'd been, how harrowing it was, and how strangely close we all felt after.

"As Bligh said, we beat the sea itself," I said.

"*Aye.* Well, I worried about you when I didn't hear from you."

"That's what Mom said. I'll be back soon."

"When?"

"In a few days."

"I'm glad. I've written some new stuff that might not be entirely terrible."

"What kind?"

"Opening monologues, to get back in practice. Sometimes it's just a few minutes of things I'm thinking about, sometimes longer."

"Can I hear some of it?"

"You mean over the phone?"

"Sure, why not?"

"All right. It's kind of rough."

"I'll be the judge of that." I took a sip of my beer, then leaned back in my chair and listened.

"Picture the old stage. Don Gold introducing me (*and now a man with a voice like butter*), and now I'm stepping through the curtains. A ridiculous grin on my face," he said, and I did just that. In his opener Buddy would always rub his hands together, or he'd push them into his pants pockets, or he'd clasp them together. He'd walk out and gaze out at his audience as though amazed all these people had assembled just for him. They'd cheer, and usually a female voice would yell, "We love you." And he'd say, "Yes, yes, I know, it's an illness."

He went on for about eight vintage minutes, with just a single clunker.

"What do you think?" he said.

"Time for the Toss and Bubble," I said.

"I thought so too," he said. "Get home safely, my boy."

29

I arrived back in New York in the beginning
of July. Within a week of my being back,
Buddy began dropping in at comedy clubs
and testing out a new sort of monologue,
along the lines of the one Claudia described,
stories about walking away from his life as a
celebrity and experiencing the world as an
unknown traveler, checking in to motels
where clerks gave him sideways glances, trying to figure out where they knew him from,
then other stories of the wise or misled souls
he met on his trip (a pack of dogs who attacked him in Yogyakarta, a twenty-foot
wave he surfed in Australia, a dream he had
about a fire overtaking the hotel where he
was staying in Delhi that turned out not to
be a dream), then a comic prose poem
about returning to New York without a
show, or a job, and having more than one
person ask him, *Didn't you use to be Buddy
Winter?* He worked in a funny bit about our

painful lunches with the young suits, and a true story about being on *The Love Boat,* and playing a widower who falls in love with Sandy Dennis, and then a few about playing the clubs around the city in the early sixties. I'd say half the time he was riveting, and the rest was a crapshoot, and when he lost the room, which he did at least twice by my count, it was because they'd been expecting punch-line jokes, not psychological theater.

He got a nice write-up in the *Village Voice,* with the headline Buddy Winter Bares His Soul.

The headline could have read, I thought, Buddy Winter Wants to Be Loved Again.

At his best my father didn't care if you liked him. If you missed his jokes, he used to think you just weren't very smart.

My second week back, Harry asked me to lunch and he sounded excited.

"Just you," he said. "I'll explain why when I see you."

We went to a dim sum place, Jing Fong on Elizabeth Street in Chinatown, Harry's favorite, and when the trays came by he kept plucking from plates of steamed or fried dumplings, and fish balls, beef balls, each better than the one before. He ordered us

Heinekens, and then he asked me about the trip. In the last month he'd grown a mustache a little like Redford's in *Butch Cassidy,* which he said his wife and Claudia had yet to fully approve.

I told him about how beautiful it was the first two days, about the dolphins, and the night sky, and then I told him about the storm, and how sick I'd gotten, how crazy it was and how unlikely it was that we'd survived. I tried to describe John at the wheel in the wind and the rain.

"Unbelievable. With this and the Peace Corps you've had a full life already."

"I almost didn't come back."

He took three pink dumplings that I think had shrimp, and then a big blob of white he said was a pork bun. Then he thanked the waitress in Cantonese.

"Impressive," I said.

"I lived in Hong Kong for a year when I was in high school."

"I didn't know that."

"My father got sent there for work. . . . Well then, so here's the deal. It's not *exactly* what we wanted, but I think it's better actually."

"What's that?"

"CBS wants Buddy to host a show on Friday nights at eleven thirty."

"Just like that?"

"We'll have to do our dog and pony, but essentially, yes. For the last eight years they've been showing *The CBS Late Movie* in that time slot. Old movies and reruns of shows like *Banacek* and *The Avengers* and *Cannon.*"

"The shows you watch when you're too stoned to care."

"Exactly. But with the movie channels like HBO and Showtime gaining more subscribers, and with the likelihood people will soon be renting whatever movies they want to watch, movies of the week are dying out."

"Makes sense."

"So I got a call this week from one of the guys we met with a few months back, remember Keith Osborne?"

"The gung-ho one."

"Yes, well, it turns out it was true. He's in big-time. He's the one who got this green-lit. I asked about five nights a week like in the old days and he said they wanted to start with Friday nights, and they wanted it to bring in some of the same viewers that *Saturday Night Live* brought in."

"It's a deal?"

"Pretty much. We go in. Go over the nuts and bolts and then we hit the floor running."

"And they're not apprehensive about his mental state."

"It's just what I told you. If we got him out there, and he looked like the Buddy of old, someone would bite. And look, if it's a hit maybe it'll go five nights. In the meantime, it's less stress preparing for one night than five."

"Buddy can play to a younger audience, certainly younger than Johnny."

"They want someone who can push the envelope."

"What does that mean?"

"They want the kind of show where sparks will fly, feathers will be ruffled. They want Buddy to get into people's faces a little. To have opinions. And there'll be a lot of new music. The kind of bands you probably listen to."

"All right.

"Have you told him?"

"I'll call him when I get back to the office."

"Why did you tell me first?"

"Because I'm sensing some hesitation with him lately, like he's doubting himself again. And I want us both in on this. I wanted you aboard first."

"When would the show start?"

"September."

"That's soon."

"You think? Time to get off our asses. Let's toast," he said, and we raised our beer bottles to Buddy.

"One more thing," Harry said. "This is about you too. They want you in on this. They like you. They like the two of you together."

My mind raced on the subway ride uptown, because our days of museums and matinees were over, and I felt in my veins the adrenaline spike I'd get when we were on nightly and constantly under the gun. They'd begun hiring staff, Harry said, and wanted from me a quick list of potential guests, including, they hoped, my former shipmate. I'm on it, I said. But was I? After L.A. I figured things would break our way, and when nothing did, I recalibrated expectations and figured it'd take a while, and maybe a long while, and now it was like getting thrown in the ocean and told to blow bubbles. Here you go, Buddy Boy, *now swim, swim!* And as the train rattled north I wondered what it meant that they wanted me "in on this," because we hadn't worked out my role if we were greenlit. (*Were these cold feet, and couldn't I just be happy?*) The goal was getting Buddy there, and then dropping him off like a parent leaves his kid at the freshman dormitory, not enrolling as the unregistered side of Buddy's brain for the next four years. And so yes, part of me was relieved, and dance-on-the-subway-seats happy, but I also felt a genuine stab of panic, and as I rolled film clips of our future good and bad, I missed my stop and wound up at the nearly empty subway station at 125th Street, at which point I had to sort myself out again and head back downtown.

30

That Sunday morning Buddy and I headed up Broadway to the holy temple of Zabar's for bagels, whitefish, and lox. He wore an old faded blue Lacoste shirt that had been washed so many times it looked like it might soon tear apart and dark blue Bermuda shorts and leather sandals he'd bought in Greece during his hiatus, and with a couple of days of razor stubble he looked like a man on vacation. I couldn't gauge his mood. We talked about our good news, but he was having trouble processing it, like it was a fish he'd caught and couldn't find the nerve to kill.

Summer in New York was cruelly hot, and the street smelled of melting asphalt and car exhaust. A boom box passed us pulsing the Stones's "Emotional Rescue," *"You're just a poor girl in a rich man's house. . . ."*

"I suppose I'm excited," he said, once the boom box passed.

"You *suppose* you are? You're back on the air," I said. "And not on channel C or J. You're on CBS."

He nodded twice and looked as though he was trying to digest food that wouldn't go down.

"To be honest . . . it's a little soon."

"Too soon? What do you mean?"

"I mean how long do we have to be up and running, six weeks?"

"Very doable," I said.

Zabar's on a weekend morning was a mob scene. We went over to the fish section and took a number. Behind the glass-enclosed counter were trays piled high with Nova Scotia salmon, Norwegian salmon, lake sturgeon, whitefish, chopped liver, capers, smoked trout, herring, borscht. The woman in front of us was eating a bagel with chopped liver and licking the sides of the bagel before taking each bite. She wore bright pink lipstick and had a hairy little dog at her side who was looking at me as though I might have a treat.

"We need to think this through, and we need to plan."

"It's only one night, and all they want as far as I can tell is you being you, your old brilliant self. You don't have to reinvent anything."

"Are you doing this with me?"

"Of course," I said, then added, "in the beginning anyway."

It wasn't what he wanted to hear.

"I mean on the show as a producer, as my able-minded muse. I need you there."

"I don't know, *do* you?"

"I can't do this without you."

"Sure you can."

"With you there I can do this, Anton. We'll make it work like we did on *The Tonight Show*. We worked so great together."

"That was all you," I said.

"But it wasn't. It was the two of us. A little more you than me."

"Untrue," I said.

"You're backing out of this."

"I'm not at all," I said.

"Then what?"

It struck me that he honestly wouldn't do this unless I partnered with him, and if he wavered they'd get someone else and we'd lose our shot. But if I said yes, I was signing on as Buddy's Boy Friday again, and I'd been increasingly convinced I needed something of my own, even if it didn't make much money, or make me famous, or even happy. We waited in silence to be served. He looked stressed and miserable, I thought, not the way someone should look after getting the sort of news he'd received. He was back on network TV. Couldn't he see how *fucking great* that was? Couldn't I?

He ordered for us, and the man behind the counter sliced the freshest, most amazing-looking Norwegian salmon, which Buddy wouldn't enjoy a bite of unless I gave him the right answer right then, so I told him, "Yes, we'll do this together."

"Okay," he said. "Then onward and upward."

We picked up a Sunday *Times* and a *New York Post* on the way back to the Dakota. The Olympics had begun in Moscow without us. They'd sealed off the capital as though they were in the midst of a military occupation.

I read from an article to Buddy, " 'The boycott was a clumsy plot that has failed, as all can see, they said on Soviet television.' They're carrying on without us as though we don't exist."

"A world without America."

"Brezhnev's dream," I said.

"Oh, he misses us," Buddy said. "You think beating Cuba and East Germany is as much fun as beating us?"

We passed the First Baptist Church, a huge turreted red-roof building that Buddy reminded me was designed by the same guy who designed the Apollo Theater, and later the Ansonia, where Toscanini and Babe Ruth once lived, he informed me for the umpteenth time, the Babe greeting visitors in a velvet bathrobe smoking Cuban cigars. It felt like Buddy was a realtor trying to sell me on the neighborhood so that I'd decide to put down roots here. Or maybe I just heard it that way. Everything about him suddenly irritated me.

At a liquor store on Columbus we picked up a bottle of champagne to celebrate — my idea — and we made mimosas. With the help of my mother and Kip, and two flutes of Moët, I got Buddy to see how lucky we were to get this shot, not to mention that after two years of hemorrhaging money he'd once again have a paycheck coming in. By that evening he was back in his TV-host brain, writing, and planning, reading the *Times,* the *Post, Esquire,* and *People* with a pen at his side to underline items to use in jokes. Before meeting with the network (in five days), we'd need to hone our sense of what we'd be, how we'd be different, and that would take work, and a little self-knowledge, and some late hours of tinkering. All within a week. We'd hit up our writers for ideas, and block out our budget, and then start reaching out to the affiliates, and potential sponsors to quiet their foreseeable concerns. And then we'd find a venue, and do a test run before an audience, and while doing all this avoid having another nervous breakdown, because that would ruin everything.

At around eleven that night I made the questionable decision to call long distance to Bermuda, thinking John would likely be up late composing. The line was scratchy, but his voice was clear.

"Hello," he said.

"It's Anton," I said.

"Anton me boy. Are you flying back down here? There's a few things I need from the apartment."

"Be there in a few hours," I said.

"It isn't the same without you," he said in a mock female voice.

"You stopped writing songs."

"Fuck no. I've got a suitcase full now."

I blurted out, "Buddy got a show."

"*Bloody* great."

"I just wanted to tell you."

"I'm glad you did."

"Well, so I guess that's our news."

"You don't sound completely thrilled."

"He said he couldn't do this without me."

"Ah, I see."

"What."

"You're worried it'll be like that *Twilight Zone* episode with the prisoner exiled on an empty planet."

"I don't know that one."

It wasn't the first time it struck me that John had watched a lot of TV over the last few years of being a househusband.

"One of the guards leaves the poor sod a robot that acts as the guy's companion, picks up his interests and tics. That's *you,* you're thinking, and all you'll do for the rest of your life is hold Buddy's hand and wipe his bum and you're worried you'll be on his deathbed laughing at his jokes and telling him how great he was and reminiscing about the day Orson Welles was on his show and said something magnificent, and all that will be true, and it will be true that his show was a great show, but where's *yours,* you'll ask. And whose bloody life will you have lived and will you wake up someday as an old man and realize all you did was work on someone else's fading dream?"

"Aw fuck."

"It won't happen. It's great news."

"Thanks I guess."

"But don't get too comfortable. I want to

take a longer voyage. Maybe to Tahiti, if you can keep from puking your guts out this time."

31

Alex insisted we celebrate in style by getting fucked up and going out to the new club he'd been frequenting, the Blitzkrieg on Thirty-Fourth and Seventh, which operated out of an old clothing factory, and had three separate floors that functioned like different clubs. The basement had bands like the Cramps, the Skirts, and the Swinging Madisons, and the floor above had a DJ spinning records, and on the floor above that one there were dangling video screens and some bigger ones with image collages, Bowie vamping in drag, bombs being dropped, demolition derbies, Nixon giving his Checkers speech, Wally and Beaver on a camping trip, Heckle and Jeckle placing dynamite in the back of a boat belonging to a droopy-faced dog.

On our way to the club we stopped at a nearby dive and had a few vodkas.

"So it's just once a week," he said.

"Which is better, don't you think?"

"I think it's great. I don't know how many people watch TV at eleven thirty on a Friday, but I certainly will."

"They watch on Saturday night. That's what they're hoping for."

"You're up against some very lame competition. There's a *Saturday Night Live* rip-off show at that time on ABC."

"Fridays." I had seen it a few times. It was an exact rip-off with skits and music and a news segment.

"So you know it. Have you watched it?"

"The bands are great, but it pretty much sucked."

"You know that they fired everyone at *Saturday Night Live*. Lorne Michaels is out, and they've got a whole new cast. From what I've heard it's a shitstorm."

"Is that good or bad for us?"

"Neither. But it's Buddy Winter. It'll be great."

"I'm going to be a full producer."

"At twenty-fucking-three."

"Freaks me out a little."

"Give me a break."

"What do you mean?"

"I mean, do you ever stop to think how lucky you've been, how many people would kill to be you? I love you, but sometimes I think you're living in a bubbled-off little castle."

"Okay."

"Good, then."

"And who nearly died twice in the last year?"

"But you *didn't,* right? And now . . ." — he pulled out a baggie containing four or five mushrooms — "time for a pre-club snack."

The mushrooms hadn't kicked in when we entered the club, which was packed with punks and glam rockers, and a few mohawks, and a sea of insanely dancing fools, which we joined. On the video floor we danced to the Jam's "Going Underground," which in that moment was the best song I'd ever heard.

At some point the chemicals hit my bloodstream, and I couldn't find Alex, and I walked by myself to the roof, where people were drinking and dancing and someone was setting off sparklers.

My eye kept dropping on something normally innocuous that I now found beautiful and odd, like the patterns of people's shirts, and the beads in a woman's hair, and the rings on a bartender's fingers, and the sound of the speakers, and the feel of the night air, and the smell of pot, and the dampness of my shirt. I'd been sweating. Bands I remember hearing: Martha and the Muffins, Joy Division, PiL, the Ramones, the Normal. I drank down a cold glass of water, and after that a shot of tequila that someone gave me along with seven other people who seemed to be celebrating a birthday. I sang with them.

Then I heard a voice with a British accent say "Winterboy." *Olive.* Her face was covered in silver sparkles, and her hair was teased out, and she was wearing a minidress and a sheer top.

Before I could answer, our mouths met and Olive pushed me against the wall and I surged with the music and felt her body up against mine.

Then she pulled back and said, "Where the hell have you been?"

32

Harry and Elliot Kaplan — who we stole from ABC the day we inked the deal — stopped by the apartment the next day to go over the media schedule, which included six different publications with whom Buddy would sit for interviews, and to work out strategies for how best to respond to questions about the breakdown and its aftermath. With a network show in development, Harry felt we should play it close to the vest, staying free of painful self-disclosure and focusing more on how great it was to be back, and our plans for the new show.

"I don't want to seem secretive," Buddy said.

"At this point I don't think that's a problem," Harry said. "People know your story."

"Not all of it they don't."

"They don't need to know all of it. It was a classic inward search. A spiritual pilgrimage. A cleanse. A reawakening. And then say something funny, so they won't feel as though you'll be doing therapeutic infomercials each week. That's pretty much it."

"Should we do a few practice interviews?" Buddy said.

"I think that would be wise," Elliot said.

We began firing questions at him, and with each one he smiled, gathered his thoughts, and gave a considered answer. Harry gave a thumbs-up after several of them but Elliot seemed unimpressed. When Buddy left the room to take a phone call, Elliot said to Harry, "You've stripped away his fire. He sounds medicated."

"*I* did?"

"All your words of caution."

"I just don't want any fuckups. Not now. Not with just a few weeks before the show starts," Harry said.

"What do you think, Anton?" They'd been looking to me to break the ties when they disagreed.

"I think he needs to be less self-correcting," I said.

"Exactly," Elliot said.

"All right," Harry conceded. "I just don't want him going whole-hog *Howard Beale* on us. We don't need anyone shooting him from the studio audience."

Buddy returned to the room, looking happily perplexed.

"Well wishes from Liz Smith," he said.

"Seriously?" I asked.

"Did you give her our number?" he asked me.

"I did," Elliot said. "You're gonna need her, and it's wise to make her feel privileged."

Harry said, "Listen, I guess you get into it a little with your answers. No more coaching. Be yourself and it'll all work out."

"I thought I was being myself," Buddy said.

"Be a little *more* yourself," Elliot said.

Buddy shrugged and said, "I can do that."

And then for the rest of our practice run he was great.

We went over the format too, and a request by the network that Elliot review the monologue at least a few hours before showtime.

"Why?" Buddy asked.

"It's just a formality. There won't be any editing. It's your show."

But we all knew it was to avoid the sort of meltdown monologues that Buddy had done last time.

I felt for him, having all of us picking at him, watching him, judging him ("like livestock at the county fair," Buddy said), rooting for him, and at the same time visibly worrying that he might combust again, or be a shell of his old self, or be better and have no one care anymore because the world, as it does, had moved on. And still, I took solace in what Elliot told us all, which was that with *Dallas* on before us, Friday nights were there for the taking, and that the network *that morning* agreed to promo Buddy during commercial breaks on three hit shows. If all went as designed, we'd own the night, and if *SNL* was as fucked up as everyone said, we might own the whole weekend.

33

The Democrats alighted on New York for their convention in August, which meant Joan and Ted would be in town and my mother would be pressed again into action, a few parties here and a trip to a day spa with Joan. In the end Teddy had won nine states and enough delegates to prove that with a marginally better performance, starting with old Roger Mudd and on the trail in Iowa, he might be headed for a win, and fine-tuning his acceptance speech. Now he was hoping for a floor fight, with a sizable block of Carter delegates jumping ship, something that was at best unlikely, and made him look like a sore loser, I thought. It was looking more and more as though Ronald Reagan, son of a shoe salesman from a small town in Illinois, star of *Bedtime for Bonzo,* and spokesman for GE, would be our next president.

The delegates partied hard regardless, as

though the world was ending. They made jokes about moving to Canada if Reagan won, and about wanting to invest in bomb shelters because of the likelihood now of nuclear war.

After her triumph at the Tavern, the rest of the campaign had been an ordeal for Joan. As his losses mounted Ted's spirits declined. He ate poorly, drank, and fell into moods, and journalists chronicled the weight he put on, his suits straining at the seams. When they posed for pictures, Ted very reluctantly held Joan's hand, or put his arm around her, and sometimes he left the stage well before her, and once while she was speaking.

"If we were to pull off a miracle and win this thing," Joan told my mother, "I can't imagine what kind of president and First Lady we'd be. He acts sometimes like he can't stand to be in the same room with me."

Teddy's last hope sank after a vote on the rules the first night went Carter's way. Teddy was gracious and said all the right things about uniting around the party and getting behind the president, and then on the penultimate night of the convention he gave the speech of his life pounding Reagan and the Republicans with such passion and precision (Where was *this* guy all these months?) that you couldn't hear him and not believe that this was what the country needed, and more so after Carter's warmed-over speech the following night. My mother's eyes welled with tears that had little to do with Teddy, I thought.

It was deeper: about the fact, I imagined, that life sometimes takes a wrong turn, and you can't will it to be any different.

"I have a very bad feeling about what's coming," she said.

"You mean Reagan."

"No," she said. "It feels like we opened the door to something, you know?"

"I do," I said.

"It's just a feeling. I'll get over it."

Joan and Ted were on the front page of the *Times,* photographed valiant in defeat. The next day he'd invited her to go to lunch with him at the Box Tree, an overpriced pretentious place in the East Forties. It was the first day of the rest of their life, Joan told my mother, with some real optimism that outside the pressures of the race they could start over again. But it turned out to be just a photo opportunity for Ted. In the pictures Joan looks lovely. She's wearing a lightweight summery dress, white with splashes of color, and he's leaning across the table in a dark suit, his thick curls combed drably back

The next evening, they held a party in their home in McLean, Virginia, and then they were supposed to fly to Hyannis Port, where they'd vacation together and plan the rest of their life, but according to what Joan told my mother later in a letter, Ted had asked the plane to make a stop on Montauk Point in Long Island. He told her goodbye, see you later, and thanks for everything, and then walked to a waiting car.

What made all this dreariness bearable was the early press for Buddy's new show. *Variety* was first, then *People,* and both pieces read like love letters. *Rolling Stone* did an interview with him. *Manhattan* magazine sent a reporter to interview him at the Dakota. People didn't like having reporters in the building. There was a mention of my living in the Dakota too, "on the dank and dimly lit ninth floor," the writer said.

Playboy ran a short Q and A with Buddy Winter, with a dashing picture of Buddy seated at a red-lit horseshoe-shaped bar. His favorite interview subjects (Alfred Hitchcock, Katharine Hepburn), pet peeves (people who hang large oil paintings of themselves in their homes), drink of choice (Tanqueray martini dry), favorite beach in the world (Waikiki), athlete he'd most like to be in his next life (Walt Frazier).

Hefner had had his own talk show, *Playboy After Dark,* which lasted two seasons and was designed to make you feel like you'd stumbled into a cocktail party that happened to have famous people who'd stand for short impromptu interviews with the host, between journeys to the bar. Hef would slide over to Roman Polanski and Sharon Tate, or Jerry Garcia and the Grateful Dead, or the Byrds, or Three Dog Night, and Hefner in a break in the conversation would say, "Do you feel like playing a song for the kids?"

Elliot said each show played to different brain chemistry. Morning shows went with coffee, weeknight shows a glass of wine. They'd run surveys, he said, and on Friday night the average TV watcher has had at least two drinks.

"How about *Saturday Night Live*?"

"Two joints."

"And while watching *Fridays*?"

"Some Quaaludes and maybe a little heroin," he said.

"What shows should you watch on cocaine?" I asked.

"An excellent question: I'd say sports but that might go badly. Too much of a jolt to the heart. Maybe you should coke up when you watch *Dallas* so that you feel like you're just as rich and powerful."

The arts section of the *Times* ran the story I liked best, because it included our stories about pitching the new show, and Buddy's joke gracing the Oscars, and then our week in L.A. The headline read: Are There Second Acts in American Life? Buddy Winter Says Yes.

34

Rachel's boyfriend, Randy, was shot in the leg one night at a bar in Flatbush. His partner was less lucky and was dragged by a car and nearly died. He'd made a run for the getaway car and got his jacket caught in the passenger-side door. The guys who did it had been arrested six and eight times respectively, for robbery and assault, and never served more than a year. Randy was furious. He was on disability and to keep busy and to stave off depression he'd been working on a few of the screenplays he'd been neglecting over the past few months. And he'd been reading, Rachel said. I had dinner with the two of them, and got an earful from Randy of how fucked up the New York legal system had become, how hard it was to get the bad guys put away.

We were at Puglia's, a favorite place of his in Little Italy. Randy walked on crutches. A pianist belted out "Buona Sera."

"It's good to get out of the house," Randy said.

His screenplays were filled with his frustrations, he said. The court cases, the stakeouts, the subway crime.

On our second bottle of wine we got to talking about the new show, and Randy asked Rachel why she never worked for Buddy, why I was the one who got to work in TV.

"I never wanted to," she said.

"Rachel ran away once," I said.

"What are you doing, Anton?"

"What? It's part of who you are."

"I want to hear this."

The waiter came by and served us family-style plates of rigatoni Bolognese and cavatelli with sweet sausage. Behind him was a man playing "That's Amore" on the accordion with a big green parrot on his shoulder. Randy tipped him, and then he pushed on to other tables.

"I ran off to Washington and marched against the war," Rachel said.

"How old were you?"

"Seventeen." This was a huge deal in our house: Rachel's year of radicalism, which launched her into her twenties.

"I marched too. But I didn't run away from home," Randy said.

"And now you're a cop."

"Go figure. You have to choose your wars carefully."

He started serving Rachel and me, filling our plates with steaming pasta.

"It's enough to feed a football team," Rachel said.

"We'll make a dent in it," Randy said, winking at me.

I remember going down to City Hall another time with Rachel and one of her boyfriends and seeing kids get beat up by packs of construction workers. The National Guard had opened fire on student protesters at Kent State. And we were just learning about the new war Nixon had started in Cambodia.

"I remember your dad was against the war," Randy said.

"He was one of the first. He went after Nixon nightly. Supposedly there were FBI agents in the audience waiting to pounce if Buddy took things too far."

"He was on Nixon's enemies list," Rachel said. "Do you remember we used to talk in code?"

"Seriously?" Randy asked.

"Half seriously, but my father was convinced they were tapping our phones," I said. "And that they were following him home after the show."

"I'm remembering a skit with Ringo playing an FBI agent."

"No, no. *CIA,*" Rachel said.

"Ringo, in a suede fringe jacket and headband over pressed slacks and black oxfords, infiltrates a party in Haight-Ashbury," I said, "where the long-haired guests all wear beads and bell-bottoms. Agent Ringo quickly falls in love with a hippie girl, played by *Laugh-In*'s Judy Carne, and has to choose whether to vacate his agency post in the name of peace and love or arrest the lot of them for plotting a revolution."

"He did one with George too."

"Harrison?"

"Yes. He's on the phone with Buddy, and an FBI agent this time bugs in. Then the agent's wife cuts in, right?"

"Yes."

"The wife comes onto the line to remind the agent to wash his hands for dinner."

"That's risky stuff, when the country's run by a thug like Nixon."

"Can you be a cop and talk like that?"

"I'm on disability. I can say whatever I want," Randy said.

The veal scaloppine came next along with some chicken Parmesan the waiter said was on the house.

"Don't expect any favors in return," Randy said.

"We won't, Investigatore Randy," he said.

"I can't eat any more," Rachel said.

"I can," I said, and I filled up my plate.

When they cleared the plates and we'd had a third bottle of wine, Rachel turned the tables on me.

"You know one reason I didn't work on the show. I didn't want being Buddy Winter's daughter to be my claim to fame."

"The way being Buddy's son was always mine."

"That's right. I used to tell people my last name was Simmons."

"Our mother's maiden name," I told Randy.

"He knows," Rachel said. She finished her glass of wine and poured herself another.

From age ten on, I lived in my father's shadow. Teachers and professors would end discussions about my work with comments about the show, or questions about particular guests, or in one instance a request for tickets and an invitation backstage, which I proudly provided, and later, when I got an A in the class, regretted because I couldn't say for sure if it was me or Buddy who'd earned it.

"You know Mom didn't set out to be the second most successful person in her family. She didn't set out to be a stay-at-home mom."

It was partly the wine talking but it was clear Rachel had things to say.

"She wasn't. She worked," I said.

"Not really. A few commercials here and there. Some off-Broadway theater. A little television. She was every bit as talented as he was. More so. He wanted to be an actor you know. And a novelist and a playwright, and he wasn't all that good at any of those things, which is why he went into hosting."

"Really. He was pretty good at all of them."

"Most of his breaks came because he was famous, and funny. Good at parties."

"And smart, no? What about the conversations on the war, and politics and books?" I said.

"He facilitates other people. You've seen him — he reads until he can fake it."

"I think there's a thin line between faking it and comprehending it," Randy said.

"That's true," I said.

I thought it was too bad Rachel couldn't see how hard it was to drop in and out of so many areas of expertise, the way Buddy could, and so elegantly hold your own.

"For you, Anton. You're his boy. His loyal sidekick. He loves you most."

"I don't believe that," I said.

Randy listened intensely and knew not to break in here. I thought they'd likely have a lively conversation about all this later in bed.

"He adores Kip, for sure, and loves me in his way. I know that. You guys are just more wound up in each other, and I'm fine not being that person, I really am. And I think it's meant that I'm further along on the path to figuring out who I am and what I want out of life. You're still a little lost in the weeds, Anton. One foot in and one foot out. And now both feet are in, right? You're right there alongside. But you know, it's his life story you're writing, and pretty soon you've got to begin writing your own."

"Thank you, wise Buddha." I was pissed.

"It's true, and you know it."

"To writing our own damn stories," Randy said and raised his glass.

"Indeed," I said.

When Buddy had been wandering who knows where in Asia, Rachel and I made jokes about him as a way of coping with his absence. Rachel wanted to get a T-shirt made that read: My Father Went to India on His Nervous Breakdown and All I Got Was This Lousy T-Shirt.

Was it like a *divorce*? we wondered. Did you get extra stuff to make up for all the shit you went through? People around us took pains to offer stories of family members or friends who'd cracked up and got electroshock, or ran off with their secretaries, or wound up on park benches talking to the pigeons. Or they acknowledged their own struggles, and their paths back to health. It was normal, they said. Everyone goes through it, they said. He'll be back, they said, in the voice people used to assure someone that a lost cat might soon turn up on their fire escape, tapping at their window.

"Listen, Anton," Rachel said. "I love you and I love Dad. It's just that everyone's so worried about him, and I'm just not. Ten years of being famous is a long time. A really long time, and whatever happens now he'll be okay. I worry about you."

"I'm fine, Rachel. You're not me and I'm not you. I make my own choices."

"If you say so."

"I can't wait for opening night," Randy said. "Will there be a red carpet? They'll all want to take pictures of the cop on crutches."

"The *screenwriter* on crutches," I said.

We then polished off the last of the wine.

■ ■ ■ ■

It's probably never a good idea to show up drunk outside the apartment building of a woman you've slept with twice but aren't exactly dating. Not at one A.M., but I was wound up from all the talk with Rachel, and I wanted to talk to someone, and I thought of Bronwen, especially since she lived nearby. I buzzed twice. She appeared at the window. "Anton!" she said. "What's up?"

"I'm sorry," I said. "I'm disturbing you."

"You're disturbing *me*!" someone yelled through the window of another apartment.

"I'll come down," she said.

In a minute she appeared in a T-shirt and gym shorts.

"Is there someone up there with you."

"That would be a yes," she said. "I haven't heard from you in a while."

"Life's been crazy."

"Tell me about it. I've got Sam sleeping in my bed."

"Sam the chef. The one you had a crush on."

"Don't fucking breathe a word."

"I thought he was married."

"He says they're on the outs."

"I just had a fucked-up conversation with

378

my sister, but I think I figured out something."

"What did you figure out?"

"You need to get back upstairs."

"He can wait."

"I figured out this whole fucking TV thing
that I ran from, and that I thought I was
trapped in, I know now that I really want to
do it. I *like* it, just not necessarily with my
father. That's all. I'll let you go back to
sleep."

She stretched and yawned then.

"Okay. I'd kiss you but I have bad breath."

"And a man in your bed."

"Yeah, well. You know. . . . Good night."

And she went back upstairs and I walked
all the way home, thinking how much I
loved the city, that I wanted to fill my lungs
with it, because soon enough I would leave
it. Not now, not in a month, but sometime,
and I wanted to hold on to the feeling I had
right then.

35

Our whole family, my sister included, rode the subway out to the U.S. Open tennis tournament in Flushing on the first weekend to watch the third-round matches. We went every year when the Open was in Forest Hills, and had seen a lot of the classic matches. Ilie Nastase beating Arthur Ashe in five brutal sets, Guillermo Vilas besting Jimmy Connors after losing the first set in 1977.

Rachel was reading an article about Buddy in *Manhattan* magazine. They included a family picture of us standing in front of the Dakota, with the caption "The Dakota Winters."

"I look bloated, like I've just had two gallons of water injected into my face," Rachel said.

"You look lovely," my mother said.

"Which sounds like you think I look worse in real life."

"I always thought that's what people meant when they said you were very photogenic. They're saying 'Wow, you're much more unattractive in person,' " Buddy said.

"No, they're not," my mother said. "Some people just look good in pictures and some don't. You for instance look very handsome in pictures."

"And quite homely in real life," I said.

"I get my picture taken a lot more than most people," Buddy said. "Lately anyway."

"The man of the moment," Rachel said.

"Mr. Winter," I said. "Is it true your daughter's face is far less bloated in person?"

"I don't know, let me see. . . . Why yes, I believe it is."

"Fuck off, both of you," Rachel said, but then smiled almost affectionately.

At the tennis center, a rep from the network escorted us in as special guests, and gave us VIP lanyards, which meant we could stroll past the guard at the Open Club, and mix with the celebrities who always packed the tournament, people like Dustin Hoffman and Barbra Streisand, Lee Majors and Brooke Shields (Kip's crush), and tennis luminaries like John Newcombe and Rosie Casals.

It was one of those blazing late summer in New York days. The sun beat down, and sweat formed around my shirt collar.

Buddy dropped by the CBS tent and talked with the gathered producers and executives who all congratulated and welcomed him. They reminded him he'd be sitting in later during the Björn Borg match with announcers Pat Summerall and Tony Trabert. I was recalling the Olympics, and how neglected Buddy felt, and how the tides had turned.

For now, he sat with Elliot — who'd scored one of those official CBS blazers — in the stadium watching a woman's match, where the twelfth seed, Virginia Wade, was getting mauled by an unseeded Rumanian.

My mother and Rachel ventured off to the food tents to buy an overpriced lunch and Kip and I went to the practice courts, where we watched the players slamming the ball to each other wearing ratty T-shirts.

Kip had gone upstate and won two small tournaments. He'd played in the qualifiers of the national clay courts, qualified, and then lost in the first round.

"Do you think of playing here someday?" I asked him.

"I'll never get close," he said.

"You're a high school junior. Who knows

how good you'll get."

He looked down at the ground, or at his huge feet.

"You know for a long time I just wanted to be better than him. I mean like this is his sport, the one he loved, and I wanted to beat him at it. And then I did, and it was sort of weird. I didn't like how it felt. He wasn't as happy about it as we both expected, you know? He's like weird that way, he forgets we're the kids and he's the grownup."

"I feel that too sometimes."

"You do?"

"Sure."

"The last time we played," Kip said, "I beat him 6–2, and he said he was going to have to face up to the fact that he'd never beat me again. I said it was okay, he could beat me at everything else."

"What did he say to that?"

"He said life wasn't a competition. And that I would win at most things soon enough."

"He's right."

"I don't know. He's good at a lot of things and he hates to lose."

"I'll tell you what, I can kick your ass at basketball any day of the week."

"Dream on."

"Tomorrow morning in the playground on Seventy-Seventh for five bucks."

"Easiest money I'll ever make," Kip said.

We watched Buddy on air from the VIP lounge, where they kept a large-screen TV in the corner of the room.

"We're joined now in the booth by one of my all-time favorite TV personalities, *Buddy Winter,*" Summerall said, "who is making his return to TV this fall on Friday nights, on his new show *Friday Nights with Buddy Winter.* Welcome to the CBS family, Buddy."

"Good to be here, men."

He wore a white Lacoste shirt over khakis, and his hair, which had been cut this week, looked clean and combed.

"Now you're a longtime tennis enthusiast and a pretty serious player from what I've heard."

"My son Kip has taken over the Winter mantle, I fear, but yes. I haven't missed a U.S. Open in years."

"Who do you like this year?" Tony Trabert asked. "Borg, McEnroe, Connors?"

"I have to go with McEnroe," Buddy said.

"The young man from Queens. He is playing hurt."

"He's a street fighter, and that's what'll win this year, I think."

Summerall asked Buddy about some of his favorite sports interviews and Buddy mentioned Namath after his Super Bowl win, Jim Bouton on the scoundrel activities of baseball players on road trips, and a storied Billie Jean King and Bobby Riggs segment during the lead-up to their match.

"You had them play Ping-Pong if I remember," Trabert said.

"I did. Bobby won that one."

"So tell us your favorite U.S. Open memory, if you will, Buddy. Anything stand out?"

"I'd have to say it was the semifinal in, what was it, '76? Orantes down 5–0 in the fourth set. Then Vilas had two match points at 5–1."

"1975. Truly one of the great ones," Trabert said.

"There was no way he could come back and then he did," Buddy said. "The crowd went nuts."

"Well then, like Orantes, Buddy Winter, who was himself down match points, has climbed right back into the big time. Welcome back. I'm sure the crowd will go nuts for you as well."

"I don't know if I was down match points," Buddy said, when he found us afterward.

"It was more like you defaulted," my

385

mother teased.

We took a taxi home that night, courtesy of CBS. Rachel and my mother were talking about gentrification. Buddy sat in the front seat talking to the driver, which he liked to do. The driver was from Yugoslavia, and so Buddy offered condolences for President Tito, who had died in May after a long illness, and whom the driver called a "great and horrible man" he hated "like an oozing sore on my heart."

I often thought that it was in dark cabs riding over the Fifty-Ninth Street Bridge that Buddy did his best interviews.

When we got back to the building and before we let the paid-for cab go, Buddy asked me, "Are you turning in?"

"Not necessarily, why?"

"I thought we might go check out some comics."

"Let's do it," I said.

We went to the Laugh Lounge on First Avenue and sat at a table set aside for us in the back of the room. Word had spread about the new show apparently, and people from the industry stopped by to introduce themselves and offer congratulations. Buddy smoked a few cigarettes, which he did only on occasion. He ordered us both martinis.

I had a sneaky feeling we weren't just

scouting, that Buddy had days ago arranged our drop-in to test out some new material, which would make this impromptu adventure all about him. But then it seemed that wasn't the case. He watched attentively instead. He liked three of the comics, and I liked one, a woman whose very funny routine was about her time as a germophobic hotel maid ("exhibit six: bathtub drains and pubic hair").

"Would you have her on the show?" he asked.

"Yeah, sure."

"That's what I think. We'll get her contact info, and maybe we'll get a chance to change her life."

I smiled.

"I still see myself in every one of them," he said, after a comic struggled through a painful run of jokes about getting dumped on the night he'd planned to propose. "It's a hard life, isn't it? You put your soul out on a platter. And you never know what kind of response you'll get."

"What if you just didn't care?"

"It'd make life easier."

"I'd want to not care what people thought."

"Good luck with that."

One of the last acts included a nod to

Plato's Retreat, that world of hairy-chested bacchanalian orgies in the basement of the Ansonia. The comic, a doughy thatch-haired guy with muttonchop sideburns, learned to his surprise that the woman rising to climax on top of him, he said, was his son's second-grade teacher. Approaching the end, she belted out, "Timmy . . . needs . . . to . . . focus . . . more . . . in . . . class . . . aaahhhhh . . . but . . . his . . . spotted leopard painting . . . ooohh *fuck me, fuck me* . . . was . . . hauntingly beautiful!"

Before the next act came out, the host said that they wanted to welcome "an old friend to the club, host of a brand-new show on CBS, *Friday Nights with Buddy Winter.*" Applause broke out. "What do you say, folks, can we get Buddy to come up here and tell us about the life of a comedy exile?"

"Aw crap," Buddy whispered, then waved his hand to feign resistance, but the crowd chanted, *"Buddy, Buddy, Buddy . . ."* until he rose to his feet, straightened his pants, killed his cigarette, and carried his drink up to the stage, like a credentialed member of the Rat Pack.

I'll acknowledge I drifted in and out of paying attention. I knew the material and from the pitch of his voice knew when to laugh. I suspect if anything he was too restrained, worried after our talk with Harry about revealing too much now that he had something to lose.

When he returned to our table, more people came by to praise his efforts, and a few of the comics slid into our booth. I recognized how much I'd missed watching people perceiving Buddy as the ticket up, and not as the ex-star who fell off a cliff.

On the cab ride home, he asked me, "How was it?"

"Your act?"

"Yes, my act."

"It was good."

"Can you be more specific? Did I go too long?"

"No, it was the perfect length."

"Meaning they had about as much of me as they could take."

"I didn't say that."

"I didn't want to do the whole nervous-breakdown-and-run-around-the-world thing, not there. It didn't seem right. I mean in the context of the show and all."

"I think it would have been fine if you wanted to go there."

"How would it have been *fine*? It could have been a disaster."

"Or it could have been real; you might have hit a chord that really resonated."

389

"So you're saying I didn't resonate."

"You did fine."

We rode through the park in silence. The driver had a sports talk show on where they were talking about the Yankees and Reggie Jackson. The host asked if Reggie was the greatest clutch hitter of all time and people were weighing in.

I thought of the first time I said something about Buddy's act that hurt his feelings. He'd asked me about a joke that had gone over fairly well, but which I hadn't laughed at and hadn't grasped. I said it sounded like an older person's joke. He'd been smiling and his face just fell, and then he got quiet. I was Kip's age. I remember thinking how strange it was to have that kind of power over him. I didn't like that he could be so vulnerable.

"*Fine* isn't good enough. Fine gets you canceled after three weeks."

I could see this turning into an argument, which would be beyond pointless.

"You were asked to pinch-hit, and you got a double."

"I guess a double's okay."

"Yes, it is. Be happy."

"The timing was okay?"

"It always is."

"Not always."

"I liked the stuff about the *Battle of the Network Stars.* And I liked the bit about the hotel fire."

"You could do my whole set from memory."

"Quite possibly."

"They liked it, that's the bottom line."

"No one heckled."

I was tired of reassuring him. It wasn't good for either of us. I thought of what the clear-minded Buddy would have talked about, that behind all good comedy was something deeper, a more pointed truth. The germophobic hotel maid was forced to stare down her fears, like Liddy strapped to the tree branch in a storm, and John at the helm of the *Megan Jaye,* and the gale winds in her story were a stranger's pubic hairs. And the orgy teacher gave the sleazy dad what he likely really craved, a woman who saw a complex genius in his troubled son.

"Was I the oldest person at the club?"

"No, there was one guy older. He came in a walker. He blew his nose for you at the end."

He smiled then, acknowledging my exasperation. We'd reached a juncture: something would get fixed here, or break.

"I think you need a personal assistant," I said.

"What do you mean?"

"Someone to do all the things I used to do," I said. "I want a different job on this show. I want to do other things. I'm a producer now. I want to produce."

We arrived at the building then.

"All right," he said. "We'll meet in the morning and talk about it."

"I appreciate it," I said.

"Do we have anything going on tomorrow?"

Without thinking I said, "Two o'clock interview with WPIX."

"How do you keep track of these things?"

"Habit," I said. "How about I don't go with you for this one."

"Good enough," he said.

36

When he returned from Bermuda, John got down to work putting an album together. He'd named it *Double Fantasy,* after flowers (very large yellow freesias) he'd seen in Bermuda, and also because he'd determined — he and Yoko had determined — that the album would be composed half of his songs and half of hers. I wasn't the only one disappointed by this news.

They worked out of a place called the Hit Factory on West Forty-Eighth.

It was arranged as a conversation between John and Yoko, his songs answered by hers.

In "Dear Yoko" he had a line straight from our trip, that when we were miles at sea, "and nowhere is the place to be," Yoko's spirit was watching over. I would argue (pointlessly) that it was his Viking ancestors or Poseidon watching over him, but it was his song, not mine. A guy named Jack Douglas, who'd worked with Cheap Trick and Aerosmith, was signed on to produce, because after being out of it for that many years they wanted someone young and current.

Fred told me John kept a tight leash over the band, which included a drummer from Roxy Music, and a bassist and a guitar player who'd toured with Paul Simon and David Bowie respectively. Yoko, Fred reported, ordered the studio to build a lounge, a "quiet room" with palm trees and a white piano, and brought in sushi and tea, and masseuses to give shiatsu massages to whoever needed one.

I heard stories of John's tirades, and the pressure in the studio, and some battles over Yoko's contributions, but all in all it was getting done. And it would be out soon in stores, and on the radio.

It felt like Buddy was moving on a parallel track, hiring writers and producers, stagehands, and a camera crew. We got a new band, and pulled from retirement our old cue card man, Les Hammond, and our velvet-voiced announcer, Don Gold, from the game show *The Know-It-Alls* ("Who knows who knows the most? Find out tonight on *The Know-It-Alls*"). We moved in to our new venue on Tenth Avenue and Forty-Seventh, a CBS studio that seated three hundred. The designers went to work on it to make it resemble our old home, with some new touches, like a larger second stage for musical acts, and seats that wrapped around in a semicircle, and aisles wide enough for the times Buddy chose to sprint through the audience, which he used to do, and wanted to do again.

They created a skyline in the space behind the stage with the view of the Upper West Side from Central Park, with a quarter moon hanging over a silhouette of the Dakota.

As for my part, I tried to carve my own path outside his immediate orbit, though I was within voice range much of the day, and met with him every morning to go over plans. But we had a staff of twenty now and there were others he could consult. It was better for morale that I not be perceived as his sergeant at arms, that I was down on the pecking order of writers and producers.

The Dakota househusbands were back to work. A few times, John gave Buddy a lift in their limo as they drove down to West Forty-Eighth. John used to joke that they were living their Howard Hughes–Greta Garbo years, stars in exile. After their stretch of hibernating, they were both out in the world again. Tuned in to the cosmos, John said.

In sorting through media requests and deciding who to do interviews with, Yoko reviewed each applicant's astrological credentials, and she recommended we do the same. Fred said she rushed to finish one of her songs to be done before a significant moon change. She beat the changing moon by a few seconds, he said.

I ran into Fred one night along Central Park South, where he was directing a fancy microphone at the clicking hooves of the carriage horses, to record incidental sound effects to be played between tracks on John's album. Next they took the mic and the high-end recording device into the Palm Court of the Plaza Hotel, where I saw him purloining the sounds of a violin and piano duo along with the muffled voices of people drinking cocktails. In the gap between "Watching the Wheels" and "Yes, I'm Your Angel," you can hear their work.

The Plaza had me picturing the Beatles when they came to New York and took over a floor of the hotel. They were twenty-three, my age, and I imagined myself being one of them, with Alex and a couple of our friends, Ted Glaser maybe and Andrew Lehr, taking the world over. Four guys, brothers John liked to say, who'd grown up near one another in hellhole Liverpool during the

Blitz, drooling toddlers when the bombs dropped, hipster teenagers when Paul turned up at that Quarrymen gig and taught John the proper way to play the guitar. George had spotted John on the bus a few times, he being the youngest by two years, seventeen when he lived above a strip club in Hamburg. Crazy stuff. Three thousand fans and a hundred journalists greeted them at the airport. They rode in four separate Cadillac limousines into the city. The Plaza desk clerk had been told to hold rooms for four British businessmen.

The next morning a lucky disc jockey named Murray the K would tour them around the city. I imagined them there in the hotel, and I thought of the scene in the posh suite in *A Hard Day's Night,* packed with people drifting in and out, John in the bathtub with his hat on, sinking into the bubbles with only his pipe sticking out. I imagine them heading out that night to 21. I can hear George with a bad sore throat conducting a phone interview with the BBC, the other three holding a press conference in Central Park, then taking a bus through Harlem.

Buddy was writing for Johnny Carson then.

I was in the second grade.

Picture me in my blue Keds and my blue wool hat, accompanying our British baby-sitter, Jenny, to the skating rink nearby and stopping within those crowds to look up at their hotel window in the hopes they'd come look out.

A Hard Day's Night came out that summer. What I loved in that movie — which I've seen a dozen times — is the chemistry between the four of them in their matching Edwardian suits and ties and dark brown hair combed forward, how they played off one another, hiding from the girls in phone booths, grilling an old man (Paul's fictional grandfather) in their train compartment, slipping into the train's luggage hold for a card game, then sliding into song.

I loved them answering questions at the snobby party.

"Tell me, how did you find America?" someone asks John.

He answers, "Turn left at Greenland."

It wasn't only the music for me; it was how I wanted to live my life. They were themselves. They weren't serving someone else's career, massaging someone else's ego. They were my age, and just *look at them,* I thought.

I was pleased to detect my friendship with John had traveled back to the Dakota with us, as I'd feared it was one of those parts of your life that would feel half dreamt afterward. But I got notes from him under my door occasionally with invitations for coffee, or a quick visit for tea and sushi, and occasionally a book about a sea voyage. He'd been thinking of Tahiti. And so each day in my minutes of free time I researched routes we might take, and I called Captain Hank one night to ask whether it might be possible to get a crew together to do this, and he was game. Of course he was.

Olive, after our wild night of debauchery that began at the Blitzkrieg and ended up in the ninth-floor stairwell of the Dakota (she did sleep over in my bed), had become what I thought about when I wasn't thinking of Buddy and the show, and all the things I needed to do, and all the people I was waiting to hear from, and the list of things I still hadn't done. She came over on a Tuesday night for a tour of the Dakota. I told her about hideouts, the secret staircases and terraces, and the corner rooms in the basement where they put old gargoyles and cornices and the old elevator cars. I'd told her at night you could hear the spirits kicking about (bullshit), and that as kids we'd pretended we lived in a castle (true), and that the courtyard was used for jousts and beheadings in early years, that the yard behind the building housed a tennis court and a croquet lawn. I told her I'd make dinner for her.

"Stir-fry right?" she said.

"What do you mean?"

"All American boys like to stir-fry. A little chicken and some water chestnuts and bamboo shoots, soy sauce and baking soda. You have a wok, am I right?"

I knew how to make a few Gabonese dishes. I said, "Poulet au Gnemboue," which my friend Gauthier had taught me.

"We'll make that then," she said.

We shopped on Columbus Avenue for chicken, palm nuts, bananas, eggs, orange juice, sour cream, and brown sugar, and then Olive picked out a bunch of stuff she said a bachelor boy like me needed.

Columbus had been run-down and dicey only five years back, and a block away on Amsterdam there were still vacant lots and run-down tenements, but now around the corner from us was a ten-block stretch of cafés and specialty shops, and on weekend nights, people ventured here just to walk up and down the street.

We went to the Korean grocer first on Seventy-Third Street, and then to two other small markets after that.

We made it back with most of our ingredients and got down to making some serious food. Poulet au Gnemboue requires you heat chicken in a large saucepan along with palm nuts ground in a blender (Gauthier used palm base, but you can't find palm base at the store), pepper, salt, green onions, and garlic.

And then fried bananas, which I'd made for my parents and Kip twice since I'd been home. You cut the bananas into slices, dip them in egg and orange juice, then roll them in bread crumbs, and drop them in boiling vegetable oil. Then add a little sour cream when they're nice and brown.

We made all this without burning anything.

"Oh my god, you've got talent," she said.

We took dessert up to the roof; a big low moon hung over the park.

"I keep thinking of that opening shot in *Rosemary's Baby,* where the building looks so haunted," Olive said.

"Not hard to do. Everyone's scared of the Dakota."

"What floor was that apartment?"

"We wouldn't let them shoot the interiors in the building."

"Why not?"

"There's a board and they're pretty protective of our privacy."

"And still they encourage celebrities to live here."

"There was a lot of debate about John and Yoko moving in actually."

"Do people like them?"

"I do. My parents do."

"But other people in the building?"

"I'd say, yes. Some people don't know what to make of her."

"How many apartments do they have?"

"I think five. She wants to buy more, and that's kind of the issue."

"She's the only woman who could have broken up the Beatles, because she actually believes she's bigger than them."

"I'm not sure she broke them up," I said.

"Seriously?"

I had the feeling I shouldn't say anything more here so I shrugged and said, "Who knows."

"You're friends of theirs."

"There's kind of a code not to gossip about neighbors."

"I love it. I completely respect that."

"Thanks."

"Do you want to hear about the Met murder?"

"I do."

Olive had been covering the disappearance of a violinist at the Metropolitan Opera.

A thirty-year-old woman violinist had been thrown down a sixth-story air shaft, and was found lying sixty feet below the roof of the Opera House. The ensuing search for the killer led to headlines about a new Phantom of the Opera. Speculation had been that it was an employee of the opera, and as it turned out it was a twenty-one-year-old stagehand from the Bronx.

"Fucking awful thing to cover," she said.

She'd also done pieces on the theft of two Picasso paintings, an Upper East Side brothel, and cockfights in the Village.

"They give you all the cheery wholesome stories."

"I know. What does that say about me?"

Fielding had an old *Esquire* with great drink recipes from an article entitled "Cocktails for the Cary Grant in You." We went back down to the apartment and I mixed Olive a Smoking Cat (wheat whiskey, bitters, bourbon, and Dubonnet) and myself a Cadillac Sidecar (cognac and Grand Marnier).

I was trying too hard to be sophisticated, I realized, but fuck it, she was British, what else was a lad to do.

She examined the black and white photos on Fielding's wall, one of which was an old photo of a dining room, with uniformed waiters and patrons in black tie and fancy dress.

"You know what it is?" I asked her.

"It looks like the dining hall of the *Titanic*."

"It's the Dakota dining room."

"There was a dining room?"

"There was indeed. A private one with waiters in white gloves and a captain in charge. And look at this." I showed her an old menu Fielding had displayed in his kitchen.

"They'd put one of these under everyone's door during the day and you could phone downstairs and make your order: Russian caviar, oysters from Prince Edward Island, stuffed quail, roasted partridge, foie gras. And the tables were set with heavy linens, stained-glass goblets and finger bowls, heavy plate silver cutlery."

"It's like a *secret society*. How many other buildings were like this?"

"I don't know if there were any. He's got lots of amazing pictures. He was the Dakota's historian at one point. Anyway, they had a staff of two hundred and forty. Maids and cooks, a seamstress."

"And a lot of the big New York families."

"He says it wasn't the bankers and lawyers. It was the world of music and the theater: the Schirmers, the Steinways. These floors were for the cooks, or people's mistresses."

"Was that how you got your place up here, as a mistress? Or would we call you a mister?"

"They call me Dr. Love," I said.

"Do they? M.D., or Ph.D.?"

Toward the end of the night we sat out on my tiny balcony drinking some kind of licoricy booze from Cyprus. I would have to travel to a lot of liquor stores, I recognized, to replenish old Fielding's supply.

"Do you know where the term Beatlemania comes from?" Olive asked.

It was after two at least.

"Where?"

"From Lisztomania, the hysterical reactions audience members had for Franz Liszt."

"The composer?"

"Concert pianist. They made a movie about this. His fans would enter a state of mystical ecstasy. They tugged at his hair, grabbed for handkerchiefs, anything, the remains of his meals and drinks. Crumbs he left on a table," she said. "Don't you wish you were a musician."

"I really don't," I said.

"You'd be worshipped."

"I'd rather worship than be worshipped," I said.

"I believe it. I like that actually," she said. "Anyway, I've been working on a story about parasocial relationships. The kind where one person extends emotional energy, interest, and time, while the other is unaware of their existence."

"Like people have for celebrities, like John."

"Exactly. But to them it feels absolutely real. It's like this. When you watch movies you get *angry* sometimes at characters, right? You feel like they've betrayed you in a scene. Or you love them for something they've done. That's what it's like for them."

"It's misplaced," I said. "Their feelings."

"Misplaced emotions are like land mines," Olive said. "Ready to blow up who walks over them."

Being famous seemed like a curse, something you couldn't escape. It followed you everywhere and you could never decide to suddenly be anonymous. You couldn't just go out to a bar somewhere and get a drink, or shop in a department store, though for minutes and sometimes hours you might slip through before someone spots you and then the jig is up. It's like being wanted by the police and your picture is everywhere, like Cary Grant in *North by Northwest* going through Grand Central Station with heads turning and the ticket master suddenly realizing, It's *him.*

37

Remember *Daktari*?

Or *The Girl from U.N.C.L.E., Love on a Rooftop, The Pruitts of Southampton*?

No?

Phyllis Diller starring as the widowed matriarch of a bankrupt Long Island society family living large in a sixty-room mansion?

The Danny Kaye Show, The King Family Show, Branded. How about *The Funny Side*? Gene Kelly's variety hour about marriage.

Laugh-In, The Flip Wilson Show, The Glen Campbell Good-Time Hour, The Paul Lynde Show, Chico and the Man, Barbary Coast, Joe and Sons, Joe Forrester, Joe and Valerie, Joey and Dad, The Joey Bishop Show, Big Eddie, Matt Helm, Harry-O, Kate McShane, The Captain and Tennille (one season), *Holmes and Yoyo, Mr. T. and Tina, Donny and Marie, The San Pedro Beach Bums* (one season), *Young Dan'l Boone, Rosetti and Ryan, Busting Loose, Switch, Logan's Run* (one season), *The Betty White Show, Man from Atlantis, The Richard Pryor Show* (five weeks).

Every one of these shows was conceived with love and ambition, pitched at a lunch somewhere, tested in advance, put into development, promoted, and cast, and then dropped into the world, into a prime-time slot, like a child dropped off at kindergarten.

Most shows die in the womb. Some last a year or two. *The Buddy Winter Show* in its first run lasted nine amazing years.

I say this now, as the great mother of mothers — CBS — gives birth to a new child.

Introducing *Friday Nights with Buddy Winter.*

In lieu of gifts, just don't change that dial when you're done watching *Dallas.*

I got swept right up in the whirl of those days wending my way through the strikes, shootings, and neighborhood identity battles in the condo-crazed city, and the ever nastier race for the White House, and the Billy Carter/Libya story getting weirder, and world events still out of control, a president plotting, one guessed, a last desperate rescue attempt for the hostages and for his second term, and then a *Manhattan* magazine story about all the top fashion models being under the age of fourteen, and well, from all this I was hammering out notes for Buddy's monologues and a few jokes, and with Elliot's guidance I was choreographing the flow of movie and TV stars and writers and thinkers and news makers, attempting on each night to create, well, a story, a narrative thread for my father to follow, and fuck if we didn't do it better than anything else on TV. The issue Harry suggested was whether it mattered on our appointed hour, Friday night, when everyone had four beers or three cocktails and some weed in them. They'd tuned in for the music and the laughs, and maybe some of them had even turned the volume down, who knows, and still, the bands were excellent: the Specials, Delta 5, Tom Petty. And I got to meet them and for a night I could pretend to be cool. John told me when I saw him in the elevator once that Buddy's guests were getting him up to speed on all he'd missed in his five years of hibernation.

Our primary headache revolved around the talent and who we could get and who we couldn't, and us wondering whether it was logistics or people not yet wanting to throw their lot in with us. Buddy wanted great talkers and thinkers, people you'd want to spend a night at a bar talking with, and he didn't care as much if they were starring in a movie that week. And Elliot said we were better off getting the hot guests and getting their best, meaning that Buddy could take the conversation where he wanted, so long as at some point he mentioned whatever it was they needed to plug. Buddy asked me for my notes, detailed critiques of his monologues and interviews, and I guess I went too far with them. I told him he was getting too esoteric sometimes for network TV and that he was losing his audience, that maybe he could take a cue from Johnny and just be funny and get out of the way, and that he didn't have to turn every conversation into a work of fucking art. Yes, I said *a work of fucking art,* in a harsh voice I didn't recognize as my own, which if you think about it was exactly what made him himself. It was like I was trying to break him down. And I can't tell you exactly why, only that I was under a lot of pressure I sensed, and that if I wanted to escape, it was better that this be a ratings success and not an embarrassing boondoggle.

I was expounding on these subjects with Kip on my balcony one night.

"You're pretty wound up," he said.

411

"What do you mean?"

"You're like Dad used to be. Like before he broke down."

"I'm nothing like that."

"If you say so."

For our third show I'd pulled out the stops to get Muhammad Ali, who was attempting to regain the heavyweight title for the fourth time in his career, this one being the toughest climb given his age, and his evident decline. We'd figured we'd get him to come on because he'd done Buddy's show before and they'd hit it off, and the two of them over the years had corresponded, and done several charity events together. After days going back and forth with his press agent, we got the bad news, that he was doing a Howard Cosell interview for ABC and wouldn't have time on a Friday to do our show. I actually kicked the phone, but then I got back on it and by the afternoon I'd booked Ali's opponent, Larry Holmes, and everyone was happy.

Elliot said it was exactly what the best producers do. They cut their losses and get the next best thing without shedding a tear.

"I don't know if you know this, but you were a big part of Buddy getting the show. The network likes you."

"I couldn't get Ali," I told him.

"Holmes is better. He's hungry and young, and he wants to make waves. There'll be some sparks with Buddy. You watch."

Holmes would fight Ali in Las Vegas for the heavyweight title a week after his appearance with Buddy. He was tall, six feet three, and though Buddy was only an inch shorter the difference seemed more pronounced on TV.

Holmes talked of his rise up the boxing ranks from unknown to the heavyweight champ. He was new enough to fame that he could walk down the street without causing a stir, unlike Frazier and Foreman, and even Leon Spinks. Ali in a crowd of people was an altogether different thing to see, he said. He'd met Ali when he was training for the Olympic trials years back and had traveled with him to Zaire for his title fight with George Foreman.

"I was Ali's sparring partner for two years," Holmes said. "You know how he is. He'd talk and talk and talk. He'd say to me, 'Come on, *earn your keep.* I'm the champ.' Now *I'm* the champ. And I'm going to do my best to kick his ass. He would have. When he was young he kicked the ass of all these old guys he was fighting and now *he's* the old guy, and I'm going to kick his ass."

"Don't underestimate him," Buddy said, as if that was possible, especially for someone who'd seen Ali up close taking Foreman down.

"He wants to take the title a fourth time. It isn't going to happen. He hasn't fought anyone real in five years. I'm still undefeated. Thirty-five fights, you know how many knockouts, Mr. Buddy Winter?"

"How many?"

"Twenty-six."

One of the other producers had come up with the idea that before the commercial break Buddy would spar with Holmes. Shadowboxing. No contact. They put on gloves. Buddy wore protective headgear and a regrettable pair of boxing shorts over his slacks. Holmes was supposed to completely miss but instead he kept slapping Buddy's head.

Not hard enough to hurt him, but it wasn't all that funny, and Buddy stopped after a while and said, "Well, that's why he's the champ."

"And why you're the *chump,*" Holmes said. It was supposed to be fun, but it sounded hurtful, and no one laughed, and then the segment ended awkwardly.

When Buddy returned he said, "Best of

luck, Larry. I hope Ali kicks your ass."

The crowd laughed, but Holmes, who watched from backstage, was pissed about it, and as he was leaving told me he wanted a written apology.

I told him Buddy was joking and had loved having him on the show, and that he said that sort of thing all the time, and not to take it the wrong way.

Holmes studied my face for a second and said, "It's cool. Ali won't kick my ass. And it won't be close. You watch. It's gonna be ugly."

Paul Simon came on too that night, promising when he took his seat that he wouldn't slap Buddy in the head. "I appreciate that, Paul," Buddy said.

He had a movie coming out called *One-Trick Pony* about a pop star named Jonah who'd fallen from stardom and was attempting to rescue his career with an ill-fated new venture.

Like Ali, I thought. And John. And Buddy. And Teddy.

They talked about artistic vision and collaboration after that, and he sang a song, "Late in the Evening," from the film.

The clip they showed had Lou Reed against type playing a shallow record producer urging Simon's character to add a string section, à la "The Long and Winding Road" and "The Sound of Silence," to a gritty song, an idea Jonah rejects on principle.

I told Buddy to ask him about the redo of "Sound of Silence," which I'd heard Simon hadn't known was overdubbed before hearing it on the radio when he was in London.

"That's actually true," he said.

"And it didn't bother you?"

"That song came out on an album called *Wednesday Morning, 3 A.M.,* which no one remembers because it disappeared, so the fact that someone bothered to bring it back to life was okay with me."

"Then it became immortal."

"A guy from the record company told me, 'Well, it isn't "Turn! Turn! Turn!" but it's nice.' "

After that show we went out to P. J. Clarke's to celebrate that we'd paced ourselves through the first few laps, and now were settling in for a long prosperous run. The reviews were positive, all of them saying Buddy hadn't missed a step, and might be even better for the rest and the perspective he'd gained. "Now we grow an audience," Elliot said.

I sat near Buddy during the first round of

drinks, and then at some point I moved to the other end of the table and then to another table altogether, so that he could bond with the rest of the crew, and with Harry and Rachel and Kip, who'd come out with us, because I'd had so much time with him, and they hadn't.

My mother saw it differently. When I slid next to her on the red leather banquette, she regarded me with what felt like disapproval.

"What?" I said.

"I've noticed something."

"What's that?"

"That you've stopped listening to him."

"Dad?"

"Yes."

"What do you mean? I've heard every story he's told a hundred times."

"And you act like you've heard them a hundred times. And you haven't, you know. He isn't boring. He says things that surprise me all the time. You used to hang on his every word."

I shook my head in denial.

"I used to love looking at your face when he spoke, and now you tune him out. And you know, Anton, he can tell. He's stopped telling you stories the way he used to."

"That's just not true."

"Isn't it? When we first sat down, he told a great story about something that happened to him on the way to the studio. Do you remember it."

"It was on the subway."

"It was as he was getting out of the subway and the guy said he'd seen the show and they walked down the street together and he gave Buddy a copy of a book he'd written."

"I guess I tuned it out," I said.

"He's noticed. He said sometimes when he's telling a story you'll get up and walk into another room. It flusters him."

"Point taken."

I sat next to him then, and he put his arm around my back. He'd been telling one of the producers about the product endorsements he had to do in the early days for Scope and Amana refrigerators. When he saw my empty glass, he flagged down the waiter for another beer, and I had to remind him to finish the story, which was about how they'd put up the wrong cue card and he'd had to ad lib. He rushed telling it for my sake.

I'd never heard it before, proving what a shit I was, and filling me with the sense of how wrong I was about a lot of things I thought I knew.

■ ■ ■ ■

I went to a different bar on the East Side the next week to see the Ali–Holmes fight with Harry and Alex.

Ali looked a step slow, like he was moving through sand, and his punches were slow as well, like he had weights on his arms. Still he'd come back from the dead before, he could do it again. Couldn't he?

"He's Muhammad Ali," Harry said. "No way he loses."

But he kept getting hit. Holmes was good, and he wanted this, wanted it bad. He wanted to knock Ali right out of the sport. I had a strange image watching the fight of seeing Buddy out there, with his shorts over his slacks, taking punch after punch.

At the end of the tenth, they called it. They should have called it sooner. It was terrible to watch in the end. Like Teddy at the Garden, Ali was done. He had a cut under his eye and a bloody nose. The greatest of all time lost every round.

38

A writer from *Rogue* magazine, a guy Olive knew, who occasionally joined her among a group of journalists who met for drinks, wrote something of a scathing cover story about John.

I heard about it from Katrina, the blonde groupie who hung out in front of the Dakota.

"People are kind of upset," she said.

"About what?"

"It makes him sound like a big phony, like he's gone back against all his ideals."

The writer purported to be a huge Lennon fan from way back. Then he lingered on all the things Yoko had spent money on. All the apartments in the Dakota, the other houses they bought, and the ones they were thinking of buying. It detailed John's voyage after he left the Beatles, his time with Janov, his battles with Paul, his craziness in Los Angeles. It really went to town on John about the Holstein cows they'd bought because Yoko figured correctly they would be a great investment, and the Egyptian art her psychic had urged her to buy.

The writer detailed his trip upstate to find the cows, how he got a local farmer to show him where the cows were, and then he talked to people about how John and Yoko never came up there, and the pastoral fantasy was just that, unreal. The point of the piece seemed to be that John wasn't who he claimed to be, or who he used to be.

There were interviews with locals who'd seen him from time to time, but he was writing about someone who didn't exist, and the real John did exist. It felt solipsistic to imagine if you didn't see someone, if he wasn't satisfying your conception of who he *should* be, that he wasn't there at all. Worst of all, he'd written the piece during John's trip to Bermuda and had speculated it was a rich man's pampered adventure. John was furious.

"Did you know he was writing the piece?" I asked Olive.

"Yeah. I guess I did, but I didn't know his angle. It is how people see him, though."

Katrina didn't believe a word of it. "They're all jealous of him, always have been, always will be."

"And you?"

"I just love him, that's all."

You are supposed to not read your press, but if you didn't you couldn't combat the mistakes, and it might end up as a tacit endorsement of lies.

It made me feel tense, I told Olive. Every day was anxiety filled because I thought someone could write a takedown, or our ratings could drop, or we could lose a couple of affiliates.

"I'm glad I don't have to open a magazine and read an unflattering article about myself," Olive said. "It's like they're perpetually in secondary school, and every day they have to check their status. No wonder they all want to escape."

We got drunk on martinis and listened to the Beatles and talked about "Norwegian Wood," which we listened to four times through. Olive claimed it was about arson.

"She tells him she works in the morning, and she starts to laugh. Why?"

"Because it'll be difficult to get up with a hangover," I said.

"And he sleeps in the bath, and he wakes up alone."

"In the bath."

"She's gone, and so he *lights a fire,* isn't it

422

good, Norwegian wood."

"You're saying . . ."

Olive smiled. "He lights her apartment on fire."

"But why?"

"Because she's gone. She just used him."

"It doesn't make sense."

"Why not? It's a love/hate thing."

"But they barely know each other," I said. "I'm not sure it's literal."

Next on was "You Won't See Me."

"This was one of Paul's Jane Asher songs," I said, because I know these things.

"That's what I always heard."

"Poor heartbroken Paul."

"She was gorgeous. Is gorgeous as far as I know. And he was the one who cheated on her. She caught him in the act."

Something I hadn't known. "When was this?" I asked.

"She came home early from a trip. It's pretty desperate what he's saying. He's going to kill himself."

"Where do you hear that?"

"Isn't that what he said? 'And I just *can't . . . go on.*'"

"He wants better communication, that's all. He says he wouldn't mind if he knew what he was missing."

"Meaning?"

"If she just answered the phone and told him what she was up to, he'd be fine," I said.

"But she hasn't told him anything. She won't get back to him and he's going crazy."

"So now it's time he set her apartment on fire."

"All their songs are ultimately about arson."

I was falling for her, I thought, and someday I'd be writing my own heartbreak song.

I told her my plan to bring them on, that John had said he'd appear with Paul, that Ringo was a cinch if asked. All we had left to make history was George.

"When would this be?"

"In a month or two. It's sort of real and not real. It would be a big deal, wouldn't it."

"It'd be great for all of them," she said. "You do realize that it's going to happen. They've all been on your father's show before. That's where they all talked about the breakup; it's like they talked to Dad, and now Dad's bringing them back for the holidays."

John brought up the article and some of the mixed reviews when I went to breakfast with him.

"The cows. Big fucking deal. We have

cows, and she sold one for $250,000. If that's the market for cows."

"It seemed like jealousy over your money."

"I don't care about money, never have, that's where they're all wrong. She cares about it, because I want her to care about it. In England you were either in the Labour Party or you were a capitalist. I grew up a socialist, but I worked for my money so I guess I'm a capitalist now. I used to equate money with sin, now I've come to terms with it. Yoko never had an issue because she was born rich, and then she was poor, and having money means you don't have to think about it as much."

I told John Buddy's story of seeing the pieces of paper in his wallet when he was traveling and thinking how absurd it was that he could trade them in for food or a place to sleep. And because there's a fifty on a green piece of paper it's worth fifty times as much as another piece of paper the same size.

"Defamiliarization," John said. "Which reminds me. I have a little present for you," he said, and he handed me passes for an hour each at the sensory deprivation tanks, where he'd previously taken Buddy.

"Take your new lady," he said. "The one I saw you with the other night."

"When?"

"Last night. We were getting into a car and you two were coming in for the night."

39

Buddy had on Peter O'Toole the next week to discuss his starring role in a new movie, *The Stunt Man,* which took nine years to get released, then became a stealth hit with the critics. I loved the conceit: a wanted criminal wanders onto a movie set and gets recruited to replace a stuntman who drowned when his car spun off a bridge. It's never clear whether we're in the movie or the movie within the movie. O'Toole plays the egomaniacal director.

Buddy asked him if he'd based the part of the director on anyone famous, Orson Welles for instance. "I don't play directors. I play *men,*" O'Toole said, and then recounted how before any film or play he locks himself away for a month and tries to absorb every word.

They talked about *Lawrence of Arabia,* and its desert locales. "I spent nine months in Jordan and Saudi Arabia, then three months in Seville and then three months in the Spanish desert, and another three months in the Sahara."

"You hated it from what I remember."

"Yes, I loathe the desert. Only lunatics and God love the desert."

"I want to go there and see it someday," Buddy said.

"Because you're a lunatic," O'Toole said.

If it was supposed to be funny, no one laughed.

"Or maybe you think you're God," he said. "Didn't I read you saying that in one of those articles about you."

"I think I said I was as funny as God," Buddy tried.

"Now that isn't funny," Peter O'Toole said.

Buddy looked nonplussed. He simply said, "In any event, it's a masterpiece, as was your performance."

"Sporting of you to say so," the actor said.

He then told a story about saving one of Buddy's rivals, David Frost, from drowning in a swimming pool once and later regretting it, which was a dark thing to say, but funny enough that it saved the interview.

Then the musical act came on, the rail-thin Tom Petty and the Heartbreakers singing "Don't Do Me Like That."

If you think it was a bad choice after the testy exchange with Peter O'Toole, consider that Petty's other hit song of the moment, "Breakdown," would have been worse.

Buddy had on Merle Miller to discuss his biography of Lyndon Johnson, and he had on John Huston (my get), and got him to tell the story of his disrupting a celebrity golf tournament in Mexico by dumping two thousand graffiti-inscribed Ping-Pong balls onto the fairway during a round, then stories of fights and car accidents and divorces, and bad financial decisions, and his days as an amateur boxer and a painter. He also had on Derek Jacobi, and Russell Baker to talk about the coming election, and Goldie Hawn, who'd just starred in *Private Benjamin* and was someone I'd had a thing for since she was the bikini girl on *Rowan and Martin's Laugh-In.*

Through all of this I followed Buddy's numbers more closely than he did, and I went to all the meetings, and I did a lot of the pre-interviews and scouting.

I found myself so wound up at the end of the day that I'd have to go out drinking to tamp down my anxiety.

"How am I doing?" Buddy would ask, expecting me to tell him he was doing great, but I kept diagnosing weak points we could work on, aspects of the show we could tighten up, or loosen up. Mostly he was as good as ever.

When Reagan won (in a landslide) for instance, he whipped up a bunch of new material. I watched him as I'd done on the plane to *The Tonight Show,* his head down, his pen flying across the page, jotting down thoughts and associations, anticipating the days after the inauguration. One idea was a skit where Reagan is visited by the ghosts of Washington and Jefferson while he's in bed with Nancy. She's wearing a sleeping mask and snoring, and Reagan is wearing dark blue pajamas reading by bedside lamp the book *Strange but True Football Stories.*

Reagan didn't have an enemies list the way Nixon did. Reagan believed he could win over his detractors and that anger and paranoia got you nowhere.

After our ninth week we lost two affiliates. Not terrible, but not a great sign. Elliot called this part of our growing pains, and that mostly we needed now to survive and then get a head of steam close to the holidays, which was when the big decisions would be made.

"What sort of decisions?" I asked.

"Nothing too big. Whether we'll live or die."

"Seriously?"

"Well, yeah. I think we'll be good. But most shows, like most relationships, as you know, don't make it. Buddy's different, but we need something."

"We're getting good guests."

"It's time to go big. Have you been talking to John about when exactly he wants to come on the show?"

"A while back."

"I don't want to wait too long on this. I want to have something to put on the table at the next meeting."

"All right. I'll find out."

"Paul said he'll come."

"Hold it. You asked him already?"

"Well, sure. You told me that John said we should ask Paul."

"He said *I* should ask Paul."

"Same thing right. We're in this together right."

"We are," I said.

"So I can go into a meeting and say we're going to rock the world by the end of, say, January. Does that sound feasible? It'll buy us ten more weeks."

"Yes, it sounds feasible."

■ ■ ■ ■

You float naked for an hour in water the temperature of your skin mixed with a thousand pounds of Epsom salts, the same composition they say as the Dead Sea, which Buddy went to in his travels. It decreases inflammation and pain, lowers stress, and calms the mind and soul. You might even hallucinate because it's pitch-black with no sound and your mind starts to make the world around you. I saw a wide calm sea, and I felt myself skim across the surface at a great speed, though in truth I was pretty still. When the session was over we were blissed out.

Afterward we rode the subway uptown and got hot buttered rums at the Museum Café on Seventy-Seventh Street, across from IS 44, which Olive wanted to know about. Why hadn't I gone to a school a mere five blocks away?

I told her people got held up at knifepoint at the public schools, that they weren't very good, which is why our parents reluctantly sent us to private schools. I made the mistake of saying "everyone did."

"Clearly not everyone," she said.

Seventy-Seventh was where they blew up

the balloons every year for the Macy's Thanksgiving Day Parade, which was in two days. I told her we could come back and watch the balloons being inflated.

"So no one went to public school?"

"There are a few really good ones," I said. "Stuyvesant and Bronx Science. And West Side High is pretty good. You have to apply to those."

"And your sister's school, Brearley, all girls, is that right?"

"Yes."

I explained there was Collegiate, Trinity, and my school, Adlai Stevenson, which were the breeding grounds for the Ivy League; Walden and Calhoun, Kip's school, were where the druggier kids went. Horace Mann and Riverdale in the Bronx were more Jewish, also places where the rich were selected and groomed. They'd eventually hire one another on Wall Street or at the big law firms.

Then some kids were sent off to New England boarding schools like Andover and Exeter and Choate. These were the coolest kids when we were young.

On Seventy-Seventh there was a welfare hotel called the Park Plaza and there had been a juice bar, the Forbidden Fruit, where junkies hung out. The block association exerted pressure and got the juice bar to close, and the hotel to move. Now it was another high-end apartment building.

I told her my sister railed about this all the time, the battle royale over the makeup of the Upper West Side.

"Have you heard what's happening in Wales?"

"What?"

"They're fighting back. Welsh nationalists have been burning down the vacation cottages owned by Londoners. They're taking pains to do it when there's no one there, and the locals admire it. It's like mythical pixies have gone out in the night and set the fires in the homes of invading rich people. They believe their culture and language are being ransacked."

"It's not outsiders here I guess."

"But it's a war all the same."

A week back I'd sent Will, per his request, a package of ideas, pitches, and rough drafts of shows we might put together including one based on Randy's experience as a cop, which I said would have to include Randy. He sent me back a letter saying I needed to move out there, and we would make things happen.

■ ■ ■ ■

But things were happening here, in bunches. John agreed "firmly" to come on with Paul. And so Elliot called Paul's manager to confirm Paul's intention to appear on the show with John, and maybe play a couple of songs.

The timing was right. And so we had news to bring to our meeting with Keith Osborne and the CBS folks, that we had John and Paul committed for a date in January, with the caveat that no one could speak of it until the New Year, not a peep, or John would back out, he said.

The result of all this was that we bought ourselves another few months, and undoubtedly more if it came together the way it appeared it would.

Around that time Alex and I went to the Bleecker Street Cinema and saw *Let It Be*. We watched it like marriage counselors, or detectives looking over a crime scene, trying to discover what happened and why, and whether it might be reversed.

Alex kept saying it should never have happened, that people missed the message of the movie.

"If you expected to see the four inter-changeable, perfectly sweet and funny guys from *A Hard Day's Night,* then you might be shocked to see that they'd grown up, and had well-formed personalities and aesthetics, and might have differing opinions as they put an album together."

"They're fighting. They can't get along."

"I was thinking about what he looked like — John, I mean. He's a fish in the water, around a healthy coral reef with a ton to eat. He's thriving. He's swimming. Right."

"Okay."

"Then think of him in that empty apartment in the Dakota, or walking out in the park. He's out of his perfect element. He's a fish on land when he's not playing music."

Paul had a clear sense of what everyone should do, and he's telling George, and George doesn't like being told what to do as though he hadn't a brain, and it wouldn't have been personal, but Paul breaks it down as such, and George feels hurt.

But "so what?" Alex said afterward. "Who cares. Listen to what they're making. Paul brings a new song in, and it's the first time anyone's heard it, and each time, there's something amazing to see it born as a thought, as a tune in his head, and then he sets it out, and the rest of them listen, and then you watch it take shape, like sculpture done by four genius sculptors."

Here's a new song, "I Me Mine," or when he lays out the notes of "Maxwell's Silver Hammer," where the fuck did that come from, and it's so perfect so good.

40

When Buddy died of cancer in 2011 we were close again, speaking by phone three times a week. In that last year he and my mother stayed with us in California, and we took walks and went out to dinner, and reminisced about *Friday Nights with Buddy Winter,* which as it turned out wasn't the end for him. In 1982 he began a six-year run on PBS where on each half-hour show he focused on a single guest, and in the case of a few geniuses (Sir John Gielgud, George Balanchine) let those interviews go for several nights. He played in tennis tournaments into his seventies. He narrated a documentary on the early days of TV, and then another on the golden age of talk shows. He appeared again on *The Love Boat,* this time with my mother. They got to be strangers who fell for each other and their improvised lines were the best ever spoken on that ridiculous show.

For years, things were strained with my father, because I needed to find a separate path and because he felt I'd abandoned him, that I had, as my mother suggested, stopped listening. When he died, I longed for my old role, and for the nights after work when we'd take over a bar and the talk would be electric, because it always was back then; wherever we went was the center of the universe.

I've been thinking of Buddy these days as I've emerged from my own breakdown, or whatever else you want to call it. I over-worked and slept too little, and like him years back, worried about the wrong things. And then I went into intensive therapy with a dauntlessly wise man named Morris at his office in Santa Monica. I felt numb the first few meetings and lost in the hours after. I then had my own version of a primal, and in those sessions talked not just about Buddy but about everything — my fluctuating relationships over the years with my mother; and Rachel, who married Randy (who wrote and produced a successful police procedural show, *The Precinct*) and worked her way up to become the first female principal at Coolidge; and Kip, who became a Buddhist and lives up in Seattle, has three kids, and still plays tennis, and who told me a while back that I needed to move up there for my sanity. I have my sanity, though, and a fetching and empathetic California-born wife (who left me once, but only for a month), and two kids who have no interest in working around celebrities.

I attended the second Obama inauguration and actually had a conversation with the First Lady about growing up on a talk show. My life has worked out largely the way I would have wanted, with a few exceptions. I've thought often about what might have happened for us had John not been shot, had someone gotten to that twisted soul before, and had the Beatles shocked the world on Buddy's stage. We'd have survived another two years, maybe more, but who knows? It's easy to say the Beatles would have saved us, and maybe they would have, maybe a lot of things. It was a year of comebacks that never materialized, and I guess they rarely do in the way we hope.

Those weeks after Thanksgiving in 1980 feel to me now like a dream. The show was coming together, John had emerged from hiding and with Yoko was holding interviews with everyone it seemed, a big one with *Playboy,* and another with *Newsweek.* He had so many plans! He and Yoko would tour with their band, and he had a play he'd written, and traveling he wanted to do, especially to Tahiti. After their reunion, my thought was that John and Paul might write some songs together again, and they'd be ones for the ages. As of December 3, Ringo had signed on to being on the show, and George was the lone holdout, but wouldn't be for long. Not with the other three pulling for this. It would be as I pitched it — the second half of the forty-two-minute concert on the roof at Savile Row that had ended because the police broke it up, and we wouldn't do a big windup for it. The network would know and the affiliates, but it would be the biggest and best secret everyone kept.

I remember a cab trip I took downtown with John on one of those perfect fall days, and his saying the best part about coming on Buddy's show would be that no one would ever ask him again when the band was getting back together.

"What I want is to outlive Elvis. To survive," he said.

"You have," I said.

"Isn't it all so fuckin' grand?" he said. "A year ago you were dying of malaria in a rancid hospital bed. Now look at you. I've sprinkled you with Beatle dust."

He said something vaguely fatherly as I

left, which was lost in the din of traffic.

I went out with Olive the night of December 8 to hear music at a new club in the Village, the Ritz, which had a cavernous dance floor, and everyone dressed in black, a lot of them wearing chains and motorcycle boots, and we all slammed into one another listening to the Flying Lizards. We left the club before the news broke out, but we could feel it everywhere around us, in the tears of strangers and the howl from down the street and in the silence from the places where music would have streamed out. Something terrible had happened, and we would never be the same again.

41

The world wept outside our building that night, wave after wave of mourners in down coats and wool ponchos and fringed denim jackets and sweatshirts, a handful in robes and slippers, old and young, faces you recognized and more you didn't from all over New York and soon from everywhere, and a few TV crews set up cameras, and a man in a wheelchair sang Beatles songs, and people embraced one another, or stood there in shock. Blood speckled the ground at the entryway. He'd been shot four times. The young surgeon at Roosevelt Hospital had opened him up and held his heart in his hand, trying to massage it back to life, but John had lost too much blood, and it was too late. At our front gate were yellow and red roses and wildflowers and photos and drawings, and messages of love and pain written out on notebook paper or posters. No one knew how close they'd been to seeing the four of them, that the shock they were meant to receive was the band back together again, which was in part my making. I'd seen it in my mind's eye, had already dreamt of it, the first of many times I would over the years.

Things we know about that last day: John got his hair cut. He did a photo shoot with Annie Leibovitz for *Rolling Stone,* the one where he was naked hugging a clothed Yoko. A reporter interviewed him for three hours for RKO Radio. When John's driver didn't show, the reporter gave him a ride to the record studio on his way to the airport.

When he left the building he signed a record for the man who killed him.

If I think of those last days I see Mark David Chapman everywhere, walking out of Central Park, entering the McBurney Y where he stayed. I see him standing outside our building in that coat and that scarf, dead inside and full of pointless rage. I can't avoid feeling that I could have done something, beat the shit out of him, or talked him out of it, or called the cops, but a lot of people feel that way.

It was startling how personally they experienced John's death, as though they'd lost an intimate friend, or brother, or lover. But they knew *nothing about him.* It made me think of Olive's riff on the misplaced emotions people feel toward stars they never met. What drove them to our front gate in anguish in a way ended his life. We love them, then we kill them, my mother said when I shared this thought with her.

Buddy's show in the following weeks found its stride. His monologues were heroically crisp and funny; we had great guests, but it had the feel of a goodbye tour, the sort athletes have in their final season. We'd meant for it to be a rebirth, not the end of the road. What made it frustrating was that we heard different things every week. A network suit would tell us we'd weathered the storm and might soon be heading toward five nights a week, and then we'd lose another affiliate, and the numbers would drop, and Elliot would warn us our days were numbered. It was like being with a girlfriend, he said, who had one foot out the door.

I suffered headaches during that period and anxiety attacks, believing it was my fault for raising our hopes.

"I can't stand the thought that he has to go through this again," I said to Rachel as we walked in the park, Buddy and my mother twenty yards ahead, on our way to the boathouse. It was close to the end.

"Go through what?"

"Losing his show again. Falling out of favor. He'll be right back where he was."

"He isn't, and you aren't."

"How so?"

"Look at him," she said, and at that moment Buddy turned and glanced warmly back at us.

"He'll be fine. You made it so. No one else would have done what you did. I certainly wouldn't have. And he made it back. He didn't want the life he had before."

"No, I guess *I* did," I said.

"I did too a little," Rachel said. "I just never said it."

I remember wandering the neighborhood and seeing the borderline businesses close and a pricey boutique opening and feeling that the city I'd known would be gone soon, or a lot of it, and I went about taking mental photographs — Grossingers Home Bakery, specializing in European-style cookies; the Avocado Tree, where I bought rolling papers and my first bong; the magazine shop where I bought egg creams; the little barbershop that had an old-fashioned bikini calendar on the wall; the gift shop where I saw a couple try to set the Guinness World Record for longest kiss, their lips swelling to the size of sausages in their fortieth hour; the

Ansonia, inside which we took ballroom-dancing classes; the Claremont riding stables, where Rachel spent all day on Saturdays and came home smelling of hay. It would all change soon, yuppie bond traders buying up apartments in converted SROs, the young and wealthy filling the best tables at Victor's, Ruelles, or the Red Baron, and browsing for designer chocolates and two-hundred-dollar pairs of jeans. And where did the old people, the crazy people, the drunks and the prostitutes, the chess-playing socialists go? The preachers and amateur politicians, the guy outside the Dublin House selling magic tricks and jokes? The West Side of our growing up had the whole world within, not just the pretty parts.

I flew out in early April, after the show ended, to Los Angeles and found a studio apartment in Venice, three blocks from Will, and we started writing together, and thinking up projects and taking meetings, which I'd become pretty good at. He was a force, like Buddy in many ways, and much sharper than he'd been in college. We were good for each other, and I thought ridiculously of John and Paul in Hamburg, writing songs together from opposing bunk beds. I spoke to Olive once a week on the phone, and then nearly every night.

I had a dream in my new home about the storm at sea, and when I woke up I was very happy, and then upset. And then I wrote for the whole day, and took a long walk along the Pacific Ocean. I wondered what Buddy was up to, and I pictured him at a movie with Harry, grabbing dinner after and sketching out a new life. It was my birthday tomorrow, I thought, and then I realized it was today, and there were messages on my phone, and I felt far away from everything then, from all I'd ever known.

ACKNOWLEDGMENTS

This book owes much to the Upper West Side of my childhood; to my parents, Heather and Joe Barbash, who moved us there just after Nixon was elected and introduced us to *Revolver* and *Rubber Soul*. Thanks to writer friends Justin Cronin, Jim Sullivan, Jason Roberts, David Mitchell, Anika Stretifeld, Dave Eggers, Jess Walter, and Eric Puchner, who encouraged me and offered wise counsel when needed.

My sister, Lisa, was a primary source of experience and wisdom, as was my stepmother, Carol Lamberg, and my godmother, Joy Boyum. David Berman, Mark Weiner, Kerstin Nash, John Swomley, and Rex Miller were able sounding boards.

Dan Chaon helped pull me from more than a few narrative ditches and has for years been a continuous source of inspiration. Joshua Blum, Ann Terry, and John Martin taught me valuable things about the world of television and talk shows in particular. Captain Hank Halsted shared some of his experiences at sea with John Lennon in two long phone conversations, though I certainly took artistic license. Joshua Wolf Shenk lent his insights on Paul and John. Steffi and Bob Berne and novelist Nina Solomon shared their thoughts on living in the Dakota and invited me inside to ride the elevators, walk the hallways, and sit in their living rooms sharing stories. Fred Seaman's book about working for John Lennon was elucidating, as were *The John Lennon Letters*, Stephen Birmingham's *Life at the Dakota*, Katharine Hepburn's *The Making of* The African Queen, and Henry Bushkin's book about his client Johnny Carson. Grant Dorsey and Brenna Wear educated me on malaria, and David Dodson and Max Mulhern taught me crucial things about sailing in the open sea. Thanks to the MacDowell Colony, Martin Lauber, and Simon Blattner, who offered me a room of my own within which to work, and to my students and colleagues at CCA who continue to inspire me.

Much gratitude to Lee Boudreaux and Dan Halpern, for first believing in the book; to Emma Dries, who helped keep me on course; to Trent Duffy, the gold standard of copy editors; and to my patient and brilliant editor Megan Lynch, for her wise and forthright counsel. Ellen Levine has been a constant force in my writing life, wise and warm, and always there. And finally to Hilary and James, who fill my life with joy and wonder.

ABOUT THE AUTHOR

Tom Barbash grew up in New York and is the author of three books as well as numerous reviews, stories essays, and articles for publications including *McSweeney's, Tin House, the Believer, Narrative Magazine, One Story, StoryQuarterly, Zyzzyva, the Missouri Review, Story Magazine, Men's Journal, ESPN the Magazine, BookForum,* and the *New York Times.* His short story collection *Stay Up With Me* was nominated for the Folio Prize, and was picked as a Best Book of the Year by the *Independent of London,* NPR, Amazon.com, the *San Francisco Chronicle,* the *San Jose Mercury News,* and was *a San Francisco Chronicle* bestseller and a *New York Times* editor's choice. His novel *The Last Good Chance* was awarded The California Book Award, was a *Publishers Weekly* and Anniston Star Best Book of the Year, and was short listed for the Great

Lakes Book Prize and the Saroyan International Prize. Barbash has held fellowships from the MacDowell Colony, Yaddo, The James Michener Foundation, and the National Endowment for the Arts.